MW01167404

Only the Beginning

Prophecy Series, Volume 1

W.J. May

Published by Dark Shadow Publishing, 2017.

ONLY THE BEGINNING

First edition. June 15, 2017.

Written by W.J. May.

Also by W.J. May

Compelled
Fate's Intervention
Chosen Three
The Hidden Secrets Saga: The Complete Series

Paranormal Huntress Series
Never Look Back
Coven Master

Prophecy Series
Only the Beginning
White Winter

The Chronicles of Kerrigan
Rae of Hope
Dark Nebula
House of Cards
Royal Tea
Under Fire
End in Sight
Hidden Darkness
Twisted Together
Mark of Fate
Strength & Power
Last One Standing
Rae of Light
The Chronicles of Kerrigan Box Set Books # 1 - 6

The Chronicles of Kerrigan: Gabriel
Living in the Past

The Chronicles of Kerrigan Prequel
Christmas Before the Magic
Question the Darkness
Into the Darkness
Fight the Darkness
Alone in the Darkness
Lost in Darkness
The Chronicles of Kerrigan Prequel Series Books #1-3

The Chronicles of Kerrigan Sequel
A Matter of Time
Time Piece
Second Chance
Glitch in Time
Our Time
Precious Time

The Hidden Secrets Saga
Seventh Mark (part 1 & 2)

The Senseless Series
Radium Halos
Radium Halos - Part 2
Nonsense

Standalone
Shadow of Doubt (Part 1 & 2)
Five Shades of Fantasy
Shadow of Doubt - Part 2
Four and a Half Shades of Fantasy
Dream Fighter
What Creeps in the Night
Forest of the Forbidden
HuNted
Arcane Forest: A Fantasy Anthology
Ancient Blood of the Vampire and Werewolf

Prophecy Series #1

Only the Beginning

By W.J. May

Copyright 2017 by W.J. May

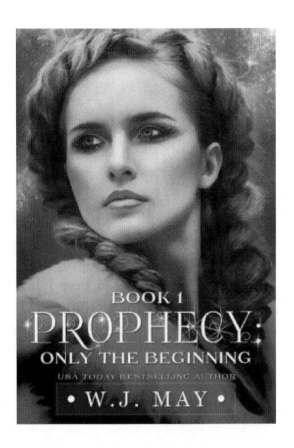

Prophecy Series

Find W.J. May

Website:
http://www.wanitamay.yolasite.com
Facebook:
https://www.facebook.com/pages/Author-WJ-May-FAN-PAGE/141170442608149
Newsletter:
SIGN UP FOR W.J. May's Newsletter to find out about new releases, updates, cover reveals and even freebies!
http://eepurl.com/97aYf

Only the Beginning Blurb:

Be prepared. There are werewolves in this story, and they are NOT friendly.
Peace comes at a price...

Rebekah and Jamie are happy, but discontent. Sometimes, it feels like everything important has already happened, that the peace their parents fought so hard to bring them is just a strange limbo they can't break out of. They want adventure, they want to make memories of their own. When a pair of new kids shows up at their school, it looks like they might finally have their chance.

It isn't long before the twins open up to the mysterious new strangers. Sharing secrets they thought they'd never tell. Asking questions they never could have imagined.

When a party in the woods leads to near tragedy, they find themselves caught in the middle of a fight they never saw coming. Trapped between two sides and put to the ultimate test.

Will they choose their family? Or their future?

Rouge's adventure may have come to an end, but the twins' is just getting started...

Loved ONLY THE BEGINNING? Find out who Rogue and Michael are in the Hidden Secrets Saga – Read what happened to send Jamie and Rebekah's life into secrecy!
You won't be disappointed!
Seventh Mark part 1 is included here FREE
Seventh Mark part 2
Marked by Destiny
Compelled
Fate's Intervention
Chosen Three
Book Trailer: http://www.youtube.com/watch?v=Y-_vVYC1gvo

Chapter 1

You know that feeling when you wake up and go through your morning routine—get dressed, brush your teeth, make toast—only to wake up again and realize that not only were you dreaming, but you have to go through the whole morning all over again?

Yeah...that was pretty much my life right now.

"—settled by trade merchants in the late1800s. While most of the progress came to a screeching halt in the Panic of 1893, we can still see evidence of—"

I sank a few inches lower in my chair and let my eyes wander over the room. Sometimes, it was hard to believe I had fought so hard for this. Fought for the right to come to this classroom every day and listen to mind-numbing speeches from teachers just as disinterested as their students. Fought to take part in a ritual that every single one of the boys and girls sitting around me would have sold their left arm just to avoid. The name itself was like a curse amongst them. Uttered only in times of great anger and stress.

High school.

A tiny moth had slipped inside the room, unnoticed by the rest of the students. My eyes followed along as it wriggled out of a crack in the window and started flying in random patterns in front of the whiteboard.

It didn't help that I had gone through all this material before. It didn't help that, in addition to having a photographic memory, I also happened to have parents who had weaponized the art of reading. Some parents like to encourage the habit? My parents cheerfully demanded it.

On my third birthday, they'd swapped out the typical *See Spot Run!* books with literary compositions of a more serious nature. Greek anthologies, Japanese poets, religious texts from all four corners of the globe. You name it—I had read it. And whether I wanted to or not, I remembered it all.

"So what do we call that economic system? Where a country hopes to amass wealth through influxes in trade?" Mr. Barrow's eyes flickered around the classroom from behind his glasses, looking for volunteers. "Also called commercialism? Come on, guys—we just went over this."

They came to rest on an unlikely candidate, but he tried anyway.

"Briana?" A blonde girl, who was secretly texting beneath her desk, looked up with a start. "Want to venture a guess?"

Her cheeks flushed bright magenta as she slid the phone up into her sleeve. "No...not really."

Barrow stifled a sigh before his searching gaze came to rest on me. "Rebekah?"

I stopped tracking the moth, and turned my eyes towards the front.

This was only Barrow's second week teaching, but already he'd figured out who his go-to students were. The kids he could count on to know the answer when the rest of the class started to flail. Mostly it was me, and this kid named Benjamin who sat in the back row chewing on his hair. On days when Benjamin was ditching—like today—it was just me.

I took a second to remember the question, then answered quietly—my eyes on my desk. "It's called mercantilism."

The class breathed a collective sigh of relief as Barrow flashed me a silent look of gratitude. It was rather expected of me by now, these little academic rescues, but the appreciation remained.

"That's right, mercantilism." He gave me a quick nod before moving back to the whiteboard. "Maybe if you spent more time listening, Miss Maven, and less time texting—you might have known it as well."

Briana's face flushed again as she dropped her phone into her bag. A boy sitting beside her rolled his eyes with a grin before turning my way. I was vaguely aware of him watching as Barrow continued the lesson, but found myself too disinterested to even glance his way.

They were all like that, I'd come to realize. They all stared.

When I first transferred into the school about five months ago, I had hoped that it would fade. That it was a simple matter of being the new girl in class, and eventually people would lose interest. But five months later, it was still going strong. And it wasn't just the boys—although they were obnoxiously obvious about it. It was everyone. Teachers included. The looks weren't unkind, but they were probing. And relentless. As if their minds somehow sensed the difference between us, although they could never figure out what that might be.

The bell rang and I pushed out of my chair with a sigh of relief. Most days, I handled the monotony a little better than this. (It was a rite of passage I'd fought for, after all), but this week things were a little different. You see, I had a birthday coming up. A big one. Eighteen. However, unlike the rest of my adolescent compatriots here, there was very little to celebrate...

"Hey! Rebekah!"

I paused in the hallway as the rest of the students flooded out past me into the sun, turning around to see who had called me. It was the boy from my class. Chris something-or-other. He was good-looking. Smart. And generally nicer than the rest. In most circles, this would make him a 'decent' guy. But in high school, the combination made him some sort of god. Between that and the fact that he was on the football team, he'd achieved idol status freshman year.

"Hey," I greeted him with a quick smile. It wasn't often that I mixed with the rest of the student population, try as they might. "What's up?"

Three little words, and the class king crumbled before my very eyes. The cool confidence shattered, the suave persona vanished into thin air.

"I was just...I wanted to..." he stammered for a second, before chickening out altogether and backing away with a self-conscious grin. "Nothing. Just wanted to say hey. Have a good weekend."

He was off like a shot before I could even answer. Retreating to a circle of jocks who immediately began speaking in hushed voices, clapping him on the back as though he'd attempted something very brave.

I watched them for a moment, tilting my head curiously to the side before heading out into the sun with an almost wistful sigh.

Five months I've been at this school. How long before the student population stops treating me like, at any moment, I might burst into flames?

I fished my sunglasses out of my bag as I slowly walked across the grass to the parking lot, sliding them up into my golden blonde hair. Thank the Maker history was the final class of the day; I didn't think I could stand to be on campus for another second.

"Hey, Rebekah!"

I lifted my hand in an automatic wave, but by the time I looked over the girl who'd said the words had already turned back to her circle of friends.

Another sigh. I quickened my pace.

It wasn't even that they were mean. Quite the contrary. I had never seen people make such an effort just to get close. The thing was—they sucked at it.

Chris was just the tip of the iceberg. It was like no one at the freaking school could manage to sustain an entire conversation before blushing, hyperventilating, or panicking to such a degree that they simply took off in the other direction—muttering some excuse about having to feed their bird.

(*Actual* story. That *actually* happened.)

Yeah, they tried all right. And I did my best to help them along. But it wasn't like there was much I could do. We were just...different. And even if I could try to get one or two of them past it, what was the point? It wasn't like I was allowed to make real friends at this school anyway...

A flurry of breathless chatter caught my attention from the other side of the lot, and I glanced over to see a group of cheerleaders falling all over themselves as they stared towards the science building.

"—can't even handle it! He's just SO freaking HOT!"

"Did I tell you that he looked at me in English today?!" another gushed importantly, waving her pink nails in the air. "Or, at least, I think he did. He might have been looking out the window instead..."

"—can't even think when he's around," Briana, the texting prom queen, was staring in a sort of lustful trance. "Just want to jump on top of him—"

I automatically glanced over, even though I shouldn't have. There was really only one person they could be talking about. Sure enough, the door to the science building opened and a breathtaking man stepped into the sun.

It was easy to see how a single glance had rendered half the cheerleading squad completely speechless. How just a flash of his dimpled grin had even the teaching staff temporarily stunned. You could almost hear the internal chanting as he walked by.

He's a minor. And a student. And a minor. And a student.

Tall. Tan. Athletically muscular, but lean. With tumbles of golden hair and ice blue eyes that seemed to pierce through whatever they touched. In a lot of ways, he looked a lot like a male version of me. As he should.

He was my brother. My twin brother. Jamie.

The second he saw me he headed across the grass at a fast pace, looking just as glad to be out of there as I was. The pack of ravenous girls followed his every move, waving to me with sweet smiles when they accidentally caught my eye. I resisted the urge to smirk, and smiled back.

They were always nice to me. In a pleading, desperate sort of way. I couldn't ever tell if it was real, or if they just wanted to get close to Jamie. I suppose it didn't really matter. The most I was allowed to reciprocate was a smile. There was no commonality, so all connection stopped there.

Still, I had to commend them for their endurance. We had been at this school five months now, and Jamie had yet to even look their way.

"Hey," he greeted me, tossing his bag onto the backseat of the car, "was your day as *thrilling* as mine?"

I snorted sarcastically. Even if Jamie and I weren't twins, we still would have been alike in every single way. He was having as much trouble with our upcoming birthday as I was.

Instead of answering, I shot a wry grin over my shoulder.

"You're disappointing your fan club." I slipped the aviators down over my eyes. "You should do another turn around the parking lot. Show a little skin. At least take off your shirt or something."

An amused frown flitted across his face as he took my bag and unlocked the door for me. "Who are we talking about?"

I rolled my eyes and climbed inside. The guy was oblivious.

It wasn't that he was lacking in confidence—don't get me wrong. When you were a hybrid descendant of both angels and werewolves, a supernatural prince descending from the most ancient of bloodlines—it was impossible not to be a bit full of yourself from time to time. But none of that translated over to girls. Truth be told, when it came to women Jamie was secretly a little shy.

As much as I'd like to tease, I couldn't really give him a hard time—I was the same way myself. We'd simply had no experience. Our band of guardians hadn't exactly forbidden it, but they'd never let us out of their sight long enough to try.

"Never you mind." I patted his head condescendingly, giggling when he shook me off with a rueful glare. "Let's get home. You don't want Dad flipping out again if we don't make it back by curfew."

Curfew.

Most people would think it implied a nighttime restriction. Be back by ten, eleven—that sort of thing. But that wasn't how it was for us. Jamie and I had curfew ALL the time. A time to be home from school. A time to be back from the grocery store. I swear they'd even timed how long it took us to walk to and from the mail box at the end of the street.

Sometimes, it felt like every single moment of every single day was exactly mapped out for us. That the beloved puppet masters holding our strings had planned them down to the second. Not that our lives were bursting with activity—quite the opposite. All those rules, all that planning...and for what? The only unsupervised moments the two of us had were driving to and from school.

Jamie's bright eyes dimmed for a moment before he nodded briskly and hopped into the car. A second later we were screeching away down the street, heading back out of town. To the castle that he and I called home.

* * *

Castle. It was another of those words, like curfew. If I were to say that my brother and I lived in a castle, most people would assume that I meant we lived in a really big house. But in my world, we tended to take things literally.

The second we pulled off the main road onto the private forested lane, I could see it. Towering above the giant red maples. High stone walls. Turrets and crenulated walkways. There was even a little fountain in the front drive.

Home sweet home.

Jamie screeched to a stop, sending up a spray of gravel in his wake. It ricocheted off the sculpted limestone—a teasing message to anyone on the inside that we were home. Sure enough, a light snapped on in an upper hallway, and even from the car I could hear my father walking downstairs.

Instead of rushing out to greet him like I usually did, some strange impulse made me hang back. I hesitated for a moment, eyes on the house, listening to Jamie prattle on about something as he gathered his things.

"Actually," I interrupted suddenly, "could you tell the others I'm going out for a walk?" Before he could answer, I shoved my bag into his arms. "And could you take that in for me as well?"

A look of surprise danced across his face before it lightened into a curious frown. One that seemed to see right through me.

"Sure, but...why? Is everything okay?"

It wasn't often I could hide things from Jamie. The guy was my other half. The person in whom I confided my wildest dreams, and darkest secrets.

Fortunately, I didn't understand this sudden curfew rebellion myself.

I brushed off the question with a casual shrug, stepping out onto the sunny driveway. "It's fine. Just want to stretch my legs a little."

His eyes flickered towards the house before he flashed me a quick smile. "Don't be long."

I nodded and headed off into the trees without a glance behind me, well aware of the casual uproar such a simple gesture would cause.

The vegetation was dense and thick, and it wasn't long before I lost sight of the house entirely. The second I did, I slowed my pace—leisurely trailing the tips of my fingers across the sunlit ferns. With every distancing step, I felt I could breathe just a little easier. With every step, I felt just a little more free.

When I came to the edge of our property, I hopped up into one of the giant trees—scaling the tall trunk in a single leap. It was something I never would have been allowed to do in public, but out here none of that mattered. I could be myself. The bark was smooth and warmed by the sun. Perfect for napping. Perfect for blissful hours of meditative thought.

I settled myself back on the branches, closing my eyes as my long blonde hair spiraled around me in the gentle breeze.

You can't blame them for being overprotective. I chanted the line over and over in my head. *You can't blame them for wanting to keep you safe.*

When it came to the strict rigidities of my life, a little understanding was required. To start, my family wasn't exactly what you'd call normal.

My brother and I were the next generation of a group of supernatural warriors. Warriors trained and bred for one reason alone. To fight a war. It was a war between angels—or Hunters—and werewolves—or Grollics. A war that had been raging on for centuries. A tangled mess of magic and pain. Both sides consumed by rage and bloodlust. Both sides suffering devastating losses as time wore on. The only strange thing about being born today?

The war was already over.

The entire driving force of the supernatural community, the fiery reason for our very existence...had cooled into a quiet peace.

The packs of wolves had settled. The bands of Hunters had gone home. A new chapter had started. One where the turmoil of the past had been put to rest. Where the magic, fang, and sword that had kept the world alive was no longer needed. Except...nothing had come up to replace them.

It was like living in an epilogue. Trapped in the afterthought of a story that had already taken place. It was like life itself had already been lived. And not by me or my brother, but by my parents and grandparents.

Don't get me wrong, I was grateful to be safe. Even though it felt like being safe and being free were opposite sides of the same coin. I was grateful for this peace they'd worked so hard to build...but it wasn't a life.

Sometimes, it just felt like waiting. Waiting in a house full of people who had cheated death so many times, they found themselves counting how many steps it took to get to the mailbox just to keep their children safe.

I turned around on the tree branch with a sigh—sprawling out on my stomach as my arms and legs dangled down the sides.

Again, I couldn't blame them. My dad had grown up in this world. Had grown up surrounded by so much bloodshed and death, I couldn't begin to imagine it. He didn't think he could even have children, until he met my mother. And, as legend would have it, the tumultuous arrival of my 'mortal' mother did nothing to ease that burden. It was when the story really began...

We'd had to BEG them to move away from their secluded house by the ocean. We'd had to BEG them to let us attend a regular school.

A regular school with regular kids. That had been our campaign slogan for the better part of five years. "But you're NOT regular kids," my father, Michael, had argued. But we wanted to be.

Growing up in the supernatural community was hard enough. But growing up with our lineage was even worse.

Children whose father was a virtual prince of angels, and whose mother held the power to destroy the world. Grandchildren of the highest ranking Hunter in the land, and niece and nephew to the highest ranking werewolf.

Power was our legacy. Dominion, our heavenly right. The ancient magic that had shaped the world for a thousand centuries ran through our veins. Our golden heads had been born specifically to wear all those weighty crowns.

And yet...sometimes I'd give it all up just to be a normal kid.

My mom got it. She understood. Having grown up with no idea what she really was, with every expectation of being a regular mortal, she knew exactly what it meant to stand out in a world where you were supposed to fit in. She understood the value of normal, and did everything she could to give it to us.

But there were limits to even what my legendary mother was able to do.

"Becka?"

Speaking of Mom...

I rolled off the tree with a little sigh, dropping to my feet in the warm grass. In all likelihood, she hadn't even left the house to call me. In all likelihood, she hadn't even raised her voice. We both knew I could hear her just fine.

"Becka, time to come in." Sure enough, I heard her closing the kitchen windows as she added under her breath, "before your father has a coronary."

A small grin flitted across my face as I began stomping back towards the house. My father? Worried about me wandering on my own?

No...

Chapter 2

The front door was unlocked, same as always. It kind of went without saying, like an unspoken rule, that no one in their right mind would ever dare attack our house. If they did, they most likely wouldn't use the front door.

I breezed inside, past the winding staircase, past the library and the foyer and the front parlor, all the way back to the living room, where my father was sitting in a tall recliner. Book in his lap. Eyes on the page.

"Hey, Dad."

He glanced over, his blue eyes sweeping me up and down in a practiced sort of way, before giving me a welcoming smile. "Finished with your walk?"

I sank into the chair beside him with a teasing groan. "Don't give me a hard time, okay? You know what other kids my age are doing right now? Sex and tattoos. And knife fights and belly dancing. Probably not at the same time, but still... All *your* daughter wants to do is take an occasional walk in the woods."

His eyebrows lifted slowly as he fixed me with an unreadable stare. "Knife fights and belly dancing?"

I jutted up my chin, unwilling to surrender an inch. "Or so I've gathered from watching copious amounts of YouTube and TV."

We stared at each other for another moment before his twinkling eyes returned to his book. I kicked off my shoes, and he automatically pushed the second mug of coffee sitting beside him towards me. Our afternoon routine.

I took it silently and gulped down half in about two seconds flat. It wasn't scorching hot the way it usually was. During my woodland excursion, it'd had time to cool. As I drank, my eyes flickered over to my father.

My parents were young.

To the rest of the world, they looked almost the same age as me—just a little bit older. My father may have been killed and reborn as an angel over a hundred years ago, but he'd stopped physically aging around nineteen. My mother had stopped at eighteen. The same age she was when she had me.

Dad was good-looking. There was no denying it. So was Mom.

My mother was pale with this gorgeous flaming red hair, but my father looked very much like me and Jamie. Blond. Tanned. The ice-blue eyes of an immortal. At this point, we looked more like siblings than father and daughter.

But no matter how young they might look, there was something different in their eyes. Something different in the way they carried themselves. You couldn't hide decades of life experience—it always shone through.

A lot of people in the supernatural community were the same way. You learned to read people based on those silent little tells, rather than their faces. The steadiness. The wisdom. My Uncle Seth, for example, looked no more than twenty years old. But he'd been alive for like, forever. Almost as old as Caleb.

"So how was school? Anything interesting happen?"

I turned quickly back to my coffee, steering the conversation towards anything else instead. "Where's Jamie?"

"He's in backyard with Caleb. Practicing."

Ah, that explained it. Why my father was sitting here, in front of the outer door, pretending to read. He was actually keeping a close eye on things.

"Is he now?" I bit my lip to stifle a knowing smile as my father shot me a look of warning. But no matter how hard he tried, he could never be stern with me for very long. Sure enough, it lasted only a moment. Then he returned to his book with a wink.

The wink was my dismissal, forgiveness, and permission. All in one.

I pushed to my feet with a grin and kissed him on the cheek. Then I yanked open the door and headed over to join my brother and grandfather out in the yard.

Jamie and Caleb were in full swing combat. Blurring over the grass at a speed which no mortal could ever hope to follow. Colors became liquid streaks. Sounds, dull vibrations through the ground. I settled into a patio chair, pulling my knees up to my chest as I watched.

Training was another one of those words unique to our weird little vocabulary. It would have struck any normal person as utterly bizarre, but to us it was as natural as breathing. As much a part of our lives as family dinners and going to school.

While it was all a bit superfluous now, there wasn't a single member of the supernatural community who didn't know how to fight. As part of what everyone considered to be the royal family, Jamie and I were fully expected to carry on the tradition. Not that we minded. It was the best part of our day.

"Watch for the cross-over," Caleb commanded, putting my fearless twin through his paces. "Careful for that left jab. Good—again!"

Training with my grandfather was like a dance. A dazzling, devastating dance. As fluid as it was precise. As graceful as it was deadly. Lose the count for even a second, and that second would be your last. Training with Caleb was pure, raw power. There was no other way to describe it. Nothing, or no one, compared to Caleb. Fighting him, even in drills, was thrilling and terrifying all at the same time.

Staring across the yard, I could see both of those feelings reflected in the face of my brother. His eyes were lit up with breathless exhilaration. Even though he was matching Caleb step for step, the older man was still gaining ground.

"Watch your feet," Caleb warned, dropping down into a low kick to sweep Jamie's out from under him. Jamie countered beautifully, flipping into the air to land on Caleb's other side. But by the time he hit the ground, our invincible grandfather was ready. "Heads up!"

A heavy kick to the chest sent Jamie flying backwards. He let out a soft gasp as he crashed towards the ground, but a second before he could hit it Caleb caught him by the arm and lifted him back to his feet.

"Thanks," Jamie panted, brushing himself off as his grandfather looked on with fierce approval. "I almost thought I had you there."

"You did well," Caleb clapped him on the back, his eyes flashing up to the patio with a mocking smirk. "Much better than your father did at your age."

I turned around in surprise to see Dad standing on the porch behind me, watching the proceedings with a twinkling smile.

"Is that right?" he queried. "I don't seem to remember you catching me or Grace before we hit the ground. I don't remember you being quite so liberal with those words of encouragement either."

Jamie and I both laughed as the adults shared a look that only they would understand. Growing up, my father always mentioned how Caleb trained us differently than he had been trained himself. When we pressed him as to what exactly that meant, he'd answered with a chuckle and, "He shows you a little bit of mercy."

"What do you think, Jamie?" Michael stepped forward onto the lawn, a casual gesture, but one that radiated power all at the same time. "Think you've got what it takes to beat your old man?"

Jamie laughed again, but shook his head. "Nah, I think I'd rather live to see my next birthday, thanks."

It was a wise move. Caleb might be indestructible—in a category all to himself—but our father was a legend. There was simply no touching him.

"Oh, come on," Michael teased, gesturing him forward. "I'll go easy."

Jamie shook his head, his golden locks shining in the sun. "I'd just as soon spar with Mom. With or without her little journal—"

"What about my journal?"

The banter was cut short as the door slid open one more time. With a sparkling smile, my mother, also known as Rogue but spelled Rouge, walked out onto the patio with my grandmother, Sarah, by her side. The men bowed their heads respectively as Jamie angled himself safely behind Caleb with a mischievous smile.

"Nothing, Mom." His face melted into a perfect mask of innocence. "Dad here was just saying how he could take you in a fight. I swore he couldn't."

I rolled my eyes and leaned back with a laugh. Very brave of him to be taunting his parents from inside our grandfather's protective shadow.

My mother smiled indulgently before turning to her husband, playing along. "Is that right, darling? You think you could take me down?"

My father's face grew tender, the way it always did when he looked at her, but he tilted his head with a cocky smile. "You never know."

She took a casual step forward, her crimson hair flaming in the afternoon sun. "Oh, honey, you should know better than that by now. I thought we'd settled this a long time ago."

"Yeah, yeah, the ultimate power," Jamie teased, his eyes sparkling. "I've never seen it."

And he wouldn't see it today either. Because my mother didn't fight with flailing fists and leaping twirls. She didn't need any of that. She never had.

It was over before we even knew it started. One second, my father was standing in front of her, his muscles tensing, as though he had a very good idea of what was coming. The next second, he was on the ground.

I leapt to my feet as Jamie's mouth fell open in shock. My mother didn't use her magic very often. And I'd never once seen it directed at another person.

"How did you do that?" I exclaimed, staring down in wonder as she reached out a hand to my father. He accepted with a quiet chuckle. "I didn't even see you move!"

"She didn't move," Michael replied, staring adoringly at his wife before planting a quick kiss on her forehead. "She spoke."

Jamie and I took a second to process this before he stepped forward excitedly, gesturing to his grandfather. "What about Caleb?"

We stared between them with wide eyes, thinking the same thing. I couldn't imagine anyone in the world getting the better of Caleb. Then again, up until a second ago I would have said the same thing about my father.

The two of them looked at each other for a moment, but didn't move. I instinctively stiffened as a wave of anticipation charged the air. But a second later, my mom flashed a quick smile and headed back inside.

"That's one fight I promised never to have." She said the words lightly, but there was a lot more to them than that.

For as long as I could remember, there had been a strange kind of tension between the two. A sort of unspoken truce: one that allowed the family to keep the peace, but had never quite blossomed into a genuine friendship.

She had been reluctant to move to Port Q not because of its public location, but because it was Caleb's house. Yet the two of them sat down for a family dinner every night. Her children spent all their time in his company.

Like most things of interest, whatever happened between them had happened before my time. There were things the older generation would never talk about, no matter how hard Jamie and I pressed. The careful ceasefire between Caleb and Rouge was chief among them.

What does it matter now? It's already all over.

A sudden wave of frustration rushed through me and I pushed to my feet. "I'll be up in my room." I tried to keep my voice as light as my mother's, but Jamie shot me a questioning look.

Caleb called out to me as I breezed through the door. "What about practice, child?" His face tightened with concern. "Jamie and I will finish shortly. It's almost your turn."

I paused for a second in the doorway, my shoulders wilting with a silent sigh. I could never bring myself to upset Caleb, no matter the reason. "I have some homework to do." I flashed him an apologetic grimace over my shoulder. "Raincheck?"

The concern melted away as he nodded with a benevolent smile. "Of course. Just gives me more time to annihilate your brother."

I rolled my eyes with a grin, disappearing into the house. The last thing I saw before I left was Jamie nervously backing across the grass.

"Annihilate? I thought we agreed to stop using that word..."

The men were much easier to fool. The women, not so much.

I hadn't even made it up the stairs to my room before my mother called out, "Becka, is everything okay? I thought you were—"

"I'm fine!" I tripled my speed, trying to get to the landing before she made it out of the kitchen and saw my face.

No such luck.

"*Rebekah.*"

My feet screeched to a halt as every muscle in my body stiffened. The full name. That one only ever came out on rare occasions. Not a good sign.

I slowly turned around, giving her my most winning smile. "Yes?"

She wasn't fooled. A mother never is. In a blur of crimson and cooking flour, she was by my side. Her gentle hands stroked back my hair as her eyes searched mine, trying to find the hurt. "What's the matter, sweetie? You can tell me."

I wanted to. I really did. But how did you explain it? How did you tell a person who had sacrificed so much, who had literally gotten themselves killed trying to give you the perfect life—that all you wanted was to get away?

Instead, I found a middle ground.

One I regretted the second I said it.

"My history class is starting a group project next week." My voice was flat, and my eyes stared into hers. "We're supposed to work in pairs. Each person takes a turn hosting it at their house."

My mother's face tightened infinitesimally as she saw the conversational cliff not far up ahead. The house rule was simple. We were never allowed to have anyone over. Ever. And we'd never broken it. Not once.

I didn't even ask the question. At this point, I didn't have to. I simply stared at her. Waiting. Feeling guiltier with each passing second.

Finally, when it could go on no longer, she bowed her head with a quiet sigh. "Sweetheart, I don't like it any more than you, but there are rules in place for a reason—"

"I've got some homework to do," I interrupted.

I didn't need to hear the speech again. In fact, I thought I might scream if I did. A look of dismay clouded her bright face, and my chest tightened with a wave of guilt. No need for her to feel terrible. It wasn't her fault. It wasn't anybody's fault. It was just the way it was.

That was the problem.

"It's fine, Mom. Really." I backed up the remaining stairs, shrugging as if it couldn't matter less. "Don't even know why I brought it up."

Before she could say anything I disappeared into my room, silently wedging a chair against the door before walking straight across the floor and pulling open the window. I was lucky. My room faced the forest, and every evening I was graced with a magnificent view of the setting sun.

The colors filled my eyes. Shimmering whites, scorched crimsons, and fiery golds, all of them melting together to crowd away the blue. I forced myself to stare directly at it, standing there until my eyes watered and burned. Then I leapt into the frame of the window and swung myself up onto the roof.

It was just as good as my tree. A place of sanctuary. One I came to almost every day to stare off into space.

Thinking. Dreaming. Wishing. Pretending I was somewhere far away.

Far from the tender, yet suffocating, embrace of home. Somewhere I could make my own memories. Write my own stories. Live my own life.

The sounds of Jamie and Caleb laughing in the backyard drifted up through the air. They were soon mixed with the soft hum of voices as my mother and Sarah made dinner in the kitchen. Every minute or so, there was the occasional flutter of paper as my father sat inside. Still pretending to read.

Just as it was yesterday. Just as it would be tomorrow.

I lay back against the cold stone and closed my eyes. Took deep breaths to slow my pounding pulse. Then took quick ones to speed it back up again.

The air around me chilled dramatically as the sun finally slipped beneath the horizon. Lights came on in the house below, and it wasn't long until I was called in for dinner. I answered robotically and pulled myself up with a silent sigh, casting one last look at the shadowed sky before going inside.

* * *

I awoke in darkness. Unable to move. Unable to see.

The air was hot. Much too hot for comfort. And thick. Scented heavily with earth. My damp hair stuck to my shoulders as I twisted and writhed in the darkness—trying desperately to find the light, trying desperately to breathe.

"Hello?!" I cried, the words landing flat just inches from me. "Hello, is anyone there?!"

It took me a second to realize my wrists were tied together. A wave of panic swept through me as I desperately tried to yank them apart—thrashing about in the tiny space. Nothing. The knots held firm.

What the hell's going on?! Where the...Where am I?!

"ANYBODY—PLEASE!" My body shook and trembled as tears and sweat poured down my face. "HELP!"

The second I thought the word, I was falling.

The wind beat around my ears, silencing my panicked scream as I plummeted through the air, grasping helplessly for anything that could save me.

Before I could get my bearings, I crashed onto the ground.

Pain above pain. It felt like every bone in my body had broken. Shattered into a million pieces. And yet, somehow, I was able to stand.

I pulled myself up with a shiver, suddenly longing for the heat. The world around me grew abruptly colder as I gazed around with wide, frightened eyes.

It looked like a beach of some kind. Miles of sand stretched out before and behind me, as far as the eye could see. It danced and hissed around my bare feet, sloping up into a forest on one side, then down into a bank on the other. And yet, there was something very important missing from the picture.

The ocean.

"Hello?" I asked again. Quieter this time. Almost a whisper. "Anybody?"

A deafening silence rang back at me. Seeping down into my very bones. I tried to take a step, but something wasn't letting me. It was like I'd been frozen to the spot. Waiting breathlessly for whatever was coming next.

Be careful what you wish for...

My eyes widened as the icy sky began to darken, blackening with violent clouds in a matter of seconds. An inhuman cry exploded from the heavens as the ground started to heave and quake. It was as if the earth was being ripped in two. The air split apart with lightning and thunder, as the very earth beneath my feet shook to the core.

I fell to my knees. Unable to keep my balance.

"Help! Somebody!"

My hands clapped over my ears, bleeding with the noise.

"JAMIE!"

I sat up with a gasp, staring at the walls of my bedroom. The lights were dim and the house was quiet. Resting in peaceful sleep. My eyes slowly adjusted as I tried to reconcile what I'd just seen with what I saw in front of me now. The slumbering night with the screaming apocalypse.

Just a dream, Becka. It's just a dream.

If only I could make myself believe that.

I was out of bed the next second, my feet skimming noiselessly over the hardwood floors as I darted out of my room, and into the room next door.

Jamie!

At this point, I didn't know if I said it aloud or in my head. Either way, I knew it would reach him. Royal legacy and eternal life weren't the only things that we'd inherited from our parents. We had our own kind of magic as well.

"Jamie!"

He leapt out of bed with a gasp, wide-eyed and shivering. His golden hair was dripping down the sides of his neck, and the front of his shirt was damp with sweat. His skin was deathly pale.

It took a second for him to get his bearings and realize I was there, but the instant he did he reached for me. I was in his arms the next second.

"What the hell was that?" he whispered, just as shaken as me.

I closed my eyes and pressed my face into his chest. Shaking my head back and forth as if I could somehow force the horrifying images away. "I don't know." A wave of chills swept through my entire body, followed by a quiet sob. "I have no idea."

But I had a terrible feeling we were going to find out...

Chapter 3

The first time Jamie and I realized we were telepathic, I'd woken from a bad dream. Well, kind of. I'd woken but the nightmare kept going, playing out before my very eyes. I'd been terrified, automatically racing down the hall to wake my twin. The nightmare followed me. It was only then I realized that I wasn't the one dreaming. My brother was.

That was the day Jamie and I decided to move our rooms closer together.

"I just don't understand. What *was* that?! We've had some funky dreams, but that...that was not normal!" The sun had risen and I was perched in the center of Jamie's bed, asking him the same question I'd been anxiously looping the last three hours.

After what we'd seen, neither of us had been able to fall asleep. We'd stuck close together, sitting arm in arm as we stared out into the dark. Horrified the dream might return. It didn't, thank goodness.

But now that the shock of the image had faded, replaced with reassuring sunlight and a rambling sister, Jamie looked as though he'd rather be left alone. "For the last time—*I don't know*!"

He was pacing back and forth in front of the bed, manically running his fingers through his hair. It was a nervous habit, and by now he'd done it so many times that the hair was beginning to take on a life of its own.

"We could ask Caleb," I said tentatively.

Jamie paused for a second, considering, before the pacing began anew. "And tell him what? That we happened to have the same bad dream?" A flicker of fear flashed across his face, but he pushed it away. "They think we're crazy enough, Becka. I don't want to add this to it."

The truth was, I didn't either.

Caleb loved us, but he was fascinated by us all at the same time. By our uniqueness. By our potential. Sometimes, that fascination seemed to crowd out some of the love. Like we were some experiment. There were odd times when I wondered if that was how Caleb had found Sarah. She'd taken our dad and his twin sister under her wing. Had Caleb been fascinated with them as well?

"You're right," I said softly, staring down the blanket. "I just thought...I don't know. I'm just scared. I've never felt something like that before. It feel real. Like it was happening. Like it wasn't a dream."

The pacing stopped and Jamie perched beside me on the bed.

To say we were close was a cosmic understatement. We were two sides of a coin. Two halves of the same heart. Eternally bonded in devotion and trust.

His blue eyes searched mine, not a shred of secrecy or shame in them. "I've never felt anything like it either. It was terrifying. I couldn't breathe, couldn't move. All I could do was stand there and..."

Our eyes locked together, reflecting one another's fear.

"...and watch the world come crashing down," I finished.

For a while, all was quiet. We sat in the center of the bed, legs folded beneath us like children, trying to figure out what to do. Then, just as Jamie opened his mouth to say something, a sudden noise broke the silence.

We turned our heads at the same time, listening as our parents woke at the other end of the hall. First came the deep voice of our father, followed by the higher laughter of our mother. A moment later, Caleb and Sarah started stirring as well in their room downstairs.

"Listen," Jamie said suddenly, talking in a quick undertone, "it was just a dream. No need to freak out about it." Our mother laughed again and he stopped using words, worried about being overheard. *Odds are, only one of us was dreaming it anyway,* he continued telepathically. *Just like last time. The other one just tuned in at the wrong time, and we both got stuck.*

It was certainly possible. Probable, even. And as it stood, I could think of no other explanation. I nodded quickly, getting to my feet.

So we just...forget about it? I asked. *Keep it to ourselves?*

Caleb's booming voice echoed downstairs, filtering up through the stone. We glanced down of one accord, then back up at each other.

"Yeah," Jamie replied softly. "We keep it to ourselves."

I nodded again, more firmly this time, then headed to my own room to get dressed for breakfast.

Weekends at the castle were a family affair. Shared meals, group activities, and most all the time in between was spent together. For a while we even started watching a movie together every Saturday night, until Caleb declared that the generational gap was too great, and refused to watch anything filmed after 1950.

It was a transformation that flat-out shocked my father when we first moved back from the ocean. Apparently, when he was growing up, 'family time' had been mostly war room strategy sessions. The first time he walked in to see Caleb flipping pancakes, he'd actually sent a picture to my aunt on his phone.

It was a 'widening of the inner circle' that Jamie and I flat-out fell in love with from the first time it happened. After years of being kept strictly isolated from everyone, save for our angel aunt and werewolf uncle, moving into the grandparents' mansion was a dream come true. And if those grandparents ceased to be bloodthirsty warriors and happened to melt into proud little puddles every time they saw us, so much the better.

But days like today—days when Jamie and I had a secret we would much rather have been discussing—the group dynamic got a little oppressive. Little being used very lightly here.

"Good morning," I said with false cheer, giving Caleb a swift kiss on the cheek as I breezed into the kitchen. The man loved Jamie like he'd personally created him, but there was a special place in his heart for me. For the youngest girl in his illustrious household. "Waffles? Delicious!"

Caleb set down the spatula long enough to give me a one-armed hug that lifted me off my feet before returning to his culinary mission. "Blueberries or raspberries today?"

I couldn't help but smile. The infamous Hunter was wearing an apron. "Surprise me."

A pair of light footfalls echoed down the stairs, and the two of us glanced over as Jamie swept into the room. He was showered and dressed, but no matter how put together he tried to make himself appear there was an unmistakable aura of guilt around him. I shot him a scathing glare from the corner of my eye, a warning to keep it together.

Who was I fooling? Jamie had always been a bad liar.

"Morning," Caleb greeted him automatically. "You look sharp."

Jamie froze in the doorway, glancing down at his clothes, then paled and glanced back up, dodging exasperated looks from me the whole time. "Uh...thanks."

Luckily, Caleb didn't notice anything out of the ordinary. Or if he did, he didn't mention it. He was too focused on the task at hand. "Do you have a waffle preference? We've got raspberries or blueberries."

"Same as you," Jamie answered automatically.

I snorted under my breath, settling down at the table with a mug of coffee. Jamie might not be aware, but that *same as you* mentality was starting to cause little sparks of tension in the house. Michael already worried that we spent a bit too much time under Caleb's influence. It wasn't because it was Caleb so much as it was that Caleb was the ultimate patriarch. The Chief Elder of the Higher Coven. In short, he was a man used to being in charge.

Except...Michael was our father. A leader in his own right. And the head of *our* family. No decision was too tough. No detail was too small. No passing thought was too random that he didn't want to hear about it personally. It was a role he wouldn't relinquish to anyone, at any time, for any reason.

It was a tricky group dynamic that was bound to cause at least a little bit of trouble, no matter how well everyone got along. The fact that Jamie had recently grown his hair to the same length as his grandfather's didn't help.

"Something smells good." Rouge swept into the kitchen along with Sarah, pouring two mugs of coffee before joining us at the table. "Waffles?"

"Waffles," Caleb answered. I noticed he didn't give her a choice.

My father came down shortly after, and together the six of us settled around the table to eat. Just like every other Saturday morning.

It was amazing how normal everything felt. Pass the syrup. Is there more cream for the coffee? Elbows off the table. We were all going through our usual lines, acting like the world hadn't been shaken to its very core. Acting like the sky hadn't just ripped apart before our very eyes.

But two of us knew better. Two of us were pretending.

This is never going to work. You and I both know that wasn't a dream.

Jamie's fork paused halfway to his mouth, but he recovered almost instantaneously. We had gotten very good at this silent communication over the years. It was rare that someone would catch us.

Eat your waffles, Becka. We'll talk about it later.

I took an exaggerated bite, and set down my fork with a loud clatter. In the whirl of conversation going on around us, no one else noticed. *We've got to tell someone. We could do it right now. Everyone's here.*

This time, a hint of frustration flashed through his eyes. *Tell them WHAT? We've already been through this. Conversation closed.*

Our eyes locked across the table, and mine narrowed into a glare. *Well, I'm reopening it! Do you know how angry Caleb would be if he ever found out that we didn't—*

"Sarah," he interrupted me out loud, ending our telepathic little talk whether I wanted to or not. "Did you want me to help plant those tulips today?"

My grandmother swept her blonde hair off her shoulders, her face melting into a warm smile. "That would be lovely, Jamie. Thank you."

That's right, I hissed in my mind. *You're just so lovely, Jamie.*

"What about you, Becka?" I looked up to see my mother staring at me expectantly. "Are you going to help your brother and grandmother in the garden? Could be fun. Get your...your mind off things."

Does she know? Realization hit me a second later. My history project. She was talking about my not-so-secret frustration over the house rules from yesterday. But Jamie didn't know that. This time, he didn't even attempt to hide his anger. He set down his coffee mug with a loud clatter and glared openly at me from across the table.

"What things, Bex?" he demanded, far too sharply to avoid raising suspicion. "What *things* is Mom talking about?"

Before I could even answer, he followed it up a telepathic reprimand.

You told her already. You little traitor! Why did you even talk to me about it if you'd already made up your damn mind?!

"I didn't!" I blurted aloud. The grownups sitting around the table shot me a strange look and I realized I'd answered his silent question, not the one he'd spoken aloud. Jamie's eyes snapped shut in a painful grimace, as I hurried to correct my mistake. "I mean...I didn't have any things. Just...uh...school stuff."

My sister is an unbelievable idiot.

"Is this the homework you mentioned yesterday afternoon?" Caleb asked with concern. "Is there something I can help you with?"

I can't even believe we're related.

I did my best to back-pedal, interrupted constantly by Jamie's silent critiques. "No. But, thank you. I think...I think I've got it under control."

I'm seriously considering strangling you in your sleep. That'll give you something to dream about—

A sudden knock at the door made us both jump.

It was a rare thing that we'd have an unexpected visitor. Usually, we could hear a car coming from the second it turned up the drive. Both Caleb and our mother gave Jamie and me another strange look, trying to understand what was going on between us. My father pushed to his feet to answer it. A second later, a flood of familiar smells washed into the house.

"Aunt Grace! Uncle Rob!"

Jamie and I leapt to our feet of one accord, racing down the hall to literally jump on our aunt and uncle the second they stepped through the front door. They caught us with open arms, laughing cheerfully as we embraced before pulling back to look us up and down.

"Now THAT is what I call a WELCOME!" Grace exclaimed, smoothing down my hair and making me do a twirl so she could see my dress. "Very pretty...and I see you're wearing those stockings I sent you!"

Jamie's welcome was a bit more manly than all that.

"'Sup, cub?" Rob ruffled his golden hair, taking great pleasure in the way that Michael bristled at the term 'cub.'

Dad had never quite gotten on board with Rob's wolfish pet names for the two of us. They hit a little too close to home. He was trained to hate werewolves.

"Look at that hair!" Rob continued, grabbing a fistful of it as Jamie laughed and ducked away. "It's down to your chin!"

"I think it's perfect!" Grace interjected, elbowing her husband out of the way to hug her nephew. "Very new-age pirate. I actually have this new styling product I've been aching to try—"

"That's okay," Jamie backed away with a little grin, sweeping it up into a quick ponytail. "I think I'll leave it alone for the time being."

"Stop trying to turn my kid into a doll," Michael commanded, scooping up his sister in a huge, ungainly hug. "You've already claimed my other one."

Grace stuck out her tongue but skipped towards the kitchen with a wide grin, taking Jamie and me along with her.

"Gracie!" Sarah jumped to her feet as we rejoined them in the kitchen, pulling her surrogate daughter in for a warm embrace. My mother quickly followed suit. "You're just in time for breakfast! Your father made waffles."

"Yeah," Grace grinned, shooting my mother a secret wink, "because the world's turned upside-down."

"I'll have none of that," Caleb said firmly, but he gave his daughter a hug before making her up a plate. "But it's good to see you, Grace. Robert."

Robert.

My poor uncle got the same treatment as my mom. Civil, but never quite friendly. Formal names. Not that Rob seemed to mind. He was too thrilled to see Caleb bustling around the kitchen to notice much else.

The eight of us sat down again, pulling up two more chairs for the newcomers. We went through all the usual conversational catch-up as we ate our way through a table of processed sugar. By the time we were finished, the coffee pot had been drained and re-filled at least five times.

"That was incredible." Rob sat back in his chair, having eaten at least twelve waffles. "Exactly the reason we came."

Sarah laughed, while Michael leaned forward curiously. "What brings you guys here anyway? You didn't even call."

Grace shrugged casually, tracing shapes into the syrupy surface of her plate with the tip of her finger. "There's weird weather at the beach today. We figured now was as good a time as any for an impromptu visit."

The rest of the table let that go without a second thought, but my head snapped up in alarm.

"Weird weather?" I asked, the picture of innocence. "What do you mean?"

Jamie shot me a sharp look, but I kept my eyes fixed on Grace. She merely shrugged again, while Rob took a sip from his coffee.

"Storm's coming. That's all."

"*Really.*" Jamie snorted.

I leaned back in my chair, shooting him a pointed look. A look that was just as pointedly ignored.

Could you be more obvious? he demanded. *Cut it out!*

But I had no intention of cutting it out. As the conversations picked back up around us, I cocked my head to the side with a withering glare.

A STORM, Jamie. They left the ocean today, because there's was a huge STORM coming. Now why does that sound familiar...?

His lovely eyes narrowed as he clenched his jaw. *You honestly think that an end-of-the-world apocalypse is barreling towards us just because our aunt and uncle said there was some bad weather at the beach? Get a grip, Rebekah!*

My mouth fell open, and I kicked his chair. *Do NOT make me sound like the crazy one here! I'm not the one who—*

"No telepathy at the table."

The two of us looked up guiltily to see our father staring at us from across the table. There was never any fooling him. Or Aunt Grace. As twin telepaths themselves, they knew every trick in the book. They'd used them all.

"Sorry, Dad," we muttered at the same time.

"Jamie started it," I added for good measure.

My twin shot me a death look, but Grace wrapped her arm around my shoulders with a twinkling smile. "Oh, come on, Michael. Even your *perfect* children are entitled to have a secret or two." She nudged me with a conspiratorial wink. "And girls are entitled to more than that."

Caleb looked highly affronted by the entire notion. "Secrets?" he scoffed. "What secrets would these two possibly have?"

My throat tightened and Jamie looked up sharply, but the adults had already moved on to other things. Only my mother remained, staring between us with a slight frown on her face. It wasn't until the conversation got lively that a sudden word jumped out at me and Jamie at the same time.

"A Hunt?" he interjected suddenly, staring from person to person. "Did you say that you and Seth were going out on a Hunt?"

"Yeah, did you?" I interjected quickly. "When's that happening?"

Michael and Rob chuckled softly as Caleb gave both of his grandchildren an indulgent smile. "You heard correctly. There's going to be a Hunt."

The heavens opened, smiling down on our graveyard of weekend waffles.

A Hunt was just about the only thing left in the world that remained of the old days. The days when heroes fought for their lives. When new destinies were carved out, and legends were born.

The peace my parents had made between the Hunters and the Grollics was generally accepted by the bulk of the supernatural community. The eternal war had chipped away at all of them, piece by piece, and the fact that the leader of the wolves had recently married the daughter of the leader of the angels helped things along quite a bit. So much so that my theatrical Aunt Grace often said that she alone was responsible for brokering world-wide peace.

But not everyone was so accommodating. There were factions of rebels and dissenters—factions on both sides—who opposed the peace. Who upheld the ridiculous notion that one race was better than the other, and neither could stop until the other was wiped out altogether.

My Uncle Seth—along with the rest of my family—stood against these rebels. Whenever a faction was located, they would organize a formal Hunt to track them down and silence them once and for all. One by one, ridding the world of whosoever dared to threatened that sacred peace.

That was the official reason they always gave. The 'keeping the peace' reason. But it didn't take a genius to see that wolves liked to kill. Hunters liked to hunt. You couldn't suppress the warrior instinct entirely, not with waffles and family movie night. If a rebel band wasn't located within a certain number of weeks they would often come together anyway to set out on a cold trail, just aching for a good fight.

"Can we go?" I asked instantly, staring around the table with pleading eyes. "Please? Can we please go?"

My father shot Caleb an uneasy look as my mother pursed her lips.

"You already basically said we could," Jamie interjected swiftly, sensing a coming rejection. "You said we could Hunt when we were eighteen. That's in just a few days."

Sarah stared between us, children she would rather trap safely in the tulip beds than allow to set foot on a battlefield. "Yes, and odds are you and your sister are going to be eighteen for a very long time. I'm sure at some point or another, you'll go on a Hunt."

My mouth fell open in dismay as Jamie pushed back his chair.

"That's not fair!" he cried. "You can't use the eternal eighteen card!" She opened her mouth to argue, and he turned to Caleb instead. "Please? You told us we could go. Don't go back on it now."

"Seriously, Caleb," I whined. "You know we're old enough to go."

"I know no such thing," Caleb said stiffly. His recent transformation from 'warrior-king' into 'grandfather' made conversations like this tricky. Back in the day, he would have sent Michael to the ends of the earth hunting some unknown evil. But his grandchildren...it wasn't the same thing. "Besides, I thought you two had homework."

Who the hell cares?

Jamie snorted into his coffee. I must have accidently said it to him, instead of just thinking it to myself. "Sorry," he apologized, wiping up the spill. "It's really hot."

It was an impasse. Kids against adults. Most of whom looked almost exactly the same age. A impasse that wasn't going anywhere anytime soon.

Grace and Sarah were avoiding looking at anyone, Caleb was hoping everyone would stop looking at him, Michael was furious that when his children wanted something they turned to their grandfather instead, and Rouge was still staring between us with that worried little frown.

Finally, it was my Uncle Rob who broke the tension.

"Ease up, kid." He casually clapped Jamie on the shoulder, disrupting his accusatory glare. "There are plenty of Hunts and we need plenty of warriors to join us. But whether or not you're old enough isn't the question." His eyes sparkled a playful challenge as he looked us up and down. "Who says you've got what it takes?"

We were out the door the next second, bounding after him as he raced across the forested yard. Halfway through he leapt high into the air, twisting and turning in the golden sunlight. What dropped back to the ground wasn't a man...it was a giant menacing wolf.

Jamie and I didn't stop to think.

We shifted right after him.

It was freedom. Pure freedom. No better way to describe it. I threw back my head with a euphoric howl and stretched out my legs as fast as they would go, nipping playfully at my brother as we chased our uncle through the grass.

The first time the shift had happened, it caught me completely off guard. I was out with my dad, bringing in bags of groceries from the car. I remember the feeling exactly. The way my body simultaneously froze and lifted, tearing itself apart and reforming into the wolf. I remember the way the ground felt strange yet oddly natural under my paws. I remember my shock and delight when I realized I was walking on four legs instead of two.

But even shifting couldn't be normal. Not for Jamie and me. As usual, the fates had another plan in mind.

Instead of changing into a regular Grollic, the magic in our blood took hold and we became something different, something sleeker.

A pure white wolf—fur as blinding as freshly fallen snow, and the sparkling blue eyes of the angel. Nothing like the fearsome beast my uncle changed into.

I remember my father dropped everything in his hands with a shout. It must have been terrifying—to see your daughter replaced suddenly with a wild dog—but he'd grown up with stranger things. Without a second's pause, he grabbed onto me with one hand and whipped out his phone with the other. My Uncle Rob showed up just ten minutes later, slowly and calmly talking me through how to change back. Aunt Grace had come with him and had the good sense to bring a robe for me to put on as well, as all my clothes had vanished. She always thought of things like that.

When Jamie changed, just a week later, he had a far better idea of what to expect. And, just like usual, or maybe unusual, he looked exactly like me.

I remember thinking that Caleb would be disgusted with me.

There was always the slightest bit of animosity between him and Rob, and I thought that would carry over into our own relationship. He was the angel side, after all. And while peace might currently prevail, the enemy had always been the Grollic.

I was so scared to face him, I ended up dodging his calls for the better part of a week. Long enough that he finally drove out to the beach house to see me. My whole body was trembling with abject fear, but the first time Caleb asked me to change his eyes lit up in wonder. I was not the beast he'd been trained to kill. I was something different.

Something better.

Coincidentally, it wasn't long after I changed that my parents finally agreed to move the family back to Port Q. I overheard the entire whispered argument, huddling with Jamie on the stairs.

"But we don't KNOW what they're going to be," my mother hissed under her breath. "We're in uncharted waters here. They need a little time—"

"That's exactly the point," my father countered. "Uncharted waters. They need to be closer to Caleb. He can help. You know he can."

Becka!

My mind snapped back to the present as Jamie streaked past me, leaping high over a fallen tree before tumbling back to the earth.

Go to the left, I'll circle round to the right. We'll get him in the middle...

He trailed off as I bolted in a completely different direction, eyes on the horizon, a surge of adrenaline pumping through my blood.

Bex!

But I didn't want to play his war games. I didn't want to prove myself to a teasing uncle who already knew I was more than up to the task. I wanted nothing more than to run. To run as far and fast as my legs could take me.

No regrets. No going back.

I made it as far as the peak of the mountain, then stopped a second to catch my breath. The world looked different through the eyes of a wolf. Full of adventure. Full of potential. I raised up on my hind legs and sent another gleeful howl ringing up through the trees. It was soon echoed by my brother. Then my uncle. Both coming out to meet me.

A wolfish smile spread up the sides of my face as I danced in place, waiting for them. Jamie was fast as lightning, but there was a chance I was a bit faster. I was just seizing upon the idea of challenging him to a race, when a sudden rustling in the trees caught my attention.

I leapt around in a second, cocking my head to the side as I stared curiously into the underbrush. It had been so soft there was a good chance I had imagine the whole thing. But I could have sworn I heard the sound of quiet breathing. Felt someone's eyes on me in the trees.

I was about to go investigate, when there was another howl. Much closer this time. I turned my head as my brother's voice called out through the woods.

Bex, time to head back! Caleb's calling.

I stared into the bushes for another moment, unable to shake the feeling that someone was staring back. Then I shook out my white fur and sprang back in the other direction.

Running as fast as I was able. Running all the way home.

Chapter 4

The remainder of the weekend passed too quickly, as it always did. I often wished the weekdays were the length of the weekend and vice versa. The best part was that Rob and Grace, in a transparent effort to witness Caleb's descent into domesticity, decided to prolong their visit for an undetermined amount of time, and Jamie and I spent every waking moment basking in their presence. When your world only consists of about eight people, you tend to latch on hard. And if those people are destined to spend the rest of eternity walking the earth at your side...?

Yeah, you could say we were close.

Homework got done in a hasty, procrastinated heap on Sunday night under the ever-watchful eyes of my father. It wasn't that school was hard, I just didn't want to be there. Neither did Jamie.

A late night of fighting and combat in the backyard around the pool house, that looked more like a cottage, left us happily exhausted and thankfully with dreamless sleep. However, Jamie and I had a hard time getting out of bed the next morning, and we were almost late to school.

I rushed through the door to my first period class, sliding a bit on the wet tile. An unexpected rainstorm had soaked the town, and the entire class—including me—got drenched with it. Colors were sharpened and smells intensified. I guess that was the wolf in me. They hit me like a wave the second I stepped inside the classroom. I held my breath a second and forced myself to relax.

It was enough to be almost overpowering, but I had long since accustomed myself to each individual scent.

Sure enough, they were all there. Ready and waiting as usual.

With one noticeable exception.

My eyes flashed up in surprise as a new scent tickled my nose. It was unlike anything I'd ever smelled before. Something that didn't seem to belong in the common-place classroom. A mixture of sugar, pine, sandalwood...and something else I couldn't quite put my finger on.

I paused at the front of the room, and looked around slowly to locate the source of the scent. My gaze drifted over the class, over the horde of faceless people I saw almost every day, before coming to rest on a boy.

Correction: the word *boy* didn't seem appropriate, even though every student in the class had yet to reach eighteen. This guy...he was clearly a man. It was written all over him.

Despite the fact that everyone's desks had been pushed into neat little lines, he was still somehow managing to sit a bit away from the rest of the class. Angled off to the side, in the far corner of the room. A look of preemptive boredom shadowed across his handsome face as he traced imaginary lines into the desk with the tip of his pencil.

I felt a breath escape my mouth and knew it was hanging open. He was hot. Incredibly hot.

For a second, all I could do was stare.

Growing up in the supernatural world I knew, I'd come to expect a certain base-line level of beauty. A standard that no one in this entire town could ever hope to achieve.

But this guy...this guy surpassed it all.

The way his dark hair fell gracefully over his eyes. The way he looked agile and strong, even in stillness. The way—even though he was looking down—the light still somehow managed to sparkle in his blue eyes.

However, the strangest thing about him by far wasn't his impossible looks, or his isolation, or his delicious smell, or even the fact that I had no idea why the hell he was sitting in my English class. It was something else.

He happened to be the only person in the room *not* staring at me.

That's got to be a first.

A throat cleared softly behind me, and I whipped around to see Ms. Hall, my teacher, looking at me with a sympathetic smile. "Are you going to sit down, Rebekah?" she asked quietly. "Or would you rather stay up here and teach the class?"

A delicate pink blushed the tops of my cheekbones as I ducked my head with a murmured apology, and headed to my seat in the back of the room. It was on the opposite side as the mystery guy, which was probably for the best. He had already started to attract all kinds of unwanted attention.

"Holy crap! How is this even happening right now?!" The whisper, quiet as it was, caught my attention, and I turned slightly to see Briana and the rest of her fellow cheerleaders scrambling in their purses for a compact to check their reflections. The lip gloss and hair crimping was soon to follow. Along with those 'ever so discreet' glances over their shoulders.

You have to be kidding me... A ghost of a smile flickered across my face as I turned my eyes back to the front, feeling quietly embarrassed for the entire female race. It was like something out of a bad movie. Something so transparent, I had no idea how they thought the guy wouldn't notice.

Except, as I glanced discreetly over, he *didn't* notice.

He kept his eyes fixed on the whiteboard, effectively tuning out the pack of ravenous women just a few seats away. It went on so long, I assumed the poor guy had to have had years of practice doing the exact same thing. Nothing could penetrate the wall. In fact, the only time he broke eye-contact with the board was the exact moment I happened to smile.

The two of us locked eyes for a split-second. A second that seemed to go on a lot longer than a second is supposed to. Then we quickly looked away. Well, I know I did. I assume he broke contact at the same moment.

For one of the first times, English—one of my favorite subjects—seemed to drag its feet through the rest of the hour. The air in the little room was too hot, almost suffocating. The smells and colors that I usually could control seemed too much. A wave of inexplicable nerves pricked at the bottoms of my feet. By the time the bell finally rang, I couldn't get out of there fast enough.

I threw my bag over my shoulder, and was gone before the rest of the people around me had even gotten to their feet. Before the boy sitting in the back of class had a chance to glance my way again.

Little did I know, handsome stranger was going to be in my next three classes as well.

Port Q High School was impossibly small, but even if it wasn't I still would've been able to find the person I needed with relative ease. *My brother.* It was raining, so he wasn't at our usual spot on the benches outside. Instead I made my way to the cafeteria, needing only a second to spot his head of golden hair.

Lovely as he was, Jamie was sitting by himself. The rest of the student population had long ago given up trying to make friends. Whenever they did, they inexplicably turned into stuttering, incoherent idiots. At this point, it was best to admire from a distance. Try to salvage whatever was left of their pride.

Hey, I spoke telepathically, sitting down beside him without a tray, *what do you say about ditching the rest of the day? Heading up into the woods?*

Jamie stared at me, but his face didn't give away what he was thinking. So I pressed on.

Dad'll flip out if the school decides to call. I'm sure we can forge a note for the office. Come on, let's get out of here.

He lifted his head to look at me, then glanced around with a rather amused smile. "Hello, Rebekah. How were your morning classes?"

A reminder that we were constantly being watched. And that it looked pretty strange if the two of us sat for the entire lunch hour without talking.

My face melted into a sweet smile, playing the game as well. "They were wonderful." *They were terrible.* "Reading through Yates was like doing it for the first time." *Instead of the five million times I've been through it before.* "I think you should seriously consider my offer."

I echoed each spoken thought with a telepathic one. Watching the corners of Jamie's mouth twitch up as he followed along with both. When I was finished, he took a fruit cup off his tray and rolled it my way. I always forgot to grab something for myself. He always remembered.

Why do you want to ditch so bad? he asked, eyebrow raised. *Just bored?*

I pulled the lid off the cup with a quiet sigh, trying to suppress the wave of inexplicable anxiety that had been plaguing me since first period. *Bored...and there's a new guy in my class who's making your darling fan club fall to pieces every hour of the day. It's getting embarrassing to watch.*

Jamie lifted his eyes, staring at me with a look of mock seriousness. *Did you tell him they're MY fan club?*

I snorted and tossed a strawberry his way. *I know, right? Loyalty doesn't count for anything around here.*

He laughed quietly before his eyes grew abruptly thoughtful. *There's a new girl in my classes as well. Beautiful. Seems...kinda lonely.*

I looked up in genuine surprise. I'd never heard Jamie call anyone beautiful in his entire life. And the lonely assessment caught me off guard, too. *Oh reeeeeally...?* Even in my head I was able to stress the word in a way that implied everything I wanted to, bringing a rueful grin to Jamie's lips.

He rolled his eyes and popped open his soda, while I tossed another berry his way. He caught it in his mouth.

Careful, I warned with a grin. *Dad'll say you're going wolf again. He'll make Uncle Rob go back to the beach.*

The two of us laughed softly, then proceeded to eat our lunch in relative silence. Actual silence, and telepathic silence as well.

My head felt like it was swimming with a mess of different thoughts and emotions, but none so specific that I was able to make out any particular thing. Instead, I just let them wash over me in a wave. Munching absently on my fruit cup, and watching as the clock inched closer and closer to the end of the day.

"So we stay?" Jamie asked with a hint of teasing and boredom in his voice.

"Yeah, I guess so. It's raining anyway." *And you stink like wet dog when you shift. For days.*

Me? Jamie's eyes narrowed as he gave me a serious look. *You should be careful. There's a funky smell coming off you that's...how should I say...putrid? I've just always been polite and not told you.*

The twitching of the corners of his mouth was the only thing that gave him away. I grabbed my tray and headed for the garbage bins to dump the fruit cup. I snuck a sniff at my armpit...just to make sure he was only teasing. Surely I didn't stink. I hadn't even shifted this morning. *Richard Cranium,* I muttered telepathically when I heard him snicker behind me. Dickhead.

Freedom, sweet freedom.

By the time the final bell rang, releasing us back into the world, I was ready to run the whole way home. The monotony had become tedious to an absurd degree, punctuated every now and then with startling recognition as

I would catch a whiff of the delightful new scent. I didn't want to smell the new boy. And yet, I couldn't stop trying to inhale his scent. I refused to look his way in the halls or any classes.

It was *exhausting*!

I hurriedly packed my bag and rushed down the hall, ready to leave it all behind me. The double doors burst open, and I headed out onto the grass.

The rain had stopped, leaving a wet world of sunshine glistening in its wake. I paused for a second to drink it all in, pulling in a giant breath of the fresh air with unspeakable relief before heading to Jamie and the car.

"Finally," I exclaimed, tossing my bag into the back seat. "Now let's get the hell out of here..." My voice trailed off as I realized my brother wasn't looking at me. His attention was focused on something else instead. I glanced in the direction he was looking. Whoops, *someone*.

Someone who had just walked out of the history building and into the sun.

And I had to admit...she *was* beautiful.

Tumbles of gently waved brunette hair. A stylish sweep of bangs that fell over an exquisite heart-shaped face. A face that seemed entirely taken up by a pair of enormous blue eyes. She looked delicate. Fragile, even. And from the way her shoulders tightened as her eyes flashed quickly across the lawn, I saw where Jamie was coming from when he called her lonely.

But the second I thought the word, she was lonely no more. The guy who had been inadvertently haunting me all day swept out the doors just a second behind her. They locked eyes for a moment, giving each other a cursory look up and down before silently heading off towards the parking lot. My forehead creased into a thoughtful frown as I watched them.

Strange...

In a way, they reminded me very much of me and my twin. Beautiful. Set apart. Every inch of them aching to be somewhere else. Somewhere new.

"Do you think that's her boyfriend?" Jamie asked quietly.

I looked up in surprise, torn away from my thoughtful contemplation. I hadn't even considered the possibility, and now that I did I found myself oddly troubled by the notion. My spine stiffened, and I climbed into the car. "Who cares? Let's go."

This day couldn't be over fast enough, and I suddenly couldn't stand to spend another second at this stupid school.

Jamie climbed into the car as well, and revved the engine to life. It was a vintage Mustang, one that used to belong to our father, and it handled like a dream. He quickly backed out of the parking space and was about to take off through the lot, when a guy flew out of nowhere and jumped into our path.

The car's brakes slammed in a screech of protest, a testament to immortal reflexes, as the guy placed his palms on the hood. A crooked smile danced across his face, and even though he'd narrowly avoided spending the rest of his life impersonating road kill he looked rather pleased with himself.

"Who the hell is that?" I exclaimed in astonishment. I probably should have known, but mortals' faces tended to blend together in times of stress. "Dickhead."

"That's Chris Harder," Jamie muttered, glaring through the windshield as a rush of adrenaline faded slowly from his veins. "He's on the football team with me." He tapped the horn lightly, sticking his head out the window. "What the hell are you doing, man? I could've hit you."

"I know," Chris slurred, walking around to my side of the car. "I'm sorry about that. Just wanted to have a word with your sister."

Jamie lifted his eyebrows slowly as I rolled down the window. The scent of beer and burgers wafted into the car.

"Are you drunk?" I asked incredulously.

Chris grinned again, tilting his head to the side as he looked me up and down. "Had to steel my nerves somehow, didn't I?"

By now, a bit of a crowd had gathered. An encounter with one of the elusive twins was an occasion all in its own right, and the dramatic manner in which Chris had decided to take his shot made it downright sensational. Even the two newcomers paused on the far side of the lot, looking over curiously as the prom king reached into the car to take my hand.

Before I could stop him, he whipped out a sharpie and started scribbling on the inside of my palm. My lips parted uncertainly, but when he finally released me he did so with a satisfied smile.

"That's my number," he said with drunken confidence, gesturing down to the chicken scratch stained into my skin. "Give me a call sometime. I'd love to take you out." He left without another word.

My twin and I were frozen in identical states of shock. Left to a literal round of applause from the entire student body. The new students standing on the edge of the lot flashed each other a swift look of amusement as I sank an inch lower in my seat.

Jamie...

"Yeah," he said quickly, shaking himself out of it, "we're going."

The crowd parted as the Mustang eased its way through. Driving with a new sort of caution, now that Jamie knew that random men might come flying out of the woodworks to draw on his sister.

It wasn't until we'd left the school far behind and headed up the old country road that he finally acknowledged the silent glare burning into face. "Okay, you were right," he conceded as we headed up the forested lane to our house. "We should've ditched."

Chapter 5

My twin brother and I may be immortal hybrids, heirs to a royal legacy, eternally doomed to live in secret—but we were still teenagers. He was still my big brother, born about two minutes before me.

And big brothers still liked to tease.

By the time we'd rolled to a stop in the driveway, he'd decided the whole incident was beyond funny. By the time we got our bags from the back of the car, it had made his top-five moments. By the time we made it to the front porch, he was seriously considering giving Chris some sort of medal.

"You better not say anything," I hissed through my teeth, catching his hand before it could open the door. "Do you hear me? Not one word!"

"Becka." His face gentled as he took me by the shoulders and stared deep into my eyes. "You're my *sister*. My *twin*. I'm not going to give you away."

"Good." I breathed a little easier as the door opened and the two of us walked into the house. Maybe he wasn't that bad. I mean, he could have beat Chris up or something. The thought of running him over didn't seem too outlandish anymore. Jamie was a good brother. I owed him one.

But no sooner had we made it through the entryway than Jamie tilted back his head and called out in a loud echoing voice, "Becka, what's that on your hand?"

I froze like he'd dumped icy water down my spine, then listened in horror as doors began opening and closing around the house, calling our family forth.

"I will *kill* you!" I hissed between my teeth.

He jogged up the stairs with a cocky smile. "You can try." Followed by laughter, he added, "If you can catch me."

Payback's a bitch, brother. Thinking fast I ducked into the kitchen, hoping to hide safely out of sight and scrub the infernal numbers off my arm before anyone else was the wiser. Unfortunately, my grandmother happened to be standing in front of the stove. Apparently getting a head start on cooking dinner.

She glanced over her shoulder as I skidded to a stop on the tile, the razor-sharp paring knife still in her hand. For a moment, the two of us just stood there. The seasoned warrior, currently battling potatoes and carrots, and the eternal teenager with a drunk boy's phone number scribbled across her arm—which she could probably smell.

She set down the knife with a warm smile. "Had a tough day a school, honey?"

My shoulders collapsed with a sigh as I slumped down across the kitchen table. "You have no idea..."

Sarah was a good listener. Always had been. Maybe it had something to do with the fact that she used to be the commander of an elite group of Hunters. Always the first to step onto the battlefield, always the last to step off it. That cool-headed quality had seeped into her very bones. Or maybe that sort of empathic understanding was simply in her nature. She had uprooted her entire life, after all. The day she found Michael and Grace, the warrior had died and the mother had been born. And now a grandmother after that.

"What is it, sweetie?" She pushed a mug of hot chocolate towards me, settling herself on the other side with a coaxing smile. "Is it something to do with those numbers you keep trying to hide?"

I stopped trying to tug down the sleeve of my sweater with a defeated sigh. Why did I think, for even a second, that might work? "This boy at school...apparently has a crush on me," I admitted, fiddling with the mug. "He gave me his number, and Jamie thinks it's really funny. That's all." I tossed the Jamie part of the sentence toward the hallway, knowing Jamie would hear it.

Sarah lifted her eyebrows slowly, but didn't press. There was a bit more to the story that I wasn't telling. That I couldn't make sense of myself. "And you're upset that this boy gave you his number?" she asked gently, trying to understand. "Or are you just upset that Jamie saw?"

"Neither. Both." I threw up my hands with a dismissive smile. "Mostly I'm just pissed that I have to scrub this crap off my hand. And arm. The guy writes like a first-grader."

She chuckled and walked to the counter to get a wet towel. "I imagine this isn't the first boy at your school to develop feelings for you. I imagine this is probably just the first one to get up the courage to do something about it."

I caught the towel, and began attacking the marks with it. "Well, bless his little heart." The ink didn't go anywhere. It simply smeared. "And bless him all over again for using permanent marker."

"If it helps, I'm sure you'll find that marker isn't nearly as permanent as you," Sarah joked lightly, returning to her vegetables. "Just give it five or six years, I'm sure it'll fade on its own."

I paused in my rhythm long enough to shoot her a sarcastic grin. "Why, thank you. You're a pillar of wisdom, you are."

"Just keep working on it." She flashed a conspiratorial smile over her shoulder. "The last thing you're going to want is for your grandfather to see..."

It was a double-edged sword, the angel blood. On the one hand, you could hear an enemy coming a mile away. On the other hand, you could also move so silently that even your own family wouldn't know you were there.

"And what is that?"

My head snapped up; Sarah trailed off guiltily as Caleb emerged from the shadows, through the kitchen door.

"What is it that you don't want your grandfather to see?"

The room went dead quiet.

It wasn't that I had technically done anything wrong. In truth, I was nothing more than an innocent bystander who was attacked with a wayward Sharpie. But when it came to things like this, facts weren't actually that important. It was the principle of the matter.

We were not allowed to mix with the mortals. End of story.

"Rebekah, come to my office."

Just five little words, but they were enough to fill me with unspeakable dread. My face paled, my head bowed, and with a shaky little nod I got up and followed him silently out the door. On my way past, I pressed the mug of hot chocolate into Sarah's hands with a fleeting look of gratitude. It was a nice sentiment, but I wouldn't be needing it. Not anymore.

Caleb's office was in the western wing of the house. A place where Jamie and I used to play when we were younger, but had little reason to visit now.

Yes, this bloody house has wings. I wasn't kidding when I said it was a castle, I joked to myself.

The two of us didn't talk as we headed through the main foyer, and down one of the lesser-used corridors. Caleb walked a few feet out in front of me as I followed obediently in his shadow. It wasn't until our destination was within sight that I thought maybe I should have sent up a distress beacon of some kind. Shot off a flare, or scribbled some hasty note for the others to find. An *'if I'm not back in an hour, my grandfather has already disposed of my body'* note.

The second Caleb pushed open the heavy doors a rush of smells poured out to greet me. I tilted back my head without thinking, breathing them all in.

Leather, parchment, cinnamon, dust...

It was an aroma that had long ago carved out a permanent place in my heart. Recalling a thousand happy memories. A thousand images of me and Jamie as kids, scampering up into Caleb's lap and pushing aside his piles of official-looking papers. Insisting that he read us fairytales instead.

The room itself was beautiful. Antique desk. Floor-to-ceiling books. Deep red ottomans that complemented the framed pictures on the wall.

At one point it must have looked highly refined, but now there wasn't a single inch of space that didn't serve as a memorial to some piano recital, soccer game, or preschool play. Caleb and Sarah had been to them all.

"Please, have a seat."

I perched nervously on my customary ottoman as Caleb took his place beside the desk. It was something I had done a million times before, but this time was different. This time, I was completely on edge.

At the very least, Caleb was merciful about it. He didn't make me wait. "Did something happen at school today?"

I got the feeling that he already knew, that he had probably overheard the entire conversation as I'd had it with Sarah, but these kinds of questions weren't to be taken lightly in our household. Our entire existence depended on complete and total secrecy. One wrong move, one slip-up, and we'd have to leave.

"A boy in my class gave me his phone number," I answered timidly. "He wanted me to give him a call sometime. That's all." I reflexively tugged down my sleeve as the ink burned guiltily on my arm.

Caleb's eyes swept over it briefly, as if he could see through the fabric itself, before returning to gaze intently at my face. "I see," he said in a surprisingly soft voice. "And what did you tell him?"

My eyes flickered up tentatively to meet his own. A crudely done papier-mâché dolphin hung on the wall just behind him. A testament to some of Jamie's early childhood art work. "I didn't tell him anything," I said honestly. "He jumped out in front of the car and took my hand through the window. I've never said more than five words to him before. And I have no intention of changing that now."

Caleb leaned back, looking pleased. The man was like a living polygraph machine. He always knew when my brother and I were lying. But on the flip side, he could always tell when we were telling the truth. "Good, I'm very glad to hear that..." A slight frown worried his brow as he studied me closer. "...but you're not." The frown deepened considerably as he shifted uneasily in his chair. "Did you...do you have feelings for this boy?"

"What—*no*," I answered quickly. It was true, I didn't. But, strangely enough, even as I sat there the face of another boy floated briefly through my mind. My chest tightened, then deflated with a small sigh. "It's just...we're always going to be like that, aren't we? Living on the outside? Coming up with excuses as to why we can't come over, why we never call. It's always just going to be me and Jamie."

"And the rest of your family," Caleb reasoned softly, but his heart wasn't in it. He'd raised children. He knew what I meant.

We lapsed into silence as he leaned back in his tall chair, studying me in the soft light. A hundred pictures hung on the wall behind him. Pictures of my eternal family immortalized in a single moment in time.

There was one of Jamie and me as toddlers, screaming bloody murder as a wave swept away our sand castles at the beach. Sarah, looking as regal as a queen. Michael and Grace flashing bored smiles as they studied on the couch.

The artful collage was punctuated with occasional pictures of sleek white wolves, leaping through the air in various states of mischief and play.

"Can you do me a favor?" Caleb circled the desk and gathered me up into his arms. Crushing the life out of me in one of those bear hugs I'd come to secretly adore. "Can you please be a granddaughter for just a few decades longer...before you start worrying about being something else?"

I laughed, wrapping my arms around his neck as tightly as I could. He smelled very much like the room we were sitting in. He smelled like home. "A few *decades*?" I quipped.

His eyes crinkled with a warm smile. "They'll fly by, I promise."

* * *

I left the office feeling considerably better than when I'd gone in. My father and I had an excellent sparring session that night. I actually beat my Uncle Rob in a wolfish race down the mountain. And I still managed to get all my homework done in time for school the next day.

About to head out to school, Caleb called me into his office again and produced a small bottle from his desk that washed all the heavy ink off my skin without leaving a trace. Apparently, my Aunt Grace had similar propositions when she was in high school. A lot.

My luck continued through the morning, when I had the perfect opportunity to get back at Jamie on our way to the car.

Hey, wait up! He stopped me telepathically on the steps, a worried frown troubling his bright face as he jogged down to meet me. *I heard Caleb called you into his office...was that all about the phone number?*

I folded my arms across my chest with a sarcastic glare. "What do you think?"

His face paled and he lowered his voice to a low undertone. "Bex, I was only teasing. I never imagined you'd actually get in trouble for it. You didn't do anything wrong!"

"Tell that to Caleb," I replied acidly.

His face paled some more. "What'd he say?"

I paused for a second, thinking fast, before the perfect revenge came to me in a moment of wicked clarity. "He screamed at me," I said in a flat monotone, lowering my eyes to the ground. "Said I was a huge disappointment. Said I couldn't go on the Hunt."

Jamie's mouth fell open in absolute horror. "He didn't..."

I nodded mutely, my eyes filling up with theatrical tears. "He said one more slip-up like this, and they're going to pull me out of Port Q. Send me back to the beach to be homeschooled."

Jamie literally flinched, looking like someone had stabbed him with a knife. His eyes tightened painfully as a look of devastating remorse swept over him from head to toe. "Rebekah, I...I'm *so* sorry," he muttered, looking about ready to throw himself off a cliff. "I never meant to..." His golden locks fell into his face as he bowed his head in shame. "I'll talk to Caleb, I swear. Tell him exactly what happened. Tell him it wasn't your fault."

A broken sob ripped through me as I clasped my hands over my face. "What's the point?" I wailed. "It's over! He *hates* me!"

Jamie's heart shattered right there on the steps. "That's not true!" he countered passionately, pulling my hands away from my cheeks. "Bex, you know that's not true! I'm going to make this right, okay? I promise! I'll talk to him! I'll give up my place on the Hunt if I need to!"

He would? Okay...now I feel a little bad.

"It's not fair," he muttered, shaking his head. "How do they expect us to control what mortals do? We don't have any power over them. If a guy literally jumps in front of the car, how can Caleb reasonably expect...expect you to...*why are you smiling?!*"

I burst into laughter the next second, wiping the tears from my face as my brother took a step back with a look of utter disbelief. "Told you I'd get even." I skipped down the steps without a backwards glance, flipping my hair over my shoulder with a triumphant smirk. "Come on, dear brother. We don't want to be late!"

By the time I got to school, I was riding a pretty serious emotional high. Colors seemed brighter. The air was crisp and charged. I even managed to ignore the annoyingly handsome new kid in my class, keeping my eyes fixed on the whiteboard with a determined smile.

By the time I headed outside for lunch, I was feeling like I could do just about anything. The world was my oyster. The horizon was within my grasp.

And *that* was when my good mood came to a screeching halt.

"Rebekah Knightly. Can I talk to you for a minute?"

I turned around to see Mr. Barrow, my history teacher, calling to me from across the grass. Beside him stood the last person in the world I wanted to see. Bathed in sunlight. Fidgeting restlessly. Looking exactly as captivating as that first second I'd seen him in class.

Shit. Shit. Shit.

I stalled as long as I could, twisting the strap of my messenger bag over my shoulder before forcing my lips up into a tight smile. "Sure."

Rule number one: Act normal. Freak out on your own time.

I jogged lightly, and then forced myself to walk back towards the building, leaving Jamie watching curiously from our bench.

Barrow smiled warmly when I got closer before turning to introduce the guy standing by his side. "Rebekah Knightly, this is Luca Kane. He and his sister are new to this school. Just transferred in yesterday."

My eyes flickered briefly over the guy's face, trying to ignore the way my heart lifted at the word *sister*, before I nodded politely. "Nice to meet you."

He nodded stiffly in return. "Likewise."

Barrow clapped his hands together with a brisk smile. "I actually called you over because Luca doesn't have a partner yet for the history assignment. I was hoping the two of you might work together."

My face blanched as my knees locked into place. *Seriously? Of all the people in the class?*

"I'm not exactly supposed to pick favorites," Barrow dropped his voice conspiratorially, "but, Rebekah, you've been so helpful to me in my first two weeks here I was hoping you could help Luca get settled in as well."

It was a kind thing to say, but if the guy felt like he owed me a debt of gratitude couldn't he show it by *not* pairing me with the dreamboat I wasn't allowed to have a crush on instead?

"Yeah, sure." I flashed another tight smile. "Whatever you want."

The teacher's face relaxed into a gracious smile, beaming out from behind his spectacles. He was younger than most. Probably a good ten or fifteen years younger than the rest of the faculty. There was an air of worldliness about him I thought had been greatly lacking in our school system, but it was paired with a tendency to stress. I wondered how long it would take for all that brown hair of his to prematurely gray with anxiety.

"Excellent." He clapped Luca on the shoulder, inadvertently nudging the two of us closer. "In that case, I'll leave you both to it. You're already a couple of days behind, so be sure to figure out a time to work after school hours. I don't want either one of you falling behind." He left without another word, whistling happily under his breath.

It wasn't until he vanished into the faculty parking lot that Luca and I finally turned to face each other at the same time.

"So..." He flashed me a crooked smile, his blue eyes dancing in the light of the sun. "...your house or mine?"

Chapter 6

"This is a complete disaster!" I slammed the door of the car, not even waiting for Jamie to get out behind me. Not even bothering to keep my voice down even though we were back at the house, within range of a dozen immortal ears.

"I don't see why it's such a big deal." Jamie slid out of the driver's seat, tossing his bag carelessly over his shoulder. "So you got paired up with this guy on some dumb assignment. It'll be over in just a few days, Bex."

My teeth clenched together as Luca's face flashed through my mind. A face as handsome as it was *completely off limits.* "Yeah? And where exactly are we supposed to work, huh?" I fixated on a lesser problem. A logistical one. "Shall I bring him back to the house? Invite him over for family dinner?"

Jamie snorted. "Maybe Caleb will make him waffles."

"Jamie!"

"What?" He backed up the steps with a grin. "You never know. I really have no idea what you're freaking out about. It's just some random guy."

Some random guy?! Had he SEEN Luca?! I rolled my eyes with a huff, and joined him on the porch. "You'd make a terrible girl."

He glanced over his shoulder, one hand frozen on the door, and gave me just about the strangest look I'd ever seen. "Okay, I don't even know how to interpret that one..."

"Just forget it." I pushed past him, dropping my things in a pile on the tiled floor and stomping up the stairs. After my fantastic day had crashed and burned, I wasn't even going to attempt following my normal routine. I knew my father was waiting downstairs. My mother was in the kitchen. My grandfather was no doubt in his office or the backyard. I knew my aunt and uncle were probably lounging in the living room, debating what movie they wanted to watch after dinner. But, for one of the first times in my life, I couldn't care less.

I shut my door with just a *tad* bit more force than was required and leapt into the air, settling down in the center of my bed. Within seconds my earbuds were in, my music was blasting, and my eyes were closed. For good measure I pressed a pillow over my face, letting out a silent scream.

I am freaking IMMORTAL! So how am I the only person on the planet who doesn't have a life?!

Another scream. This one had a little bite to it.

Just focus on your breathing, Becka. In through the nose, out through the mouth. Rinse and repeat. Over and over.

It should have worked. It always did in the past. On those rare moments that my 'perfect' life of doing absolutely nothing crept up and caught me off guard, this breathing ritual was always enough to calm me down.

But this time, it backfired. The second my eyes were closed and my mind was clear, a certain face floated into my mind. A face so utterly mesmerizing that I realized I hadn't really stopped thinking about it since that first day.

My door opened and closed quietly behind me. Even with music blasting into my ears, I could hear it clear as day. There was a soft creak of the floorboards under careful feet before the mattress tilted beside me.

"Rebekah?"

I should have known that Caleb would be the one to come up and talk to me. Since we'd moved away from the beach house just a few short months ago, the man had captured my entire family in a loving stranglehold. One he fully intended to keep for the rest of eternity.

The earbuds came out and I slowly sat up on the bed, hugging my knees to my chest as my hair spilled down miserably around me. "Sorry," I murmured, trying to preempt any questions he might have with a deflective apology. "I'm just...not feeling that well."

A pathetic excuse. One that Caleb saw through at once, but he didn't press for more. He simply nodded, then patted me gently on the back. "How about a little sparring session. Just you and me?" he suggested gently. "Winner shaves the loser's head."

A faint smile ghosted across my face. The words sounded ridiculous coming out of Caleb's mouth, mostly because they weren't his own. He had overheard Jamie and me saying the exact same thing a few weeks ago, and had *lost his mind* before he realized we'd only been joking.

For a second, I was almost tempted. Spending time with Caleb always cheered me up, and sparring was just about the only thing in my entire life that gave me even a taste of adrenaline. And it might get my frustrations out.

But even as I sat there, the smile slowly faded and died.

"What's the point?" I stared down at my blanket, slowly unwinding a stray thread. "Why even teach me how to fight?"

Caleb was a kind man, but there were certain things about which he would never compromise. Upholding traditions was high on that list. "We must always be ready," he replied.

Words I'd heard a thousand times. I'd never questioned them until now. "Ready for what?" I mumbled, well aware that I was sounding more and more petulant, but too upset to care. "Everything has already happened."

Caleb softened, his arms opening wide. "Come here, child."

I scooted into his arms without another thought, leaning my head against his chest as all of the pent-up troubles and frustrations I'd been keeping locked down came pouring out of me all at once. "I'm sorry, it's just...sometimes I feel so OLD already. Like the entire world has already passed me by. The chapters are closed. The stories have already been written. Everyone's destiny has already been fulfilled, and Jamie and I are just sitting here, waiting for a future that's never going to come."

It was strange talking about feeling old to a man who bested me by centuries, but Caleb seemed to understand. He gazed intently into my eyes as I bowed my head, letting the words tumble out.

"And even though we don't belong to the old world, it's like we can't belong to the new one either. We can't talk to anyone. We can't make any friends, make any plans. We're just...out of place. Sidelined. *Eternally*." Never had I hated that word like I hated it in that moment. A flash of genuine anger sparked in my eyes, and I threw up my hands in despair. "And to top it all off, I'm going to fail my history class!"

It was at this point that Caleb pursed his lips with a little frown. He seemed hesitant to interrupt, but as the final lamentation echoed out between us he cocked his head to the side with a quiet question. "...you're going to fail history?"

My face screwed up as a burning tears glistened in my eyes. "No. I don't know. Probably." I took a breath to steady myself, and let it out in a shaky sigh. "We're doing this huge project. It accounts for thirty percent of our grade, and I can't even have my partner over to the house to work on it with me. Because, heaven forbid anyone finds out I'm a freak!"

Freak was a word that was banned in our household. It had been ever since I could remember. Our magic was a gift, not a curse. Our heritage was a blessing, not a burden. These were the phrases by which we lived.

"Rebekah," Caleb reasoned quietly, "you know that's not true."

The tears spilled over as I gazed up at him, feeling truly heartbroken inside. I didn't know what it was that had triggered the sudden rush of emotions. Was it the culmination of over a decade of angst? The fact that I'd recently developed my first off-limits crush? Or was it simply that I had a birthday coming in a few days...and it was going to be my last one?

"We're not aging anymore, Caleb," I whispered, unable to even look him in the eyes. "Jamie and I have been keeping track of it, checking desperately for any changes. There aren't any. We've just stopped."

We all knew it was coming.

While my twin brother and I might be a rarity amongst those already unique, our immortality was never a question. The only uncertainty was when exactly the two of us would cease to age. Sarah thought we might get to grow up as much as Caleb. My mother was secretly hoping that we weren't going to age any older than her. And whatever my father and Caleb's opinions were, they kept it to themselves.

But sure enough, the time had come. It appeared that I was destined to be eighteen years old forever. Gifted with life everlasting, yet very much alone.

"You're sure?" Caleb's eyes glittered the way they did whenever he discovered something new about me and Jamie, but he kept the emotions carefully to himself.

My chest tightened so fiercely it felt like I couldn't breathe. But all I did was flash a quick smile, shrugging as if it couldn't matter less. "Looks like this is going to be our last real birthday after all." I said the words as casually as I could, but each one cut into me like a knife. Immortality could be a beautiful thing...*if* there was a point to it. A basic direction, some kind of purpose. A reason to get up every morning.

Without that...it was nothing more than a cage.

An eternal cage.

Caleb sat quietly for a long time. Each of us staring off in opposite directions, lost in thought. Then, without any warning, he turned back to me. "Ice cream."

My head slowly lifted as I stared at him in surprise. "What?"

"Ice cream," he repeated firmly. "That's what we need here."

Without any more explanation than that, he got off the bed in one swift motion and took me by the hand. A second later, we were heading back down the stairs.

A little smile spread up the sides of my face. "Being a grandfather really has softened you," I teased quietly, weaving my arm around his chest in a one-armed hug. "You know that, right?"

"I know no such thing," he retorted stiffly, but when he glanced down he gave me a wink. "Go outside. I'll pull the car around front."

I did as I was told, digging the toe of my boot into the gravel driveway as I waited with a childish grin. No one knew how to take the reins like Caleb. And no one else knew exactly how best to cheer me up.

"Where do you think you're going?" my father called as he walked around the side of the house with a smile. Judging by the grass stains on his pants and the errant twig caught in his hair, I gathered he and Jamie had already been training. Or, more likely, he and Rob found an unsupervised moment to try to cheerfully beat each other to death. "Another walk?"

Before I could answer, Caleb's Bentley whipped around the corner with a metallic screech. The passenger door flew open, and I slid inside with a grin.

"We're going out to get ice cream," I replied, buckling my seatbelt while feeling decidedly smug. "Caleb's idea."

"Ice cream?" Michael shook his head as an astonished sparkle danced across his blue eyes. "Is that right?"

"What?" Caleb demanded, revving up the gas.

My father folded his arms across his chest with a faint grin. "Did you ever think that maybe, if you'd taken me out for ice cream every now and then, I wouldn't have rebelled against you and sided with Rouge?"

I stiffened, but Caleb merely laughed—a deep, rumbling sound that always seemed to pleasantly surprise those people who heard it. He reached down and ruffled my golden curls with an affectionate smile.

"But then we'd never have this one, would we? Or her brother."

My father and I shared a quick grin before he took a step back, patting the hood of the car. "Bring me back a cone."

"When you go through an existential crisis, then you can have a cone, Michael," Caleb answered sternly. "Not a second before."

The two shared a fleeting smile. Saving the world hadn't been enough?

Without another word we were flying down the gravel driveway, racing down the forested road at breakneck speed. Driving was the one thing that my parents had flat-out refused to let Caleb have any part of teaching us. The man was a menace. And Jamie and I were far too impressionable as it was.

It wasn't until we'd gotten on the main road that Caleb turned to me with a relaxed smile, completely ignoring the way we barreled past a logging truck who was forced to swerve onto the curb.

"So—have you decided yet?"

"Decided what?" I waved apologetically to the man in the rearview mirror. "What kind of ice cream I'm going to get?"

Caleb shot me a quick look before turning back to the road. "What day you'd like your history partner to come over."

Chapter 7

I stood in the middle of my bedroom. Still as a statue. As if my feet had been glued to the floor. I stopped breathing. Didn't blink. Simply stared across the room, my eyes burning with unspeakable intensity.

My closet stared back at me. Winning our silent war.

Why is this so impossible?

My aunt was a clinically diagnosed shopaholic, and my family had a discretionary spending budget larger than most countries. Translation? I had clothes. I actually had very nice clothes. A lot better than anyone else in this small town. And yet, I somehow couldn't find a thing in the world to wear.

Jamie! I sent up a telepathic SOS as loud as I could. *911! I repeat: 911!*

Less than a second passed and my brother was flying into my bedroom, his golden hair streaming out behind him as he skidded to a stop. "What is it?!" he gasped. "What's wrong?!"

I gestured helplessly to the closet, the contents of which had been thrown haphazardly all across the room. Even having meticulously gone through each combination, I was no closer to finding a solution.

"It's a lost cause," I croaked.

It took him a second to follow along. As close as Jamie and I were, he was still a teenage guy. And teenage guys wouldn't necessarily think to translate *911 emergency* into something having to do with clothes.

"What's a lost cause?" He glanced twice between me and the closet, growing more confused with each past. "Did you...did you get *robbed*?!"

As much as I hated to admit it, the assumption wasn't that much of a stretch. The virtual explosion of clothes left few alternatives.

"I have nothing to wear," I answered miserably, sinking onto the bed. *All evidence to the contrary.*

Jamie opened his mouth to reply, then closed it carefully as a pair of silk stockings slipped off the ceiling fan and fell onto his shoulder. "Becka, do you...*like* this guy?"

I felt all the color drain out of my face. The two of us had spent almost eighteen years together. Eighteen years in close confidence, talking about anything and everything under the sun. And yet this was uncharted territory for us. It was uncharted territory period.

Jamie's eyes burned holes into me as he stared intently. He opened his mouth, about to say something else, when I cut him off.

"No. Of course not." I turned my face away, letting my long curls spill down to hide my blushing cheeks. I just...haven't ever had a friend over." I watched him from the corner of my eye.

A legitimate excuse, but not good enough to fool my brother.

Jamie crossed his arms over his chest, suddenly looking a lot taller than he had just a few seconds ago. "He's not a friend. He's a mortal. A random student you got paired up with on a random project. Nothing more."

There was an edge to his tone, and whether or not it was intended the words stung. And sounded eerily familiar.

"Aw thanks, Caleb," I replied bitingly. "I think I know the speech by now."

Jamie flushed but stood his ground. "It's like you said: we've never been allowed to have anyone over. I know it's a first and it's exciting, but I don't want you to get your hopes up and then be disappointed. Especially not our senior year. Especially not by that guy."

My eyebrows shot into my hair, and without meaning to I stood and copied his stance. Arms folded across my chest. Shoulders defensively squared. "*That* guy?" I repeated incredulously. "And what the heck is so particularly bad about *that* guy? At least he didn't throw himself in front of our car just to try to give me his number."

Jamie clenched his jaw, but gave nothing away. "I just don't like the look of him."

Oh, really? Well, if you're going to play the obnoxiously protective older brother, then I'll play the smug and superior little sister! "Well, you certainly liked the look of his sister."

A devilish gleam flashed through my eyes as I watched the words take effect. The transformation was instantaneous. The anger melted into an eager sort of surprise. The suspicion, into lighthearted curiosity.

"His *sister*?" Jamie repeated, unable to keep a smile from creeping up the sides of his face. "I figured the two of them were dating."

"Nope." I shook my head and turned, with determination, back to my wardrobe. "Siblings."

I let him mull that over while I focused on my closet. What did one wear to a study session? Was it school-time casual? Just a shirt with jeans? Or maybe you were supposed to go a little nicer? Sundress with cute flats? Or maybe I was just overthinking this entirely and it couldn't matter less...

Jamie stood quietly behind me, not saying a word or offering any help in any way.

"What do you think about this?" I held up two shirts for Jamie's opinion, both of which would be paired with dark jeans. One was a light lavender color, sleeveless, but with an overlay of lace. The other was a deep blue, almost the exact same color of my eyes.

He glanced at both of them briefly before his girl-induced grin faded back into a brotherly scowl. He rolled his eyes, as if it couldn't matter less, and swept back towards the door muttering under his breath, "...have to teach you what *911* means..." He peeled the stocking off his shoulder and dropped it on the floor. "...doesn't involve your wardrobe..."

He had almost reached the door, when he paused suddenly and snatched something off my bed. A ghost of a smile flickered across his face before he tossed it casually into my arms. "Wear this."

The next second, he was gone.

Leaving me holding a chin-to-the-floor parka that revealed not a single inch of skin. It even had a hood.

...*Typical.*

* * *

Two hours later, I had left the closet and stood glued by the window. My room had been cleaned spotless, my piles of rejected clothes safely hidden away. I'd spent so much time in front of the mirror that even my flawless Aunt Grace would have been proud.

Strangely enough, despite all my preparation I'd kept it relatively basic. Dark jeans, a simple blouse, and just a touch of mascara to highlight my already overly-dramatic eyes. The only fanciful part of the entire ensemble was my necklace. An exquisite opal dangling from a delicate silver chain. It was breathtaking, yes, but hardly unusual. I wore it every single day.

My long golden curls were loosely swept back with a jeweled clip that allowed them to waterfall down my shoulders, and after an agonizing decision I had thrown on a pair of sparkling ballet flats right at the end.

Barefoot is too casual. Don't want to be too casual.

I'd spread my history notes in an arc across my desk, and all the related text books had been carefully stacked in the center. A cup with two pencils sat right on the other side, and just in case we needed more to work with I had pulled out a stack of empty notebooks as well.

I was ready.

Or so I thought.

The second I heard tires turning up the gravel drive my heart went into overdrive, then suddenly stopped. There was a whole other list of things I'd forgotten to do. Precautions I'd forgotten to take. People I needed to hide away lest they send my unsuspecting crush running for the hills.

My crazy family...

"Hey!" I streaked downstairs, calling out as I ran. "Hey, guys!"

There was no answer. Everyone else in the house had spent the last two hours putting up with my fretting and pacing, and had long since turned to other things. Things that didn't involve my high school history project, and the fact that I couldn't decide between two different pairs of socks.

By the time I made it down to the living room Caleb and Jamie were reclining on one of the couches, engrossed in what had to be one of the most bizarre inter-generational exchanges I had ever seen.

"Snap-talk, you called it?"

"Snap-chat," Jamie replied patiently. "Look, this is the app, right here." He held up the phone and took a quick photo of the both of them. The screen lit up as he played a moment with the filters before a happy little beep sent it shooting off into space.

Caleb was nonplussed. "Then what happens?"

Jamie angled towards him on the couch, unable to understand how his grandfather was failing to miss the fun. "It's done. Now it just disappears."

"You've got to be kidding me."

"It just goes to the person you're sending it to, and disappears."

Caleb threw up his hands, looking furious that he'd wasted the last ten minutes of his life on his grandson's nihilistic telephone app. "What the hell is the point of that? *It just disappears.*"

"It doesn't need to have a point. It's supposed to be—"

"Who've you even been texting?" Caleb interrupted. When Jamie didn't reply, he pressed again. "Who's important enough you want to hide your conversations from us?"

Jamie's face fell a little, as he glanced sullenly down at the screen. "...Rebekah."

I was the only person he ever texted. The only other number in his phone besides the rest of the people living in the house.

Under normal circumstances, I'd have found the entire thing quite funny. But on this particular occasion, I was able to focus only on one thing.

"Guys!" I tried again to summon their attention. "Seriously, can you—"

"—just don't understand your entire generation," Caleb continued with his usual regal arrogance. "Posting locations and private information on the internet. And now this. A picture that vanishes ten seconds after you—"

"Oh, I'm sorry," Jamie interrupted with a grin. "I'm sorry that we've progressed past the carrier pigeons you used when you were growing up."

"Hey, you two!" I waved my hands in the air. "I need to—"

"Carrier pigeons!" Caleb repeated with a rueful chuckle. "Just exactly how old do you think I am?"

Jamie shrugged innocently. "Dad told me you were spawned some time during the Bronze Age."

"MICHAEL!"

Before I could get a word in edgewise my father sauntered into the room, my Aunt Grace tight on his heels. Their white-blond hair was windswept and wild, and they were clutching a razor-sharp javelin in each hand.

"What's up?" he asked casually, leaning against the door.

Caleb bolted forward on the sofa, his dark eyes dancing with rage. "Did you really tell your son that I was some kind of Cro-Magnon?!" he demanded. "Some kind of evolutionary mishap that spent most of his time carving cave drawings and learning to make fire?!"

Michael and Grace exchanged a swift glance. Followed by a shrug. "I honestly thought that was the case," he replied.

"Yeah," she added, "I always pictured that myself."

Caleb was beside himself. "You WHAT?!"

Sensing a pending apocalypse I leapt in between them, keeping my other ear on the progress of the car the whole time. "Guys, please! This isn't the time for—"

"Rebekah?" Sarah's voice called out from the kitchen. "Honey, I didn't know what your friend might like to eat, so I just roasted a whole pig. Is that going to be okay?"

I turned in what felt like slow motion, a look of pure horror twisting my face. "You roasted...you did...what?!"

Before she could answer a monstrous Grollic crashed through the door, its sharp claws skidding across the hardwood floor.

"Oh good, Rob," Michael began conversationally, "there you are. We were just discussing Caleb's origins. So how far back would you guess he dates? Are we talking Spanish Inquisition? Or all the way back to the Jurassic Age—"

"ENOUGH!"

Every inch of my body was shaking as the cry rang out through the air. Each of the conversations in the room came to a dead stop as my family slowly turned to face me. Even the giant wolf sat back attentively on its heels.

"You cannot do this!" I shrieked. "You cannot behave like this! We're about to have a guest! My very FIRST guest, and this supernatural circus act has got to DISAPPEAR!" My curls quivered down my back as I thrust an accusatory finger at each one of them in turn.

They all stared back, not bloody moving.

I glared at each one. "You! Stop antagonizing Caleb! You're lucky he doesn't throw you off the northern turret. You two! No medieval weapons! Grandma! Under absolutely no circumstances is it okay for you to roast an entire pig! And YOU!" I spun around to the wolf, glaring up into its yellow eyes. "I don't even know where to START! We cannot have a WOLF in the middle of the LIVING ROOM!" My shoulders rose up and down with quick, hyperventilating breaths. "Shift back IMMEDIATELY, and for the love of all that is good and holy you had better FIND YOURSELF SOME PANTS!"

My voice echoed in the charged silence. Bouncing back again and again.

"I mean...*honestly*! Are you guys trying to give me a *heart attack*?!"

No one moved. No one spoke. Then, after what seemed like a very long time indeed, Jamie's face cracked into a smile. "Uh...yeah. Kind of."

I blinked, staring around the room in a daze.

"...what?"

All at once, the silence shattered as half a dozen voice rose up in loud, raucous laughter. A wave of incredulous disbelief swept over me as my entire family abandoned their positions and came up to hug me, one by one.

"You looked a little wound up, sweetie." My father gave me a wink as he tugged the end of one of my curls. "We thought we might help you relax."

"I told them not to do it," Jamie said loudly.

Grace shoved him with a grin. "Yeah, right; it was your idea."

They passed me around a little circle, each one of them offering their own unique condolences before, finally, only Caleb was left.

"Go open the door for your friend, Rebekah." He hugged me tightly, then gestured to the foyer. "He's almost here."

I nodded quickly, but then leaned in to give him an extra embrace. "Thank you," I whispered. "Thank you for letting this happen."

It had been his idea to propose such a thing, there wasn't a doubt in my mind as to that. And it had been his influence that saw it through. No one else would have the clout to make it happen.

He nodded stiffly, but his eyes were twinkling. "Go to the door, child."

A wide grin stretched across my face as I spun on my heel and raced out to the foyer. It wasn't until I was halfway there that I glanced back around. "But seriously..." my eyes leveled with my grandfather's, "...don't tell him you don't know how to work a phone, okay?"

"Just go."

Chapter 8

By the time I got to the front door, the house was quiet once again. I didn't have to look behind me to be certain that the living room had discreetly emptied. That the wolf had shifted back into a man. That the javelins had been put away, and everything looked exactly the way everything was supposed to.

Just a normal house. One that happened to bear an uncanny resemblance to a European castle, but still. Just a normal family. One that happened to look a little too much like Viking gods, but still.

Just a normal study group.

You can do this. Just act like a completely different person, living a completely different life, trapped in this completely different reality. Piece of cake.

There was a knock on the door. I counted to five before pulling it open with what I took to be my best 'normal' smile.

Luca was on the other side.

There you are.

For a second, all we did was stare. His dark eyes took in every detail of my face, while I looked back at him in breathless anticipation. You could hear the wild pounding of two hearts as time itself slowed down to watch.

Then a soft throat cleared from somewhere inside the house, and I broke out of my momentary trance.

"Uh...hey." I glanced down quickly, spilling my hair to hide my blushing cheeks. "I'm glad you found the place okay."

Luca hadn't moved. Not an inch. He just stood there, backlit with a golden halo of afternoon sun. "Found the place? It's a little hard to miss." His eyes flickered from the engraved archway, to the high stone towers, all the down to the golden fountain bubbling cheerfully in the drive.

A heated flush of embarrassment swept over me, and for the first time in my life I was suddenly ashamed. Ashamed of the beautiful place where I lived. Ashamed of the decadent palace tucked away in the heart of the woods. "I meant the turn-off," I muttered, wishing I could come up with anything better to say. "It can be tricky if you've never been here before."

A strange expression flickered across his face. One that I couldn't for the life of me identify. Then his lips turned up in a crooked grin. "So...can I come in?"

"Oh, yeah." I opened the door farther. "Sorry, please come in." *Great job, Bex. Invite a guy over, and the first thing you do is block the doorway. On a side note: you should have gotten rid of the fountain...*

I caught another whiff of that delicious scent as he swept past me. The one I hadn't been able to get out of my head since that first day I walked into English class and it bowled me over. My hand froze on the door as I pulled in a silent breath, savoring every second of it. Then I followed him inside.

He had paused in middle of the foyer, tilting his head back to stare at the high stone ceilings, his worn boots planted on the checkered tiles. I flushed again, embarrassed by the extravagance of it all, but at that point there was nothing I could do but watch as he took it all in.

Most people took a second when they first stepped inside. Most people needed a second. It was the kind of place that demanded it. The kind of place that had never once failed to impress.

Until now?

A faint shadow flickered across Luca's handsome face before settling in his eyes. There was an almost imperceptible tightening of his jaw, followed by a little crease in the center of his brow.

"All this is yours?"

The question threw me off guard. That wasn't a normal thing to ask, was it? I had invited him to my house. So, of course he knew this was where I lived.

"It's my family's," I answered swiftly, eager to move on to other things.

For whatever reason, I felt like he was getting angry the longer he was standing there. I didn't know why, and I didn't know how to make it stop.

"Your family's..." he murmured, still looking around.

I was definitely right about the anger thing. It was one of the first clear-cut emotions I'd seen from the guy, but only because it was too much for him to hide. It was like a literal cloud of dislike swept over him, stiffening him from head to toe as he rotated in a slow circle upon the marble tile. It was a dislike that didn't leave his face when he finally turned his eyes to me. "Must be nice."

Okay, I might be slightly lacking in experience but we definitely aren't following the normal script, right?! This is getting super weird, right?!

Our eyes locked, and for the second time in just a few minutes I found myself unable to look away. It was like some kind of energy was holding me there. A magnetism I was unable to overcome.

"Sometimes it is. Sometimes...not so much."

The answer surprised the both of us. Him no more so than me. Why had I just said that? I certainly hadn't meant to—it just popped out. But even more startling than the confession was the sickening realization that it was true.

A wave of panic washed over me as I suddenly remembered the other pairs of immortal ears in various rooms throughout the house. Each of them able to hear our conversation as if they were standing right beside us.

"My room's upstairs," I blurted, shattering the awkward tension as best I could. "We can work up there. It'll be quiet." *Or you can just kill me now, save me from making a total idiot of myself.*

The harsh edges of his face softened the slightest degree as he stared down at me fidgeting nervously in the entranceway. All my cool preparation and calming pep talks had vanished the second he deviated from the expected script, and it was all I could do to keep my head above water.

"Sure," he said quietly. "Let's go upstairs."

He followed me without another word. Up the winding staircase. Under the crystal chandelier. Down the hallway lined with priceless paintings. All the way to my bedroom at the end of the eastern wing.

I rushed the entire way. Wanting to avoid as much of the finery as possible. Sensing that it offended him in some way. But whether or not that was true, he kept his opinions to himself...shutting down to a flat, robotic affectation as he followed along in my footsteps.

That is...until he stepped into my room. Then he came alive again.

Only, this wasn't anything like how he was downstairs. This time, his lovely eyes brightened with the hint of a genuine smile.

My room may have been clean, but it was hopelessly cluttered. Dizzily disorganized. A far cry from the rest of the house which gave off an air of almost clinical perfection. There wasn't a square inch of space that didn't bear testament to some random family outing, or errant childhood thought, or whimsical collection I'd started, then forgotten completely just three days later.

A hundred quotes and poems and paintings were plastered on the wall. A tiny weapons collection was mounted on an ancient chest in the corner. An army of dreamcatchers dangled from the wooden headboard of my bed.

It was the only place I had in the world that was entirely *me*. A little sanctuary from the realms of both the humans and the immortals.

"Radiohead?"

I glanced over my shoulder to see him staring at a poster taped on my wall. It was a crumpled beneath a frame of glass. Smeared with a dozen inky fingerprints and smoothed awkwardly flat.

"Yeah." An automatic smile lit my face as I remembered. "I went to this concert with my brother. Things got a little crazy."

It was one of the only times that Jamie and I had been allowed to go anywhere other than high school by ourselves. That alone had made it a memorable night, worthy of a permanent place on my cluttered wall.

"Oh, yeah? Do tell."

My head snapped up in surprise to see Luca staring at me expectantly. I had said it merely as a passing answer, but he was just getting started. With a little grin, he kicked off his shoes and settled in the middle of my bed like it was the most natural thing in the world, folding his hands behind his head as he leaned back to look at me.

"Let me guess—backstage, VIP passes? Selfies with the band?"

I couldn't tell if he was teasing, or if maybe the beautiful guy from my English class was just a dick. He was impossible to read. All I could do was stare helplessly into those hypnotic eyes, wondering what was going on.

"No, actually." A hint of frustration sharpened the edges of my words, giving them a little bite. "We were in the mosh pit by the stage. A fight broke out and some guy dumped his beer all over me. That's why the ink on that poster is smeared."

"Princess was in a fight?"

My lips parted in surprise, and he flashed me a caustic grin. Was he serious? Lying on my bed? Giving me condescending nicknames?

"Princess started the fight," I corrected sharply.

It was true. In my over-enthusiasm to get to the stage, I had accidently elbowed a couple of drunks in the face. One drunk turned on another, and the next thing you knew the entire thing had dissolved into a glorified food fight.

My eyes narrowed and I was about to add something like, *and it's none of your damn business* when, all of a sudden a burst of clear, sparkling laughter echoed in the room. It caught me completely by surprise. Destroying my anger and quickening my heartbeat all at once.

I had never seen him laugh before. I had barely seen him smile.

"Is that right?" His eyes twinkled bright with mischief as he stared up at me. "Goldilocks here starts a fight in the middle of a mosh pit? I hope you at least took one of those scythes along with you. Stashed it in your purse…"

I glanced back at my weapons chest in shock. For the last two hours, I had debated stashing it in Jamie's room, but in the end I'd decided there wasn't any harm in leaving it. No one in their right mind would look at it and assume it had any practical use. At worst, they'd think it was a bit eccentric.

"You know what a scythe is?" I asked in surprise, unable to contain the question. His eyes flashed up to mine, and I was quick to apologize. "Sorry, I've just never met anyone else who does."

It wasn't the sort of thing you could just find on the street. In fact, Caleb had purchased it from a Greek museum just to add to my illustrious collection.

"Television," Luca replied simply, peeling himself off the bed. "So what else do you have in there?"

Before I could stop him he crossed the floor and knelt to open the chest, letting out a low whistle as his eyes flickered from piece to piece. The metallic glint reflected in his eyes as he reached down and pulled out a fourteenth-century halberd, one of the more gruesome weapons in the bunch.

"This is beautiful," he murmured, turning it over in his hands. "Did you reinforce the grip here?"

The question broke through my confused little trance, propelling me forward to join him on the floor. "My uncle did. It was a birthday present." I reached out a tentative finger to point out a trail of miniature markings carved into the blade. "Do you see the writing? It originally belonged to a member of the German royal family."

I had always found that an interesting detail. Luca, apparently, did not.

"Royalty, huh?" His fingers tightened upon the handle. "That figures."

There was a silver flash, and next thing I knew the blade was spinning absentmindedly in his hands. A gesture as effortless as it was lethal.

What the hell?!

My body instinctively stilled as it sliced the air just a few inches away from my arm. I had trained with the halberd many times. I knew exactly how dangerous it could be in the wrong hands. Even more so in the right hands.

"Is that why you got it?" Luca was unfazed. Twirling the deadly weapon as casually as if it was a pencil. "Because of the royalty thing?"

Faster and faster it spun. Blurring silver in his distracted hands.

"You see it in a movie somewhere and order it online?"

Faster and faster.

"Or did you just—"

ENOUGH!

With a burst of blinding speed, my hand shot out and caught the weapon by the blade—stopping it mid-swing. The sharpened metal hissed to a stop as Luca and I locked eyes.

The room fell deathly quiet, then slowly, ever so slowly, he released the handle.

"I got it because it's in mint condition. *Not* because it belonged to royalty." I put it back in its sheath, maintaining eye contact the entire time. "I went to the concert because I like the music. Not because I had backstage passes. And I live in this ridiculous house because it's the one my grandfather built, it's where my family is, and I have nowhere else to go."

The chest slammed shut between us, locking with defiant *click*.

"Now, can we get started on this project? Or do you want to sit there and keep tearing apart my life?" *Judging me like you think you know me.*

For once, the guy with all the cocky answers had nothing to say. His lips parted, but not a single word came out. In the end he merely bowed his head and nodded, gesturing silently to the desk.

Without another word, the two of us settled down to work. Passing the books between us, looking up only with the occasional nod in affirmation or shake of the head as one idea was passed over for another. The minutes on the clock dragged by as, slowly, uncomfortably, we made our way through the piles of material and sorted it into a workable outline.

The entire time, I was trying not to cry.

I should've known this would never work. I should've known it was a stupid idea from the start. The guy thinks I'm a spoiled brat. A stuck-up princess who lives in her castle in the woods and doesn't talk to the other students. I'm surprised he even agreed to be my partner. Barrow probably forced him.

A silent sigh wilted my shoulders as my pencil trembled over the page.

Jamie knew this would happen. He tried to warn me. Why didn't I just listen? There's a reason we don't mix with these people. Maybe I should just—

"What's this?"

I jerked in surprise, then looked over to see him frozen on the other side of the desk, staring down at something in his hands. Something that held his complete and absolute attention. His fingers traced gently up the sides, and without seeming to think about it his lips curved up in a little smile.

"Let me see?" I phrased it as a question, reaching out my hand.

But whatever it was, Luca had no intention of surrendering it. He simply held it up, angling it in my direction so that we could both see.

"Did you draw this?"

My throat tightened as my entire body locked down in horror. It seemed those notebooks I'd brought over weren't completely empty after all. It was an old sketch. The kind of thing I used to do all the time. The kind of thing I still did in secret, sitting out on the roof, gazing up at the stars.

"No, I..." The automatic lie died on my tongue as my cheeks blushed a delicate shade of pink. "Yeah, actually. A long time ago."

The years might have passed, but the drawing always remained exactly the same. A bizarre self-portrait. The picture of a girl who sat drawing herself on the roof. Who was drawing herself on the roof. Who was drawing herself on the roof. The picture got smaller and smaller every time.

"It's incredible," he said quietly, studying it with a thoughtful eye. Gone were the sarcastic defenses. Gone was the inexplicable bitterness and rage. The boy sitting beside me suddenly looked his own age. "And sad."

Sad?

He was always saying the very last thing I expected him to say. The very last thing in the world I had a prepared answer for.

It was a girl sitting on a roof. Stargazing. Drawing. A pensive smile on her face. Who in the world would look at it and think it was sad?

Except, of course...he was right.

I had been crying the night I drew it. I cried every night I drew. Feeling like the walls of the world itself were closing in. Forcing me to become smaller and smaller, just to fit inside the lines.

"I'm sorry for the way I acted when I first got here," he said suddenly. "I haven't been having the easiest time...settling into Port Q. It wasn't my idea to move here. None of this...none of it was my idea." He set his pencil down with a little sigh, running his hands back through his hair the same way I'd seen Jamie do in a million moments of stress. "Olivia and I are just trying to keep our heads down," he continued softly, unwilling to meet my eyes. "Counting the days to graduation."

I stared at him curiously. Just as baffled by the sudden change in tone as I was by his strange behavior when he first walked in. "Olivia?"

"My sister," he said quickly. "Well, stepsister. She's the only family I have left. Our parents died in a car crash a few years ago."

Another shocking confession.

One second, we were awkwardly outlining the rise of industrialism in the Civil War. The next, we were sharing personal tragedies. Pulling tear-stained pictures out of notebooks long forgotten.

"I'm so sorry," I murmured, shaking my head as an unexpected wave of sympathy washed over me. "Family is...is everything. I can't even imagine."

His eyes flickered up, and he gave me a sad smile. "You close with yours?"

My face warmed with an automatic glow. "Yeah, we're close. Sometimes it feels like they're the only people in my entire world." I laughed lightly, a laugh that didn't quite hide the bitterness just underneath. "I have a brother, Jamie. He's my best friend."

Luca nodded with a little frown, trying to place him. "Tall? Blond? He's on the football team?"

"That's the one."

Another nod. "He looks like you."

I laughed lightly, doodling absentmindedly on the edge of my notes. "He should. We're twins."

"Twins," Luca chuckled, leaning back in his chair. "That explains it."

"Explains what?" I asked.

He flashed me another grin, his eyes dancing with mischief. "Explains the look on his face when that guy tried to jump into your car the other day."

For the second time in just a few minutes, my face blanched in complete and utter mortification. I should have known that little encounter was going to come back and bite me. The entire school was buzzing with it the next day. "Oh, crap. That."

He laughed again. A sound so free and unrestrained that, before I knew it, I was smiling as well. "You can hardly blame a guy for trying."

"*Yes*, actually, yes I can." I tossed an eraser at him with a grin. "If he colors on me with permanent marker, then I most certainly can."

"Hey, no harm done. It all came off, didn't it?"

Without seeming to think about it he reached over and took my hand, turning it over as he searched for any lingering ink. His long fingers smoothed down my own, lacing briefly in between them before we lifted our heads to look at each other at the same time.

"Sorry," he muttered, releasing me the next second and turning to gather up his things. "I should actually get going. Liv will be here any minute."

Speak of the devil...

As if on cue, the doorbell rang. First once, then twice more, incessantly.

He rolled his eyes, stacking the piles of notes into his bag. "She can get a little impatient..."

"That's fine," I said quickly, helping him pack as best I could. "My brother can let her in."

Jamie! I called telepathically. *Can you get the door?* There was a rustle of fabric as he paused a movie in the next room and got to his feet. *Thanks!*

My hands never stopped moving, and I looked up a second later to see Luca staring at me curiously. It was only then that I realized the rather odd way that all must have looked.

With a look of the utmost innocence, I voiced my request again. Out loud, this time. "Jamie, can you get the door?"

There was a pause in his step, before he continued jogging downstairs. "Sure."

I could hear the smile in his voice, even from here.

A second later the door pulled open, and a feminine voice echoed up the hall. It was followed quickly by my brother's.

"Well, thanks for the invite." Luca swung his bag over his shoulder, getting to his feet. "I think we got it mostly done."

"Yeah." I tried to hide the disappointment in my voice as I realized he was right. "I think we did."

He paused for a second, then shot me a sideways glance. "That being said, it is *thirty* percent of our grade. Want to meet up later at my house? Smooth over any rough spots?"

A flutter of excitement danced in my eyes as I tried to keep as casual as him. "Yeah. That's probably for the best."

"Better safe than sorry, right?"

"Right."

We stood there for a second before turning at the same time to hide matching grins.

"In that case, I'll see you soon." He slipped on his shoes and headed for the door. "I'd better save your brother from my demented sister."

I laughed quietly and followed him down the stairs. Sure enough, Jamie and Olivia were talking by the door. But it certainly didn't look like either one of them needed saving from the other. Quite the contrary. I had never seen that particular expression on my brother's face.

Olivia was even lovelier up close and in person. With tumbles of soft brunette waves, and eyes so bright they seemed to light up the world around her. Eyes that were staring at my brother like he was her own personal sun.

Luca cleared his throat quietly, and the two of them took an automatic step apart. The boys sized each other up in a way that was half-friendly, half-appraising, before Jamie held out his hand with an easy smile.

"Sorry we didn't get the chance to meet. I'm Jamie, Becka's brother."

Luca shook his hand firmly, matching him smile for smile. "Luca. Olivia's brother."

There was a bit of a warning in the way they said their sister's name. A warning so ludicrous and transparent that Olivia rolled her eyes and gave me a conspiratorial grin.

"It's nice to meet you," she said to me.

I grinned back. "Nice to meet you as well."

Olivia didn't shake. She hugged. Pulling me in for an unexpected embrace that was just as sweet as it was surprising. As I glanced up at Jamie through her waves of hair, I could see him secretly coveting one as well.

"Did you get everything you needed done?" she asked her brother.

Their eyes met, and he gave her a swift nod.

"Almost. Just have to nail down a day with Rebekah to finish it up over at the house." He flashed me a quick smile. "Friday work for you?"

This time, it was Jamie and I who exchanged a quick look.

Not only was Friday already booked, but the odds of me being allowed to go to a mortal's house were just about as slim as Caleb spontaneously turning into a Grollic. I was already pushing my luck having the both of them here.

Fortunately, I had a built-in excuse.

"Actually...Friday is our birthday." I cocked my head at my twin, then turned back to Luca. "Sorry about that. Maybe we could finish at school—"

"Happy early birthday!" Olivia exclaimed, officially claiming the title of the sweetest person I'd ever met. Jamie was clearly smitten. "Eighteen?"

"Yeah," he nodded, "you?"

"Still seventeen." She pushed Luca playfully on the shoulder. "But Luca's almost nineteen already. He loves to lord it over me."

I laughed. "Jamie's the older twin. Never lets me hear the end of it."

Luca smiled, and tilted his head at me appraisingly. "So what about on Thursday then? I can text you my address."

I hesitated a split second as a telepathic warning rang out in my head.

Don't make any promises you might not be able to keep.

Jamie and I locked eyes, and I nodded swiftly. We followed them outside towards their car.

"Uh...yeah. Definitely text it over, and I'll check to see if I'm free." I tried to hide my nerves. "My dad has pretty strict rules about that sort of thing."

"Oh, I totally get that. Our guardian is super strict, too." Olivia looked towards the house as well before giving Jamie a sideways glance. "Well, if it helps, your brother could always come with you. To avoid the whole 'you can't be alone with a guy' thing."

Jamie looked like he thought this was a great idea. The two of them shared a secret smile before he nodded innocently in my direction. "I'm free Thursday."

What happened to 'don't make any promises you might not be able to keep'? I silently demanded. He avoided my gaze.

"Cool," Luca said, shooting his sister an exasperated look. He turned back to me and held out his hand. When I did nothing but blankly stare back, his eyes danced with a little grin. "Want to give me your phone so I can program in my number? That way you can tell me if Thursday is going to work."

"Oh, right. Sorry." I whipped it out the next second and handed it over, trying to tune out my obnoxious twin's telepathic laughter. Luca's fingers flew over the keys at the speed of light as his lips twitched up in a mischievous grin.

"Or I could always just scribble it down on your hand," he said innocently. "I'm sure there's a Sharpie somewhere in my bag—"

"You've made your point," I snapped, elbowing Jamie as his laughter echoed out into the real world as well. "I'll text you as soon as I know."

Luca nodded, then surprised me by pulling me into a quick, one-armed hug. "Try, okay?" His gaze burned into mine, holding me completely captive. "I had fun today. Probably the most exciting since coming to Port Q. It'd be cool to do it again."

By the time I recovered my senses, he was already pulling away. Olivia hopped up on her toes to give Jamie a quick kiss on the cheek, and the two of them got into their car without another word.

Leaving my brother and me rooted to the spot.

"Is that a blush I see?" I teased under my breath as the engine sprang to life. "Could my brother possibly be blushing?"

"Shut up. You're one to talk." He waved goodbye and walked back into the house without another word. Probably to start coming up with a plan to convince Michael and Caleb to let us both loose on Thursday afternoon.

The front door had already closed when Luca hopped back out of the car and jogged over. His dark hair spilled into his eyes, and he answered my look of confusion with a charming smile. "I almost forgot to tell you something...the girl in that drawing was really beautiful. But she hardly does you justice."

My mouth fell open in surprise as I stared up at him. "How did you know that was me?"

His fingers reached out and grazed the tip of my necklace, sending a cascade of electric shivers racing down my skin. "Same pendant." He tilted his head suddenly, staring at me with a thoughtful smile. "Same eyes."

Olivia honked impatiently, and he backed away with a grin.

"See you at school, Rebekah."

I nodded mutely, watching him go. He was already back in the car with his feet up on the dash by the time I called out, "It's Bex!"

Chapter 9

For the first time in longer than I could remember, I was actually excited to go back to school. I got up far earlier than usual the next morning, soaking in a freesia bubble bath to calm my nerves before toweling off quickly to begin getting ready. The clothes were carefully selected. The makeup, flawless. The hair, given free rein to tumble down my back in a cascade of golden curls. In a completely uncharacteristic move, I actually sprayed on a hint of perfume—the secret bottle I saved for special occasions.

By the time I finally got downstairs, I was expecting to find my brother waiting impatiently by the door. But Jamie was nowhere to be found.

"Jamie!" I called, tapping my foot with manic energy against the checkered tile. "Come on down, we're going to be late!"

There was a brief pause, followed by a telepathic reply.

In a minute...

My head snapped up curiously, and I doubled back up the stairs to see what was taking so long. After a brief search I found Jamie in the bathroom, staring uncertainly at his reflection in the mirror.

"Do you think my hair's too long?" he asked when I rounded the corner.

I stopped short. Unable to reconcile what I was seeing. "...what?"

"My hair." He lifted his chin with a slight frown to examine it from another angle. "Do you think it's getting too long? Should I cut it?"

My lips parted in surprise, then closed again with an affectionate smile.

I couldn't remember the last time Jamie had asked for my opinion on anything to do with appearance. Not since his Lion King t-shirt phase when we were about four years old. To be honest, I couldn't remember the last time Jamie had even looked in a mirror.

"Your hair?" I stalled for time, fighting back a sisterly grin.

It was bit on the long side, like our grandfather's, falling down to the edge of his jaw. A unique look, but to be honest the whole thing fit him like a glove. He looked like one of those pictures you'd see in old Greek mythology books. The guy holding a spear, leaping high into the air to slay a dragon. Or the guy on a heavenly chariot, riding forth to drag out the sun.

Bronzed, athletic body. Shining blue eyes. And a sunlit array of golden curls. It was easy to see why Olivia had been so taken with him.

"Nah, it looks good." I jumped up to ruffle it for good measure, earning me an instant scowl. "You should leave it."

He studied my face for a second, as if I might be lying to deliberately sabotage him, before shrugging it off like it couldn't matter less. "Cool. Whatever."

If I was a better person, I probably would have let the subject drop. He was obviously feeling nervous and insecure, which was not only adorable but incredibly out of character. Yes, I should probably have let it drop. But as a little sister, there are certain things you really can't let slide.

"So...this wouldn't happen to have anything to do with seeing Olivia at school today, would it?" I asked slyly, swaying back and forth in the doorway.

"No." He glared defensively. "Are you wearing perfume?"

"No."

We stared each other down for a second, neither one surrendering an inch, before our mother's voice echoed up the stairs.

"Guys! You're going to be late!"

The sibling stare-off ended, the anxious preening came to a close, and the two of us made our way downstairs and off to school.

It was a short drive. Maybe just ten minutes or so. But for whatever reason, today it felt like we would never get there. Neither one of us said much in the car. We kept things light and specifically avoided the bathroom incident and any mention of the Kane siblings. But when we finally rolled into the school parking lot, Jamie pulled into the empty space next to their car.

"See you at lunch." He was out of the car before I could even reply. Heading off towards the math building, even though I knew economics was his first class.

Curious, I pressed my face up against the window and watched him breeze confidently across the grass. Only someone who knew him very well could see the nervous way his fingers were drumming against the strap on his bag.

Was he meeting Olivia? Had the two of them worked out a place to—

"You coming out? Or are you just hiding from drunk football players?"

I jumped a mile as Luca's grinning face appeared suddenly in front of the window, jerking me out of my thoughtful trance. How was it possible that he'd managed to sneak up on me? I must have been more out of it than I thought.

"Hey." I climbed out of the car with a shy smile, reaching into the back-seat to grab my bag. "Sorry, I was just...thinking."

"About me, I hope."

My eyes lifted in surprise as Luca took my messenger bag and swung it over his own shoulder. When he saw me watching, he flashed a wink.

"I'm kidding, Bex. Relax."

It was the first time he'd called me by my nickname. Now that I thought about it, it was the first time anyone outside my family had called me by it. My heart quickened with a little flutter and I suppressed a smile.

"I was kidding about the football players, too," he continued. "Rumor has it your brother gave them a scary little warning. Half the team quit."

I stopped dead in my tracks, staring up in shock. "Are you serious?!"

He let me hang for a minute before letting out a burst of laughter. "No, I'm not serious." He chuckled again, gesturing me forward as we walked across the grass. "You're pretty out of it this morning, you know that?"

Too bad all my preparation didn't stop me from being a socially clueless idiot. "Sorry." I shook my head, pushing my golden hair behind my ears. "It's just...it's just been a weird week."

He glanced at me out of the corner of his eye, his handsome face melting into a thoughtful smile. "Good weird? Or bad weird?"

Our eyes locked, and I bit my lip to hide a grin. "Too soon to say."

"Oh really?" His eyebrows arched and he offered his arm with a theatrical bow. "In that case, allow me to try to tip the scales."

I giggled softly and laced my arm obligingly through his. "And how do you plan on doing that?"

The morning sunlight caught in his hair, haloing it around his face as he glanced down at me with a mischievous smile. "I have one or two ideas..."

* * *

A new student in a small school was already enough to cause a social frenzy. When that student happened to look like Luca, the frenzy escalated to epidemic proportions. When that same student managed to breach the invisible divide and make contact with the school's resident goddess?

...it was unlikely the student body would ever be the same.

"Do you think they're dating?"

The whispers came from every possible angle as Luca and I headed down the hallway to our first-period class. Echoing back louder and louder as people peered around lockers, and stood up on their toes to get a better view.

"Of course they're dating. Look at them. Who else would they possibly want to date in this school except each other?"

Faster and faster the rumors swirled. Louder and louder the speculation.

"—like a pair of freaking movie stars. I'm thinking of starting a blog—"

A familiar voice rang out amongst them. None other than Briana, queen of the cheerleaders. Head of the Jamie Knightly fan club.

"I don't know about dating," she whispered authoritatively. "Rebekah's always seemed really shy. But they're definitely sleeping together."

Not dating, but definitely sleeping together?! How the heck did that work?!

There was a hitch in my step as my eyes widened in disbelief, but Luca pulled me gently along. Pursing his lips and bowing his head to hide a smile.

"They're an excitable bunch, aren't they?"

I flashed him a nervous look, worried he might somehow think I was enjoying all the attention, but one look at his face told me that wasn't true. He might come off as standoffish and abrasive to everyone else, but there was a softness in his eyes when he looked at me. A quiet protectiveness that I'd never seen before. That never really went away.

"It's high school," I murmured, doing my best to avoid the stares. "And you're the new kid in town. What do you expect?"

Much to my surprise, Luca laughed again. Quieter, this time. So quiet that only I could hear it. "Sorry to burst your bubble, but I'm not the only one they're staring at." His eyes twinkled as he looked me up and down, taking in every single detail with the sweep of his gaze. "But I doubt that's anything new for you. I bet you and your brother get people staring at you all the time..."

It was strange, the way he said it. Not as a compliment, but more as a thoughtful observation. One that bordered almost on sympathy when he saw the way I chafed against the spotlight. Stranger still that he included Jamie.

"Yeah, it...it hasn't always been easy, going to this school." I tossed back my hair with a quiet sigh as we neared my locker. "We were only allowed to start coming here a few months ago, and it hasn't really died down since."

Luca paused, leaning up against the lockers with a curious expression. "*Allowed* to start coming here?" he quoted with a frown.

My hand froze halfway to the lock. Eighteen years of living in the shadows had taught me better than that. Eighteen years in isolation had hardened me against such casual truths. It was a stupid mistake. And one I couldn't afford to make again. Not if I wanted to stay at this school...

"We were homeschooled for a while." I shrugged as if it was no more casual than that. "Didn't want to..." I trailed off as an electric light flashed suddenly in my eyes.

There was a chorus of giggles, and the next thing I knew Briana and her group of followers had disappeared into the girls' bathroom.

"...unbelievable."

I didn't know what was worse. The whispers, the stares, or the fact that some of the bolder upperclassmen were actually snapping what they obviously thought to be 'discreet' pictures with their phones.

The entire thing was an adolescent catastrophe.

But the most memorable moment by far came when Chris Harder—the prom king turned Sharpie attacker—solemnly left his group of wide-eyed jocks and came to join Luca and me by the lockers.

"Hey." He ran a bashful hand through his hair, glancing between us without looking us directly in the eye. "I just wanted to say...sorry. The other day, I...I didn't know."

My face blanked as a look of utter amusement danced in Luca's eyes.

"I'm sorry?" I tilted my head to the side, trying to understand. "You didn't know...what exactly?"

Chris blushed as Luca literally bit down on his lip to keep from smiling. "I didn't know about this—you two." He gestured quickly between us, unable to hide the look of wistful bitterness that flashed across his face. "I wouldn't have given you my number otherwise. I didn't know you were taken."

Taken?! I felt like I'd been slapped in the face. My jaw dropped open as my entire body locked down in baffled disbelief.

This couldn't be happening, could it? Chris, Briana, the entire rest of the school. Had they all taken some kind of group narcotic, and I was just bearing witness to the surreal effects?

We were WALKING TO CLASS. Not kissing. Not cuddling. Not holding hands in the parking lot. WALKING TO CLASS.

What the hell are they thinking?!

But then, just as I was about to say as much, the strangest thing happened yet. In a move that was as deliberate as it was utterly mischievous, Luca reached over and slipped his arm around my waist. "Thanks, man." His eyes twinkled as he gave Chris a triumphant grin. "I really appreciate that."

Okay, I was baffled before. Now? I was flat-out stunned.

I simply didn't know what to do. I had never been in this kind of situation before, had never imagined it was remotely possible. All my skills, excuses, and clever deceptions failed me in one fell swoop. Leaving me lost and completely defenseless. In the end, the only thing I could manage was to stand there—frozen—and watch as Chris returned to his friends. Probably to confirm the rumors that Luca Kane and Rebekah Knightly were officially an item.

It wasn't until the bell rang and the hall emptied of students that I finally snapped out of my paralysis, gazing up at Luca with wide, unfocused eyes.

"Why'd you do that?"

His arm was still wrapped around me. It was a fact I was hyper-aware of with each passing second. The heat from his body seeped through my thin shirt, warming my skin as that intoxicating scent threatened to overpower.

For a second, he just stared at me. Then his fingers tightened and the edge of his thumb grazed along my ribs. "I did it for your own good." The warmth of his breath tickled my cheeks as he leaned towards me with that twinkling smile. "Consider that your get out of jail free card with the rest of the football team..."

* * *

It was, without a doubt, the best day I'd ever had at school. For the first time, I didn't feel like I was trapped outside, looking in. For the first time, I felt like I was the in on the action. In on the secret.

Luca and I sat together in every class. The teachers didn't seem to mind, and the students were more than willing to make room. It was like seeing the two of us in such close proximity was giving them some kind of contact high, just from lingering close.

The only teacher who seemed to realize that the class had played an unspoken game of musical chairs was our history teacher, Mr. Barrow. His eyes swept briefly over the room, lingering a second on me and Luca, before he returned to his lecture with a little smile.

The hour passed quickly and the two of us were already halfway out the door on our way to lunch, when he called suddenly out to us.

"Mr. Kane."

Luca stiffened slightly as he paused in the doorway. His hand tensed on my back before he turned around with a tight smile. "Yes, sir?"

Clearly, he expected Barrow to demand some kind of update on our project. Require assurances that we wouldn't be late in presenting it, just because we'd been paired up a day or so later than the rest. At the very worse, he feared our young teacher might assign even more work in his first week.

But Barrow did none of those things. He simply flashed us both a warm smile before he cocked his head towards the calendar hanging on the wall. "Just wanted to remind you about the solstice party this weekend. I'm sure you're very busy, settling in, but it's not something you'll want to miss."

I paused a foot or two behind Luca, staring curiously at the teacher. "Solstice party?"

Luca's eyes tightened for a split second before he flashed me a quick smile over his shoulder. "Mr. Barrow invited me as a welcome when I first transferred over. Ran into me in the office, and said I should go."

Well, that was very nice of him.

I smiled brightly at Barrow, still alight with curiosity. "What is it?"

"It's just a group of friends getting together to celebrate the alignment of the planets." He turned to the whiteboard, and began wiping off his lecture notes. "Apparently, it was a longstanding tradition of this town—one that the locals have tried to keep up over the years. Now, it's nothing more than a huge party out in the forest near Interstate 12." His glasses caught the light as he turned back to us with a warm smile. "You should come, too, Rebekah. It's all ages." A look of amusement danced across his face as he picked up his leather satchel. "Perhaps Luca could take you. Since the two of you seemed to be joined at the hip..."

With a soft chuckle, he swept out the door, leaving us both in a charged silence. After a few seconds, I chanced a sideways glance at Luca.

"...I think that was for bastardizing his seating chart."

Luca looked down in surprise before his face lightened into a smile. "Yeah...I think you're right."

He took my hand and led me down the hall to our lockers and then to lunch.

It was a nice day outside, so I wasn't surprised when Jamie bypassed the cafeteria at lunch and settled instead at our favorite picnic table outside. I was surprised, however, to see that someone was sitting there with him.

"I should have known," Luca muttered under his breath, staring at his little sister with a brotherly scowl. "She wouldn't shut up about him the whole way back from your house."

My heart leapt with excitement at the words, and I couldn't resist a smile. "What's so wrong with it? They look cute together."

They certainly did. I couldn't think of a time that I had ever seen my brother look so happy. His entire face was radiant with it. Casting off a golden glow as the afternoon sun danced around him and sparkled in his eyes.

As for Olivia? She looked just as enchanted as Jamie.

The two of them were angled towards each other at the table. Not quite touching, but close enough that every move was deliberate. Every tiny gesture was done with the other in mind. A tray of food sat untouched before each of them, but they couldn't care less. They only had eyes for each other, lost in their own little world.

"What's wrong with it?" Luca replied caustically, shifting uncomfortably in place. "She's my little sister. Emphasis on the *little*."

I snorted and returned my eyes to the table.

Brotherly instincts aside, he was right. There was something wrong with it. In fact, there were a whole host of things that were wrong with it, things that Luca and Olivia could never understand.

The line between mortals and immortals could never be crossed. Our unholy secret could never be revealed. And while Jamie and I might enjoy the occasional sunny afternoon playing footsie under a picnic table, such a thing could never be allowed to last.

But for now...what was the harm?

"Olivia seems sweet, but she's almost eighteen." I gave him a nudge and the two of us started across the grass. "I'm sure she can handle herself."

Luca cast a long-suffering look towards the heavens before letting out a little sigh. "That's exactly what I'm afraid of..."

The happy couple didn't even look up as we joined them at the table. Not even with a telepathic nudge from me. It wasn't until Luca literally dropped his bag with a crash in between them that they sprang apart with a little jump.

"Bex!" Jamie leaned back in surprise, looking like he'd just woken up from a very long sleep. "Sorry—I didn't see you there."

My lips curved up in a smile I made no effort to restrain. "Yeah, well, you looked a little distracted."

He blushed furiously and lowered his eyes to the table, scooting over automatically to make room for me beside him on the bench. On the other side of the table, Luca and Olivia were having similar problems.

"Hey there, sis." Luca's eyes flashed a silent warning as they locked onto hers. "Having a good time?"

Her face tightened with a dainty scowl. "Well, I was before you so rudely dropped your stuff in the middle of the table." She shoved it defiantly onto the grass, maintaining eye contact the entire time. "Oops."

Jamie and I glanced awkwardly at each other before he did his best to break the ice, pushing out the bench for Luca to take a seat.

"So how are you liking Port Q?" He glanced quickly between brother and sister as Luca sank stiffly onto the bench. "Olivia tells me it's a lot different than your old school."

Luca shot him a tight smile, one that didn't reach his eyes. "Did she now?" He turned that same icy smile onto his sister, freezing it in place. "And what else did my dear sister tell you?"

Much to my surprise, the cold words had no effect on her whatsoever. In fact, they had rather the opposite effect. The second Luca was done speaking, she threw back her head with a tinkling laugh. A sound that softened her brother in spite of himself, and brought an automatic smile to Jamie's lips.

"You're one to talk." Her eyes sparkled with mischief as she shot me a conspiratorial grin. "I just spent the whole morning listening to rabid teenagers raving about Port Q's new power couple, Rebekah Knightly and Luca Kane."

This time, it was Jamie who sprang to action. His head snapped up in alarm as his blue eyes burned suddenly into mine. "What?"

As if the verbal question wasn't enough, it echoed deafeningly in my head.

WHAT?!

I winced automatically, bringing a hand up to my temple as if to protect myself from the telepathic reverberations in my brain.

"It's just a joke," I said quickly, trying to ignore the way Luca and Olivia were staring curiously between us. "Luca just said it to get Chris Harder off my case when he came up to me today. That's all."

Jamie's lips thinned into a hard line, as his eyes flashed a warning.

...that had better be all.

Enough with the telepathic reprimands!

"I said that's *all*."

It came out a little louder than I'd intended. And a little sharper. To be honest, I hadn't meant to say it out loud at all. But I hadn't quite been myself since that first moment Luca slipped his arm around my waist.

There was a moment of awkward silence before Olivia cleared her throat dramatically and shifted the conversation forward.

"So...how about this weather, huh?"

Jamie and I chuckled appreciatively as Luca gazed thoughtfully across the lawn, his eyes coming to rest on a trio of guys tossing around a football.

"Nice day for a game," he murmured, almost to himself.

"Do you play?" Jamie's face brightened with sudden interest as he looked Luca up and down, assessing him in a whole new light.

"I used to," Luca answered, unable to keep the wistful note of longing from his voice. "Back at my old school. Not so much anymore."

"Well, you should play for us." Jamie didn't miss a beat with the instant invitation. "The season started a few weeks ago, but it shouldn't be a problem."

Luca couldn't help but laugh. A little taken aback by the unhesitating hospitality of it. "What are you, the team captain or something?"

Uh...yep. Voted unanimously his first day.

"It's a group effort," Jamie said dismissively, shrugging it off with an easy smile. "I can set up a tryout if you're interested."

Typical of Jamie to shy away from the praise. That kind of modesty was one of his more endearing traits, one he was completely oblivious to himself.

Even Luca softened a bit before returning his smile. "Yeah, that would great. Thanks, man."

"Don't mention it." Jamie unscrewed the top of his water bottle before rolling a fruit cup automatically my way. "I'll get your number from Liv. Text you the time and place."

A sudden silence fell over the table as Luca looked up with a chilling stare. "And how do you have Liv's number?"

Jamie froze dead still, looking as caught off guard as I probably did when Luca wrapped his arm around my waist in the hall. His lips parted uncertainly, and for a split second he looked about ready to deny the whole thing.

Then Luca leaned forward with a chuckle and clapped him on the arm. "Relax, man. I'm just messing with you."

Jamie let out a silent breath as Olivia and I both started laughing. The sun peeked out from behind the trees as the four of us settled in for what had to be the best lunch the students of Port Q High had ever seen.

* * *

They were perfect. I was utterly convinced. After just forty-five minutes of sharing a meal, I was convinced that Luca and Olivia Kane were perfect.

What was more—they were perfect for *us.*

Each exactly suiting our personalities. Each providing our exact balance. It was if they had been handpicked in the heavens and sent just for us. The only connection my brother and I had to the outside world.

There was only one problem...

"How can she be mortal?"

It was the first thing Jamie or I had said since getting in the car that afternoon, and I looked up with a start to see him staring blankly ahead.

"You've seen her, talked to her..." His eyes tightened as her lovely face flashed through his mind. "How can she be mortal?"

The words touched a dark place in my heart, and instead of answering I folded my arms protectively across my chest as the car pulled into the drive.

As soon as it did I was spared a response entirely, as something caught our instant attention and delight. There was another car parked in the driveway, wedged snugly in between Grace's and Caleb's. A car that looked far too flashy to follow the 'keep a low profile' rule. But, then again, the man who drove it didn't exactly follow that rule either.

"Uncle Seth!"

We called out before we'd even rolled to a stop, leaping out of the car and racing forward as a handsome man made his way out of the house.

He was flanked on both sides by members of our family, and his face lit up with a wide grin as he threw open his arms. "And how are my favorite surrogate niece and nephew?"

We skidded to a stop with a grin, thrilled beyond words at yet another treat this magical day had in store.

"What're you doing here?" Jamie asked excitedly. "We weren't expecting you for another few weeks."

"What am I doing here?" Seth repeated with a devilish smile. "Well, it's funny you should ask..." He glanced over his shoulders at both Caleb and Michael, both of whom met his eyes with a little nod. "There's evil afoot, children. It's time for a Hunt..."

Chapter 10

Faster than even Caleb's immortal eyes could see, Jamie and I flashed to either side of Seth. Both of us flat-out begging without a hint of shame.

"Can we come?!"

It was impossible to gauge who said it first. We'd both blurted it out at the same time, swarming our honorary uncle to such a degree that he had to stand on tiptoes just to lock eyes with our parents over Seth's head.

"Well someone's a little over-eager," he chuckled, easing us back a step so he could get some room to breathe. "Been cooped up here a little too long?"

My mother rolled her eyes as she and Grace joined the men out on the front steps. "You have no idea. I can't remember a time before they both started asking. I'm pretty sure it was Jamie's first full sentence."

Seth laughed again, looking us over fondly. While he wasn't technically family, there were few childhood memories Jamie and I had in which he hadn't played a major role. From ballet lessons to soccer games, the man had been there for them all. Always with a different woman on his arm.

He was on the Higher Coven with Caleb—a job that kept him busy and travelling—but whenever he had a few free days to spare he spent them with us. Without complaint. Without question.

"Shit! You've grown up!" He ruffled Jamie's hair with a grin, sizing him up and down. "Facetime didn't do it justice. You're just as tall as me! And Becka..." His lips pursed into a wicked smile as he looked past me to my father. "You're going to have trouble with this one. Got a little heartbreaker on your hands."

Dad cleared his throat purposely. "You're her uncle—"

"Honorary uncle. I—"

"Don't change the subject!" I demanded, refusing to let him off the hook for even an instant. Plus, we all knew Seth had a thing for the ladies. He'd lost his soul mate, you could say, and had been dancing with all the ladies till he found a new one. I would never be an interest for him. However, that didn't stop him from teasing my father. "You have to let us—"

"—come on the Hunt. Yeah, I heard you." He raked his fingers through his dark hair, letting it spill back across his face. "But what's the rule on that again? That you have to be eighteen?" His eyes twinkled merrily as he looked us both up and down. "Still look seventeen to me."

"For a *few more days*!" Jamie cried in exasperation. "Please, Seth. Come on! You know Caleb will listen to you."

Our grandfather cleared his throat with a little smile. "*Caleb* happens to be standing right here."

"Seriously, Seth—*please*?!" I grabbed his arm, standing on my toes to make him look me in the face. "You can talk to Michael."

"Your *dad* also happens to be standing right here," Michael interjected with a bemused grin. "And if you think for even a second that I'm going to take parenting advice from a man like your *Uncle Seth*, then you've completely lost your minds."

"I have no idea what you're talking about," Seth countered with a lofty grin. "I would make a terrific parent, had I ever fathered any children."

My mother laughed shortly, shaking her head. "Who's to say that you haven't? A guy like you?"

Before he could defend himself, Grace joined in. Her long blonde braids making her look like some kind of Viking princess. "There's probably a small army out there by now. Enough to populate their own island."

My father shook his head gravely, joining in on the fun. "Little bed-hopping miscreants. Arming themselves with coconuts and spears in their quest to find their lost father..."

An involuntary shudder rippled through Seth's shoulders. "Now that's a chilling thought."

"That's enough!" Jamie turned to his uncle with a truly heartbreaking expression, the kind that could melt just about anybody. "*Please*, Seth? We'll do anything you want. Anything you say. We'll *help*, I promise."

"You're our only hope, Seth," I added with an exaggerated whimper, a picture of tragedy as I laced my arm through my brother's. "The rest of them clearly don't believe in us. But there's a chance you still do."

There was a soft chorus of sarcastic laughter behind us, but Jamie and I kept our eyes on the prize. Hoping beyond hope that our uncle would crack.

He did so with his own unique style. His eyes sparkled as he looked over our shoulders with a little grin. "Well, actually..."

WAIT, WHAT?!

A wild cheer echoed through the trees as Jamie and I promptly lost our minds. Unable to believe it could be true. Unable to sit still for even a second.

It wasn't until Caleb put a heavy hand on our shoulders that we were able to calm down enough to take a breath.

"To shift out of excitement, pups, this is *probationary*," he cautioned sternly, staring at us in turn. "For the next few days, we're going to try things out. Up your training regimen. See what you both have to offer. *If*, at the end of that time, your father and I are satisfied with what we see then we can talk about the Hunt."

Jamie and I couldn't nod fast enough. Any faster and our heads might fall off completely. But now that our grandfather was finished, Michael stepped forward to take his turn.

"This is nothing like those romanticized stories I know you both have rattling around in your head." His voice was soft, but powerful. In a lot of ways, it was a hell of a lot more effective than Caleb's. "This is serious. This is life or death. One wrong move and I'll be bringing you back to your mother in pieces."

The cartoonish nodding stopped as Jamie and I stared back at him with impossibly wide eyes. The two of us had dreamed about the Hunt ever since I could remember. We'd pretended to be its champions as children in the sandbox, acting it out with toy soldiers and sticks. In all that time, it had never once occurred to either of us that we would be in any sort of actual danger.

We knew it was dangerous, of course. Hunters and Grollics lost their lives every time. But for whatever reason, we had always assumed we would be somehow above that. That our charmed life would carry over and we would fly into battle on the wings of all our powerful legacy, high on the adrenaline and the thrill, untouched by the actual grisly bloodshed. A pair of golden warriors, nothing holding us back.

Those images went up in smoke the second my father opened his mouth.

I felt Jamie stiffen beside me, and we reached out at the same time to take each other's hand. A silent promise was made. Unheard by any of the adults standing around us. More holy than any vow they'd ever taken.

We would keep each other safe, my brother and I. The same way we'd always done. The same way we'd continue to do.

You and me. Now and forever...

I shot him a glance from the corner of my eye. Our eyes met for a fleeting moment and he squeezed my fingers, finishing the silent oath.

...and any forevers after that.

"So, what's it going to be?" Seth's eyes lit with excitement as he looked between us. "You two need another telepathic moment, or can we get started?"

* * *

It was training unlike anything I'd ever experienced before. Training the likes of which I could not imagine.

Every muscle was screaming in protest. Every battered bone ached for relief. And yet, I kept pulling myself off the ground. Pushing myself past my every limit. Reaching forward with every ragged breath.

"Again, Rebekah! Again!"

My hands flew up to protect my face as Seth launched himself towards me. The wind whipped around my face as I tried my best to deflect his savage attacks. At this point, I wasn't even worried about attacking myself; I would simply settle for having all my limbs by the time we went in for dinner.

"Good," he complimented as I blocked a lethal kick delivered at blinding speed, "that's really good, Becka."

He isn't even out of breath! How's it possible that he isn't out of breath?!

"Don't patronize me," I panted, picking myself up off the dirt. "Give me your best shot, old man."

He threw back his head and laughed, waiting with everlasting patience as I dragged my weary body slowly forward. "You don't want me to do that."

No, probably not.

"But you really are doing well, Becka." He tilted his head speculatively as he looked me up and down. "It might seem hopeless, but try to remember that you're sparring against the best warriors in the kingdom. Your father is a legend in his own right. Caleb has never been beaten. Your Uncle Rob was named Alpha for a reason, and me? Well, I don't have to tell you about me."

Without another word, he lashed out three times in quick succession and I was down on the ground once more. Panting for air and trying not to cry. My eyes squinted into the light as a hand reached down to help me back up.

"My point is...not all your fights are going to be like this. You learn from the best. You'll grow to be the best."

Or die trying.

On the other side of the field, my brother wasn't having much better luck. In fact, it might have actually been worse for him. He was with Caleb.

There was a blur of golden hair as he crashed into the ground, hard enough to leave a small crater where he landed. Caleb's hand didn't shoot out to catch him this time. The training wheels were off and we were on our own.

A soft gasp escaped his lips, but he said not a word of complaint. Merely picked himself back up with the same fire-eyed determination as I had myself.

Caleb waited until he was standing, then took a step forward. "What did you do wrong?"

He was relentless. And terrifying. But that's why he was the best.

Jamie wiped a smear of blood from his forehead, trying as best he could to keep it together. "I didn't watch the left—"

"You didn't watch the left," Caleb interrupted before he could finish. A streak of black flashed through the air, and the next second my brother was lying on the ground once more, clutching his shoulder in pain. "The *left*, Jamie. Better you learn the lesson from me than from a rogue Grollic."

Jamie panted and pushed himself gingerly to his feet, cradling his injured arm protectively against his chest. "Y-Yes, sir."

Caleb nodded, pleased with his compliance, then strode forward once more, a predator hunting his prey. Jamie caught me watching, and sent me an agonized message.

Bex, quick! Shoot him!

A tired laugh rose up in my throat and I hurried forward, coming to stand in between them. "Why don't you pick on someone your own size? Or you scared to fight a girl?"

Caleb straightened up immediately, then a booming laugh rumbled out of his chest. A laugh I was well used to, but made Seth look over in surprise. All at once the warrior was put on the shelf, and our grandfather was back. His knuckles stained with streaks of our blood. "Not so easy fighting in the real world, is it?"

My eyes flickered around the field with a touch of irony. I'd have to disagree with him slightly as to the definition of the 'real world.' The top branches of one of the towering maples was cracked in half from where Seth had used it to launch himself into the air. "Are you stalling?" I deflected with a grinning sneer. "Come on, show me what you've got."

Caleb smiled indulgently as Seth openly laughed, twisting the top off a flask he pulled from his jacket pocket. "Not lacking in confidence, this one…"

There was a sudden rustling of grass as another voice echoed out over the lawn. "Now this is more like the Caleb I remember. The one I grew up with."

Jamie and I turned automatically as our father walked forward, surveying the grisly training ring with a thoughtful smile. His eyes swept automatically over his children, checking for damages, then he gestured Jamie forward so he could examine his arm.

"It's a sprain," Caleb said dismissively. "Nothing more than that."

Michael never lost focus, running his fingers delicately over Jamie's shoulder. "Oh. *Just* a sprain? Do you want to tell his mother that?"

"It's a shame we can't just fight like her," I piped up suddenly, remembering the way my mother had leveled the battlefield with just a soft flutter of her lips. "If nothing else, it would certainly save a lot of time…"

Caleb moved forward with a serious expression, unable to joke when the stakes were so high. "Your mother, like all the rest of us, started developing her power by centering her emotions. By focusing the latent power inside of her to project onto the outside world."

Jamie and I gazed back with blank stares. I was sure I'd read half of that on a fortune cookie somewhere. And I had no possible idea how I was supposed to apply it to my own life. Finally, when the silence drew on longer than was allowed, I gave my twin a discreet nudge.

"Sure," he said quickly, nodding along. "Of course."

This time, even Caleb had to smile. He did so while removing his silk tie, which he had actually been fighting with the entire time. Jamie and I trained in grass-stained athletic gear. Caleb did it in cufflinks. When he was finished he held it up in the air, dangling it down like a ribbon.

"Blindfolds."

Um...what? Did I just hear that right?

"That's impossible," Jamie countered, tilting his head to the side with a dubious frown. It was, wasn't it?

Caleb only smiled. "Michael."

Without another word, my father walked forward into the ring. He didn't seem surprised, he didn't even hesitate as Caleb wrapped the soft fabric around his eyes. Then, without a moment's pause, the two began to fight.

My jaw dropped open as my hair whipped around my face, flying back and forth with the sheer speed of it. With the sheer force.

I had never seen anything like it. Not in my entire life. Sure, I'd seen my father and grandfather spar from time to time, but it was nothing like this. It was nothing that could even touch this.

This was pure devastation.

Pure power.

They flew around at such a velocity, that before long there were mere streaks of color where the people were supposed to be. Violent collisions shook the air every few seconds, but they were almost instantly paired with equally raucous laughter. It was the laughter I didn't understand.

"Getting slow in your old age!" my father called with a grin, ducking into a crouch as Caleb's fist swung into the air above him before leaping around for an attack of his own. "Sarah would be ashamed."

How he was managing to fight, I would never know. The man couldn't *see*, for Pete's sake! How was he even staying on his own two feet?!

"If I'm getting slow, then you're getting rusty." Caleb kicked him in the center of the chest with the force of a small diesel truck, somersaulting him backwards. "Where's that flawless technique I taught you?"

"I'll show you."

With no more warning than that, my father flipped into the air. So high that he momentarily blocked out the sun. Jamie and I gasped in unison, and Seth let out an appreciative whistle as he rocketed down with a spinning kick.

It caught Caleb right in the throat. Or at least...it should have.

Faster than the eye could see his hand shot out and caught Michael by the ankle, stopping the savage momentum with a single flick of his wrist. My father froze on one leg—his other held high in the air—and took off the blindfold with a flushed smile.

A smile returned in full force by Caleb. "And *that* is how it's done."

There was a round of applause from the porch, where the women had come out to watch. Jamie and I stared in shock for another second before racing forward, desperate to try out the blindfold for ourselves.

I was only a step behind him, but came to a sudden pause when there was a vibration deep in my pocket. I pulled out my phone to see a text from a number I didn't recognize. It had to be Luca.

Where are we at with Thursday? Can you come?

The breathless excitement died in my eyes as I looked down at the screen. I hadn't asked my parents yet about my study session with Jamie over at the Kanes'. But I had a pretty good idea what they were going to say.

"Hey, Dad?"

Michael turned around and jogged over, his white-blond hair still standing up where the blindfold had held it at bay. "What's up, sweetie?"

I hesitated, turning the phone over and over in my hand.

"Do you think...do you think that I could go to a study session for that same history project over at Luca's house? His sister'll be there, too," I added quickly. "And they invited Jamie along."

Michael paused for a moment, glancing down at the phone before his face softened into a gentle frown. "Two times with the same mortal?"

"Yeah, but he's my history partner." It sounded rather lame when compared to 'mortal.' "We almost have it done, we just need a bit more time."

My father looked at me for another moment, both worry and sympathy battling it out behind his eyes before he made it my choice. "I'll tell you what, you can go out on Thursday or you can stay here and train."

He didn't need to finish. If I went out on Thursday, there would be no reason to come back and train. There would be no Hunt to train for.

I hesitated only a moment. Hesitated as Luca's magical smile flashed through my mind. Then I came to my senses, and tucked it safely away.

"I'll train."

Michael kissed me on the forehead, steering me back towards the ring. "That's my girl."

Chapter 11

Sometimes you have to risk what you want in order to gain what you want.

Or something like that. I gave up my Thursday night with Luca so I could chase after a bigger prize. Well, sort of. Luca wasn't a prize I was after. At least that's what I tried to tell myself.

Then again, we were talking about the Hunt. *THE HUNT.*

Every second Jamie and I weren't at school, we were outside in the grass ring—getting beaten down by either Caleb, or Sarah. Or Dad. Or Seth. Even Mom. Our training sessions with Rob were a bit different—they tended to be on all fours—but were no less brutal than the angelic death dance being taught to us by the other members of our family.

I had never been more exhausted and more exhilarated in my entire life.

The lessons had a way of taking hold of you, seeping deep down into your bones in a way that surpassed instinct and skill. In a way that simply became a part of who you were.

It wasn't long before Jamie and I found ourselves on the offensive. Not only dodging our elders' attacks, but countering them with attacks of our own. Attacks so fantastical and deadly, sometimes I didn't believe I was actually the one doing them until my feet landed back on the ground.

But of course, training life at home was only one half of the world I was balancing.

The day after Seth arrived, Luca came up to me at school.

"So what's the story with Thursday?" He took my book bag and swung it routinely over his shoulder, like it was an everyday occurrence. "Why can't you come over? Did you ask your parents?"

My throat tightened as I bowed my head. It a testament to how utterly infatuated I'd become, that even with the prospect of a Hunt I was still torn to pieces that I wasn't allowed to go to Luca Kane's house later that week. "I did, actually." With a grimace of apology, I forced myself to look him in the eyes. "It's not going to happen, Luca. I'm sorry."

Much to my relief, he didn't seem the least bit upset. Instead he shrugged it off with an easy smile, wrapping his arm around my shoulders. "No worries. Some other time." His fingers played with the lace fringe on my shirt as he gave me a little squeeze. "At any rate, it gives me more time to brush up on my game. You coming to my tryout?"

Jamie had made good on his promise. The day after the four of us ate lunch together for the first time, he went right to Mr. Barrow—who was filling in for the football coach—and asked if Luca could try out for the team. Barrow had agreed and set up a tryout for Luca on the field. It was football. It shouldn't have been a big deal that he was trying out but, somehow, the issue felt like it was important. Kind of like an initiation of some sort.

"Wouldn't miss it," I said with a grin, leaning into him as we passed a horde of giggling girls on the way to class.

I'm not going to lie, I'd been skeptical about the whole 'pretend couple' thing at first. Well, let's be honest, I was secretly thrilled, but skeptical. As it turned out, it had to be one of the best things that could have happened since I started high school. While I couldn't wait to go to a school that was inside our house, I also felt like I lived in a looking glass.

Before Luca, not a week would go by that I didn't get a slew of unsigned notes, or letters, or flowers stuffed nervously into my locker. That some random guy I'd never talked to before would profess his undying love, and then proceed to follow me from class to class.

But those days were long gone.

Now, the only communication I got from the opposite sex was when they paused to open a door for me, or move out of the way so I could pass them in the hall. It was like Luca had created some kind of invisible force field, and not one of them was brave enough to cross.

Of course, that wasn't the only thing I liked about our silly little game. Pretending to be dating Luca Kane came with other perks as well.

The best one being...*Luca Kane.*

If I had thought that my initial infatuation with the guy would be a passing thing, I was obviously mistaken. If nothing else, those feelings had only gotten stronger. Growing more day by day.

And it wasn't just his looks.

Although, I was having a consistently impossible time tearing my eyes away from his face. It wasn't just that jaw-droppingly gorgeous body, or those hypnotic eyes, or the sexy dimples when he smiled.

It was just...Luca. *Sigh...*

With just a bit of careful prodding, I was able to peel away the rough exterior. See past the standoffish demeanor he presented to the rest of the world. There was a softness behind those guarded eyes. A captivating light that drew me ever closer, unable to tear myself away.

It was crazy. It had only been a few days, but they'd had a profound impact on me.

A change that I could feel down in my very bones. Immortals didn't warm to people very easily, it wasn't in our programming, but Luca didn't seem to fit any of those rules. Even though he had come out of nowhere, I instinctively sensed that he would be important. Even though it had only been a few days, it was like I'd somehow known him my entire life.

I did question the coming out of nowhere. Could he be here for a reason? Was he really mortal? I mean, I could smell a wolf a mile away. I pushed the issue aside. Luca wasn't immortal. Nor was he a wolf. He just happened to be an extremely hot guy who was interested in me.

So I now looked forward to going to school the way most kids would look forward to throwing a party, or going to Disneyland. Every second I wasn't training away to earn my place on the Hunt I spent thinking about Luca. Each night when I lay down to go to sleep, his was the only face I would see.

It made keeping myself from turning into a bumbling idiot every day at school a real challenge, but strangely enough I seemed to be getting better at that as well. It was as if my short, but intense training sessions were starting to give me a newfound confidence. Making me feel comfortable in my skin in a way I'd never felt before. (It was a change that couldn't have come at a better time, because Luca was making me feel all kinds of things that I had never felt before.)

For the first time in my life, I started asking myself the same kinds of questions I knew only from magazines or hearing actresses say on TV.

Was I ready for a boyfriend? Was I ready to have sex? How far was too far? Did he like me as much as I liked him?

Would my family bury him in the forest if they ever found out?

Unfortunately, that last one was all me.

It was a nerve-wracking little game, especially with the Hunt finally within my grasp, but one that was well worth the risk.

As it turned out, Luca and I weren't the only ones playing...

"Olivia's going to sit with you during Luca's tryout, okay?" Jamie appeared out of nowhere as I walked across the grass, falling into stride beside me with a huge grin. "I think she's secretly hoping Luca's going to fail. Something about controlling that ungodly ego..."

It was Thursday afternoon. The day before our birthday. The day of the big football showdown. We could finally see a light at the end of the tunnel. A merciful end to what had to be the longest week of our lives, and both Jamie and I were giddy with the excitement of it.

"Just be careful out there today," I reminded him quietly. "You and I have been programmed into overdrive lately. The last thing you want to do is explain how you ended up throwing the defense halfway across the field."

Jamie shot me an arrogant smile, completely unconcerned. "You know I don't get near the defense, right? I'm the quarterback."

I cocked my head with a little frown. "But then how do you make all the baskets?"

"*Baskets?*" He stopped in his tracks, turning to me with that look of exasperation that only a brother could ever give. "This is football, Bex. There are no baskets, just touchdowns. How many times do I have to...you're just messing with me, aren't you?"

I jumped up with a grin, deliberately tangling his curly hair. "Yep! But thanks for man-splaining football. It was highly entertaining."

He chuckled, and the two of us continued walking out to the field. "You are the very worst..."

I grinned again, but as we got closer it faded into something stern. "I'm serious, Jamie. Don't be cocky. Don't be flashy. Just keep your head down and throw the ball. It's not like we can just turn these lessons on and off."

"I know," he interjected excitedly, completely missing the warning, "and we've only been at it a few days. Imagine how we're going to feel after a few weeks! A few months!" He dropped his voice so as not to be heard, eyes dancing as he considered the possibilities. "Just think of Caleb. It really explains him, doesn't it? The guy has had centuries to perfect his skills."

He certainly had. And look at what he'd become.

"I wonder what kind of people we're going to be after that much time..." I mused quietly, lifting my eyes to the horizon.

It wasn't a subject we liked to dwell on. When you're seventeen years old and completely isolated save for your sibling, the concept of 'eternity' isn't exactly a welcome one. I couldn't remember the last time Jamie and I had even discussed it. And somehow today, in light of the present circumstances, it seemed even worse than usual. We were going to be eighteen tomorrow. The same age Mom turned when she got the journal. Same year she found out she was the Seventh Mark. The seventh child, whose real name was Jamie, but had been called Rouge instead. Benjamin or Jamie was the name given to the seventh to stop the curse.

But that was a whole different story. A hidden secret one might say. A saga.

A soft sigh breezed by my ear and I glanced over to see Jamie staring blankly into the trees. It was the same look he'd gotten a lot this past week. A look of profound sadness, paired with the most unbearable powerlessness. Until recently, the two of us had never latched onto anyone. Now that we had, every second was tainted with knowing that we'd eventually have to say goodbye.

"So you're ditching me with your girlfriend, huh?" I asked with a teasing grin, making a deliberate effort to brighten the flailing conversation.

"She's not my girlfriend," he replied swiftly. It looked like that was going to be the end of it, until he shot me a sideways glance. *But I kissed her.*

I stopped dead in my tracks. "You *WHAT*?!"

The people walking behind us had to quickly veer off to avoiding crashing into me as I froze in place, openly gawking at my big brother.

Jamie glanced nervously around before grabbing my arm and pulling me forward. "Would you keep your voice down?"

I would try, but I refused to be distracted. My entire would had flipped upside-down in a single instant, and I was unable to understand how my twin was possibly being so calm.

"You *kissed* her?" I hissed. Half to confirm that's what he had said, half to give myself time to process the information. "When?"

He blushed a million shades of red. "After school. I don't know—what does it matter?"

"It matters *because you kissed her*!" I grabbed onto his arm, pulling us both to a stop. "Do Mom and Dad know?"

"Are you kidding?!" He yanked his arm away fiercely, his face growing pale just at the thought. "No! And they're *never going to know*. Promise me!" His eyes burned down into mine.

I nodded quickly. "Of course I promise. It's just...this is big, Jamie." Despite all the things working against it, my face lit up in a genuine smile. "You *kissed* her."

That had never happened before. For either of us.

An echo of that same smile danced across his face, undermining his every attempt to keep it under control. "Yeah, I kissed her. Can we just let it drop already? I'm already regretting telling you."

"Fine, I won't say anything." I zipped my lips and skipped along beside him as we headed to the field. "...about the fact that you kissed her."

A reluctant grin spread up the side of his face. A grin that grew thoughtful as he gazed down at me in the sun. "Just...sit with her, okay? I want you to get to know her. It's important to me."

I blinked up at him, unexpectedly touched that he desired my approval. "Then it's important to me." I slipped my arm through his, grinning ear to ear as he walked me to the bleachers. "Is she meeting me here?"

"Yeah, right after class." A whistle sounded in the background, and he turned his head towards the grass. "I've gotta go. See you after!"

"Good luck!"

Without another word he jogged off across the field, and I climbed up into the empty stands. Both of us spinning from what we'd just said. Both of us secretly worrying about all the things we'd yet to say.

The last bell of the day came and went, but Olivia didn't appear. I sat waiting, scanning the field and watching some of the school doors as time ticked
by.

I sat down on the bleachers, waiting and looking. Part of me had a feeling
that she wasn't going to show up. I was about to send Jamie a mental note
when my father walked up and settled beside me on the bleacher.

"Dad!" I looked up in surprise. I glanced around, making sure no one was
within earshot and Olivia wasn't on her way over. "What're you doing here?
I thought you were supposed to be trying to get a lead on the Rebel Faction
with Seth."

Jamie and I had taken to calling the factions of rogue Hunters and
Grollics the Rebel Alliance. We'd thought it was very clever, but that bit of
levity had been quickly shot down by the older members in our group.

"And miss a chance to watch my son play football?" Michael leaned back
with a contented smile. "Not a chance. Seth can handle it."

And that's one of the reasons I love you, Dad.

The two of us shared a little grin, and settled in to watch as the boys ran
out onto the field.

At first, it was just some basic warm-up drills. A lot of passing back and
forth, with some laps around the field. It was easy to see Jamie was a little
more wired than usual, but he handled it well, making sure to keep pace with
the rest of the team and not exceed them too spectacularly.

To me, it could not have been more boring.

That is, until Luca jogged out onto the field.

"That's the guy?" Dad asked with a little frown. I thought we were too far
away for him to get a good look, but what he did see he wasn't happy with.
Plus, Dad was immortal; he had eyes better than almost anyone. "That's the
guy who came over? Whose house you wanted to go to?"

"Who?" I tried to downplay it, but Luca wasn't making it easy. The
second he was on the field, he took off his shirt. Revealing just a tight-
fitting workout shirt below, deliciously stretched over his sculpted muscles.
"Uh...yeah." I shrugged as if I hadn't even noticed him. As if I hadn't been
staring in a daze for the last five seconds. "That's Luca."

Dad shot me a dry look before returning to the practice. "Uh-huh."

I didn't know much about the old coach but Barrow seemed to be doing a good job, putting them through their paces. After a few minutes, he divided them up into groups of four before calling Jamie and Luca over to him. Together, the three of them headed to the far end of the field for, what I could guess, was the tryout.

Come on, Luca. You've got this.

In hindsight, I don't know why I was even worried. Luca handled each drill like a pro. Running farther and farther down the field as Jamie threw him the ball. His legs blurred with the speed of it, and he caught each pass with effortless grace, reminding me very much of my own brother.

It quickly became apparent he was going to pass with flying colors, and before long the two boys digressed into a friendly competition. After just a few minutes Jamie joined him on the grass, and it was Barrow throwing the ball while they raced against each other to catch it.

The sounds of their laughter echoed up and down the field as they battled back and forth, trying to one-up each other. One of them would leap into the air, the other would dive to the ground. One of them would throw it back over his shoulder, the other would do it with his eyes closed.

The entire thing was going brilliantly, until one fateful moment.

The moment that things accidentally went a little too far.

I watched like it was happening in slow motion. The way Barrow pulled his arm all the way back, his face screwing up with concentration as he aimed for the sky. The way Jamie's heels sent up little sprays of dirt as he flew across the grass, his feet barely skimming the surface. The way his eyes dilated without thinking as he leapt into the air—higher than could be ignored, higher than could possibly be explained away. And finally, the way he flipped effortlessly back to the ground, the football tucked safe in his arms.

Only to straighten up and see the entire school watching.

The smile faded slowly from his face before dying in his eyes. The ball went loose in his grip as an eerie hush fell over the stands. Adults around the field stopped talking. The team went quiet. Even the cheerleaders paused their incessant jabbering to turn around and stare.

Jamie, what have you done?

My blood ran cold as I perched on the edge of the bleachers, every inch of my body tingling with an electric sort of readiness as I waited for the other shoe to drop. I hardly dared to look at my father, but when I finally chanced a peek at him in my periphery I was surprised to see that he wasn't looking at Jamie. He was looking at Jamie's coach.

"Get off the field, get off the field..." I whispered it repeatedly under my breath, too shaken up to use my telepathy. "Just get off the damn field..."

But Jamie was frozen in place, trapped under the terrifying spotlight of a million probing eyes. All the color seemed to drain out of his face, leaving it a deathly sort of pale as he took half a step backwards, poised to run.

Then a loud burst of laughter shattered the silence.

"Dude! That was awesome!"

Jamie jumped as if he'd been shocked as Luca strode casually across the grass, clapping him on the shoulder with an easy smile. The two locked eyes for a moment—one terrified, one completely calm—before Luca eased the ball from his hands.

Then, as if nothing at all out of the ordinary had happened, he began tossing it playfully into the air. Chattering on all the while. "...reminded me of this play I saw Elway do a few years back at the Super Bowl in Colorado. Do you remember the one I'm talking about? It started with this defensive blitz, and then..."

The longer he kept talking, the more the rest of the people watching instinctively relaxed. A strange sort of crowd mentality took over, and the second they saw one person dismiss what had happened they were able to dismiss it themselves. After a few seconds, tentative conversations started up again as people returned to what they'd been doing. A few seconds after that, the entire thing was forgotten.

Well...not by everybody.

"Rebekah, get your things," Michael muttered, never taking his eyes off his son. "We're leaving."

I nodded silently and did as he asked, following him obediently down the bleachers to the grass. But my gaze stayed locked on Jamie and Luca, standing in the middle of the field. Jamie had yet to move, and Luca had yet to stop talking. They simply stayed where they stood.

It wasn't until Michael pointed to the ground near his feet that Jamie jerked out of his horrified trance.

"I'm sorry, I...I have to go." A faint tremble ran through his body as he tore his eyes away from his father and turned to Luca instead. The latter was watching him with a strange sort of steadiness, a silent yet inexplicable show of support.

"No worries." His eyes swept Jamie up and down in a quick study, casual but careful all the while. "You okay?"

"Yeah, fine." Jamie was coming out of it quicker now, running his hands back through his hair as he pulled himself together. "Thanks, Luca." He flashed him a tense but grateful smile, then took off jogging across the field to where Michael and I were standing on the sidelines.

It was easy to see the fear on his face as he came closer. Waves of panic and remorse rolled off him, and by the time he reached us there was not an ounce of color left on his face. It was shock white.

I lowered my eyes to the grass as he stood, trembling, in front of our father. There were few absolutes in our world, few lines that you could never cross. He'd just crossed a big one. What happened next was anyone's guess.

"Dad, I...I'm so sorry," he began quietly. "I didn't mean to—"

"Get in the car." My father's voice cut through the air, sending a host of chills rocketing up my spine. This wasn't going to be good at all.

Jamie visibly flinched, then bowed his head, pulling his keys out of a pocket in his bag.

"Not that car. Give those keys to your sister," Michael instructed in that same terrifying calm. "You're riding with me."

Without a word, Jamie dropped the keys in my palm and followed my father across the lot to visitor parking. Leaving me to gather up the rest of our things and drive his car home.

I did so as quickly as I could. Torn between being thrilled that I wasn't about to get one of my father's infamous lectures, and feeling protective of Jamie all the while. As I swung both bags across my shoulder, my eyes flickered to the other side of the field. Did Jamie have a football bag I needed to grab? He was wearing a bunch of padding stuff and holding his helmet, but was there more? I gazed around and caught Luca still watching.

He met my eyes with a sad little smile, and lifted his hand in a wave. I stilled for a moment, staring back in a daze before lifting my hand as well.

A second later, I was racing to the student parking lot. *Screw the football bag, if there is one.* I hurried to toss my things in the back of the Mustang before diving inside. My father's sleek Porsche was already pulling out onto the road, but even an entire parking lot away I could hear him shouting.

Another belated shudder, and I threw the car into gear.

I knew something was about to hit the fan.

If only Jamie's little mistake was the worst of it. If only the little mishap on the field had been the end. But, unfortunately, I had a feeling things were just getting started...

Chapter 12

The mistake on the football field was just the start. More was to come. I was sure of it.

It happened the very next day. Right in the middle of our history presentations.

I'd shown up late for school, missing my first few classes. Not because of any special birthday surprise, but became my entire family was still on lockdown from the incident at the football tryout.

Happy freakin' birthday.

Michael had ranted and raged. Caleb had followed soon after. My mother didn't say a word, although her troubled silence was probably the worst of all. It lasted for well over two hours, until the adults had finally scolded themselves quiet. Then my Uncle Rob piped up with an ill-timed joke, asking if Jamie had at least caught the ball, and the entire thing started all over again.

Sports had always been a touchy subject in our house. At least since Jamie and I had been around. Not just because they could be seen as an unnecessary risk, but because of the rather controversial way in which they'd gotten started.

Jamie had tried out for the team in secret, then promptly panicked when he was picked to play. In that panic, he'd taken his permission slip to Caleb instead of Michael, hoping for an easier sell. Unfortunately, our father had been sitting in the office at the time and things hadn't gone well.

When confronted, Jamie had tried to defend himself.

"What was I supposed to do?" he exclaimed. "What are *you* going to do if the school calls for a parent- teacher conference, huh? You look the same age as me! I have to put Caleb's name on these things—"

"Caleb is not your father!"

That ended the conversation quickly.

But yesterday, Jamie had been in luck. After tearing him to shreds, the adults had decided that it would look too inconspicuous if he were to be pulled suddenly from the team. Luca's inexplicable save had salvaged the situation for now. As long as nothing else happened to raise alarms, we would be okay.

Unfortunately, that plan was about to go up in smoke. I should've seen it coming. I should've been more prepared for it. Except I wasn't...

"—which reflect the parallels to Marxism we can see today."

Luca and I gave each other a quick nod, then looked out at the rest of the class as we finished our presentation. True to form, they stared back in a lusty daze, not taking in a word we'd said even though their eyes were locked on our mouths the entire time. It wasn't until Mr. Barrow started up a pointed round of applause that they snapped out of it and began clapping along.

"Very good," he congratulated, gesturing us back to our seats. "That was very good. Thank you. Now, who's next?"

We walked quickly through the rows of desks, settling down in our usual seats at the back of the class. Briana and Chris were up next. After our performance, they looked nervous to be taking the stage.

"Hey, beautiful, is your brother okay?"

I turned my head sharply as Luca whispered to me under his breath. It was far too quiet for any of the other students to hear, but that didn't stop my heart from pounding against the walls of my chest. "He's fine. Why?"

The first three rules of having a secret life were all the same.

Deny, deny, deny.

Luca's eyes rested on me curiously before he lifted his shoulders in a dismissive shrug. "He looked pretty shaken up yesterday, that's all."

That's a bit of an understatement. "He's fine," I said again, more believably his time. For good measure, I paired it with a winning smile. "I think he just twisted his ankle when he came down. Caught him by surprise." *And that's a terrible excuse.*

Luca stared at me for a moment before his face lightened with the hint of a smile. "Yeah, that must have been it."

I turned my eyes deliberately back to the front as the next presentation began. This one was a study of inventions ranging all the way back to the late1800s. To help them out, Barrow had been kind enough to dig through the town archives and provide props.

"Flash photography was first created in 1887 by Adolf Miethe and Johannes Gaedicke," Briana said loudly, picking up an old camera and passing it around. "It was later revised by a man named—"

"You should take him to see a doctor."

I twisted around in surprise to see Luca staring at me with that same twinkling smile. The one that lingered in my mind long after it had faded. "What?"

The camera was getting closer and closer, passed from person to person as it travelled between the desks.

"Jamie." The corners of Luca's lips twitched up as he leaned back in his chair. "The last thing he wants is an injury right before the start of the season."

What was he talking about...? Oh, right. "Uh, yeah." I tucked my hair nervously behind my ears, hoping he would just let the subject drop. "I'll tell him."

Luca's quiet laughter came to an abrupt stop as the girl sitting next to him handed off the camera. He took it delicately, turning it once over in his hands before his eyes flickered up to me. A faint shadow passed across his face, one I didn't understand, before he offered it out with a smile.

At this point, I could not be less interested. I turned the antique camera over in my hands, pretending to examine it, while really, my mind was racing on to other things.

Why isn't Luca letting this go? And why exactly did he have to get involved in the first place? It was far too deliberate, the way he stepped in to intercede on Jamie's behalf. The timing seems... a little too perfect, the performance a little too scripted, and the look on his face says he knows more than he's letting on.

A realization was forming in the back of my mind. But I refused to acknowledge it. I wasn't ready—yet.

But what on earth does he think he knows? A person was either a part of the supernatural world, or they weren't. It wasn't like he could just—

My hands jerked of their own accord, and I looked down in surprise.

"What the hell?"

At first I thought I'd just gripped the camera too hard. Things like that tended to happen when I was distracted. But what started as a strange tingling sensation in the tips of my fingers soon sharpened into a white-hot burn. A burn that laced its way quickly up my arms.

I dropped the camera with a quiet shriek. At least, I tried to drop it. It was as if the metal had melted into my skin. A wave of panic swept over me, followed by an instant wave of pain. The burn crept higher still and I shrieked again, rocketing back in my chair as the edges of my skin started smoking.

"Rebekah?" Luca leapt up in alarm, trying to yank the thing free. "What's going on?! What's happening?!"

Mr. Barrow rushed over, pushing Luca aside as he wrestled with the camera himself. "Hold still! It's okay, just hold—"

There was a sudden flash as his flailing hand came down on the lever. A wave of powder exploded in the air, blanketing the both of us in a silver cloud.

That's when I screamed for the first time.

It was pain unlike anything I'd ever felt before. My entire body was alive with it. As if I was being pressed too close to a flame.

But the screaming wasn't out loud. It was just inside my mind.

JAMIE!

Not two seconds later, my brother burst into the room.

I shuddered to think how fast he must have raced out of his own class, but at the moment I couldn't have cared less. My skin was on fire. Nothing else mattered.

"Bex!" He tore through the rows of students, sliding to his knees at my side. His eyes flickered incredulously over the silver dust sprinkled across my face and hair, over the antique camera clutched between my sizzling fingers. Acting on impulse he tried grabbing it out of my hands, but dropped it a second later with a yelp of pain. The smell of burned flesh filled the air as a splash of blood splattered down upon the tile.

"I can't breathe!" I whispered, crimson tears spilling down my face. When the flash had gone off, I'd inhaled. It was inside me, eating me alive. Whatever the powder inside was, it had started burning the inside of my lungs. "Jamie, I can't—"

There was a loud bang as the door burst open again.

Only this time, it wasn't my brother who'd come to the rescue. It was my father.

"Dad?"

Jamie and I said it at the same time. Shocked beyond words to see him there, but relieved as hell at the same time. Part of me should have registered not to say the word 'Dad.' We should have called him Michael. He was too young-looking. I didn't clue in; I was too busy trying not to breathe, or gasp a shallow breath without screaming.

Michael's eyes swept quickly over the four of us—me, Luca, Jamie, and Barrow—before he blurred through the scattered desks and knelt by my side. Without a second's pause, he took off his jacket and wrapped it carefully over the camera. "Hold tight, Rebekah." Bracing me with one hand, the other wrenched it away.

I let out a soft cry as the skin peeled away from my fingers, leaving them bloody and raw. But no sooner had the blood hit the floor than I was up in my father's arms. Streaking out the door with Jamie hot on our heels.

No explanations. No looking back.

* * *

By the time we made it back to the house, my hands had already healed themselves. But the shock remained, along with the continual falling of tears. Jamie had texted the rest of our family from the car, and no sooner had we reached the porch steps than the front door burst open and they came pouring outside.

"I'm sorry! I'm sorry!" I wailed, reaching out for Caleb with a sob.

He grabbed me without a second thought, lifting me up in his arms. One hand stroked the back of my head as the other wrapped tightly around my ribs, rocking and soothing me all at the same time.

"There, there child," he murmured, kissing my forehead as the tips of my shoes brushed back and forth across the porch. "There's nothing for you to be sorry about. You did nothing wrong."

Maybe so, but I still couldn't manage to get a handle on myself. Another frightened sob ripped through me and I buried my face in his shirt, my damp curls soaking through the expensive fabric.

My father had pulled over the second we were off the main road, and grabbed a water bottle from the backseat. With incredibly gentle hands, he'd poured it carefully over my face—letting it rinse away the burning powder, while shielding my eyes with the back of his hand.

Strangely enough, it didn't seem to burn him. Even when Jamie and I had been hit with an instant reaction.

Thankfully, there was a second bottle of water in the trunk and he repeated the process again and again. Trickling it over my hair and face until there was nothing left but tender, pale skin.

"What happened?" Caleb demanded, glaring over the top of my head.

My father's eyes burned as he dropped something I couldn't see onto the ground. Something that shattered upon impact. "They were passing around an antique camera in class. The kind that used silver nitrate. The flash went off in her face."

Well, that explained it. Only wolves were susceptible to certain chemical compounds. As hybrids, Jamie and I were vulnerable. My father's angel blood left him immune.

"Why were you even there?" Jamie murmured, still in a daze as to what had happened. "You came in just a second after I did myself—"

"It doesn't matter," Michael replied swiftly. "You know realize the two of you can never go back to that school. Ever."

It took a few seconds for the words to sink in. A few seconds, but when they were over everything had changed.

"Wait...what?" Jamie backed away, as if he could feel each word in addition to hearing them.

I peeled myself slowly off Caleb and went to his side. "You can't...you can't just take us out of school. We're in the system. People know us there."

"I'm on the football team. We have friends..." he trailed off at the look on my father's face. A look as decided as it was unyielding.

The decision had already been made. And it was very much final.

"Dad, please." My voice cracked as I stared into his blue eyes. "I'm sorry about today, but we can find a way to fix it. We'll be more careful, I promise. Just please—please don't take us out of school."

Michael was unmoved.

"Yesterday, your brother jumped twenty feet into the air, and today, you touched a camera that melted off your skin. You're *done* with school."

Even though we were out in the open air, it felt like the walls were inching closer. A door closing shut. Forever locking us on the wrong side.

"Caleb, please," Jamie begged, unable to keep a note of panic from his voice, "talk to him—"

"How can I," Caleb answered briskly, "when I agree with your father absolutely?" The two of us wilted before him as he stared sympathetically into our eyes. "I'm sorry, children. We gave it a try, but that school is no place for you. It's better that you stay here. With your own kind."

"Mom and Dad went there. They met at school. Grace did, too. They had risks—"

"That we learned from," Caleb cut me off. "I didn't want you there in the first place. We all knew it wasn't going to work out. It was just a matter of time."

Jamie shut down. Every muscle locking into place as he bowed his head in defeat.

But I wasn't giving up so easily. In just a few hours, I'd be eighteen years old. Able to make my own choices. Able to decide for myself.

"I don't care what you say." I jutted up my chin, glaring back the tears as I wiped a leftover smear of blood from my face. "I'm going to school tomorrow—"

"You called me Dad," Michael interrupted sharply. "Both of you did, the second I stepped inside the room." He straightened to his full height, staring down with the wisdom of centuries, even though his body was forever frozen at nineteen. "How are you going to explain that?"

Words failed me. Solutions failed me. He was right. There was no explaining that away. There was nothing left to be done.

The dream, as magical as it had been, was over.

* * *

Seconds ticked by as I realized there was no going back. This was it.

"Let's go inside for your birthday," Michael muttered under his breath, glancing towards the house. "Your mother made a cake..."

We followed him inside, Caleb flanking our backs.

No one spoke. There was nothing left to say.

Dinner turned into a subdued affair. Jamie and I went through the motions: robotically swallowing the food, forcing polite conversation, blowing out the candles after everyone sang. But there was no life behind it. No sense of spirit or hope. All that was gone now. Taken away as we were permanently imprisoned in our magnificent house.

The second the festivities were technically over, Jamie and I headed upstairs to go to bed. Neither one of us felt much like celebrating, and to be honest there was only so long we could keep our emotions at bay.

I locked myself in the bathroom to take a long relaxing shower as he headed down to the weight room to punch the bag until it broke. By the time I got out and headed to my bedroom, all of his school things had been thrown carelessly into the hall, like he couldn't stand to look at them another second.

No doubt Sarah or someone would throw them away by the time he got up the next morning, sparing him from having to do it himself. But I couldn't help but stare wistfully as I leaned against the wall.

Wondering what had happened after we'd left. Wondering what was going to happen the next day. And the day after that.

A soft sigh escaped my lips as I turned on my heel and headed to my room. But just before I could slip inside, there was a knock on the front door.

I paused, curious to know who would come by this time of night.

"Hello?"

I paused mid-step as my Uncle Seth's voice echoed up the hall. I glanced down the stairwell.

He'd come home.

He'd missed all the drama the past two days, having been away tracking down leads on the faction the Hunt aimed to destroy. When no one answered him he stuck his head tentatively inside, two tiny presents clutched in his hands.

"Caleb? Rouge? Anybody?"

I was about to go down and answer, when a pair of heavy footsteps walked towards him from the downstairs hall.

A second later, Caleb's hushed voice whispered up the stairs. "Those can wait until tomorrow, Seth. The children are already asleep."

"At ten o'clock?" Seth sounded surprised. "It's their birthday. They didn't want to stay up a little—"

"They weren't in the mood to celebrate," Caleb interrupted, sounding abruptly tired. "Michael pulled them out of school today."

"Permanently?" Seth sounded shocked. "Why? What happened?!"

"It's a long story." Caleb deliberately lowered his voice, indicating for Seth to do the same. "Let's just say, they're not going back."

There was a pause, followed by a low whistle.

"Well, shit." Seth was the only one who was either crazy enough, or brave enough, to curse around Caleb. "That's terrible. How are they taking it?"

"Jamie threw a tantrum. Rebekah's pouting." Caleb sighed as if the entire ordeal was exhausting. "They're kids. They can't possibly see the bigger picture at their age. They're taking it like kids."

Oh, we couldn't, could we? My eyes glowed with anger as I backed slowly into my room. *We dumb kids just threw tantrums and pouted, is that right?!*

I closed the door silently behind me before falling onto the middle of my bed in a rage. Ironically, I was somewhere very much between pouting and throwing a tantrum. Not that I was going to admit that to anyone. How could they do this to us?! How could they keep us here?! Presume to know what was best?! Make the choice for us?!

We were ADULTS now! It wasn't up to them. It was up to us! And I, for one, wasn't going to stay locked up in this crappy house forever.

No sooner had I thought the words than there was a buzz in my pocket. I glanced down in surprise, wondering why Jamie had texted instead of just telepathically calling me, before I realized that he was no longer the only person in the world who happened to have my number in their phone. It wasn't Jamie.

Sure enough, it was from Luca. A simple text.

You okay?

I sighed as my hair spilled down over the screen, before texting a reply.

Fine. But not sure when I'm going to see you again. My dad's pulling us out of school.

There was a brief pause, before a message lit up the screen.

...All because you took a bad picture?

I grinned in spite of myself. Only Luca could find a way to make a joke about the fact that a camera nearly melted off my hands.

Lol, this is serious. We're officially out. Today was our last day of freedom.

Another pause. Followed by a cryptic answer.

Well the day's not over yet...

Five minutes later, I was flying down the hall to Jamie's room. My feet ghosting across the hardwood floors. The door was closed but unlocked, and I slipped inside without a sound.

"Hey," Jamie sat up slowly on his bed, "what's up—"

I clamped my hand over his mouth. My eyes glowing with excitement.

How would you feel about going to a little party? I grinned wickedly. *Maybe, our own birthday party?*

Chapter 13

"You sure this is a good idea?" Jamie nervously glanced around as the two of us ventured cautiously into the trees. "Sneaking into the forest. In the middle of the night?" A branch creaked softly behind him and he jumped a mile. "If our life was a movie, this is the part where the audience would be screaming that we're both idiots who deserve whatever's coming."

"Except it's not a movie, and we're going to a *solstice* party. Come on, Jamie. It's our birthday! What do our parents and family do? Basically ground us for being...teenagers!" I tried to hide behind anger but I wasn't sure if Jamie was buying it. "What's the worst that could happen?" Bold words, but I pulled my jacket tighter as I said them, walking surreptitiously closer to my brother. "Besides, we were invited by a *teacher*. What could be more respectable than that?"

A trio of bats screeched through the air, freezing us in place.

"Well," Jamie whispered, "considering the fact that we no longer *have* teachers, I'm not sure it really applies."

I gulped silently and nudged him forward. He shook his head. Another push and the two of us started moving, albeit at a much slower pace. "I thought you were the guy here," I muttered.

"What the hell is a solstice party, anyway?" Jamie asked after a few more minutes of wandering. Every shadow reached towards us, and every whispered sound made us jump. "It sounds like the kind of thing where we're supposed to bring packets of henna and sit together on pumpkins."

A nervous grin flitted across my face as I discreetly took his arm. "Actually, from what I've been told it sounds like the kind of thing where we're supposed to take off our clothes and dance naked under the stars."

127

He stopped dead cold, staring down at me in the dark.

"I'm kidding."

For another twenty minutes we wandered through the trees. Both taking turns looking behind us to see if we were being followed by one, or all, of our family. Getting away without getting caught seemed odd. Not that we'd ever tried before. We'd never disobeyed like this. *Focus, Becks. It's just a party. Normal things teenagers do.* Twenty minutes to figure out we were going the right way. Not so long in the real world, but it felt like a small eternity in the dark. By the time we finally saw lights in the distance, we'd both discreetly armed ourselves with sticks. As it turned out, having superpowers didn't make much of a difference in the adolescent mind. Too many movies. Too much television.

"Mr. Barrow invited you here?" Jamie asked doubtfully as we got closer, peering through the trees with a little frown. "To this?"

I hated to admit it, but I kind of understood his skepticism. From the looks of things, it wasn't a solstice party so much as a woodland rave. There were flashing neon lights, buckets of dry ice, and an intricate sound system blasting music into the trees. An enormous bonfire roared in the center of the clearing, and someone had even managed to throw a disco ball over the branches of one of the ancient trees towering up above. The moon reflected off its silver mirrors, raining down sparks of metallic light on everyone scattered blow.

"Well...this is it." I spread my arms uncertainly, not sure whether that was a good or a bad thing. "Consider it my birthday present to you."

There was a violent retching sound, and the two of us froze in place as a man stumbled out of the bushes and threw up just inches from our shoes.

"Really?" Jamie was deadpan. "I didn't get you anything."

The rest of the party looked to be more of the same. Drunk and stupid. A waste of time. I was on the verge of just grabbing my brother and walking away, when a sudden voice rang out through the trees.

"Rebekah? Jamie?" We looked up at the same time to see Mr. Barrow walking towards us, a beaming smile lighting his face. "I thought that was you! I'm so glad you made it out!"

He looked as happy and relaxed as I'd ever seen him, finally free of the professional shackles The glasses were tucked safely away in his pocket, the tie nowhere to be seen, and it was easy to see that the wide grin most likely had a lot to do with the five or six beers he'd already consumed. Or more. Who was counting?

"I'm actually particularly glad to see you, Rebekah." His forehead creased with concern. "I wanted to make sure you were all right after what happened in class today."

My spine stiffened as a wave of ice-cold dread coursed through me.

Of course he would mention that—what was I thinking coming here?! And the party's probably full of more kids from school! "Oh, that..." I stalled for time, tucking my hair behind my ears as I sent my brother a telepathic SOS. "That was actually just—"

"Severe allergic reaction," Jamie intervened smoothly, flashing his coach a distracting smile. "Looked a lot worse than it was."

Much to my surprise, Barrow didn't question a word of it. He merely chuckled—taking two drinks off a passing tray and pressing them into our hands. "That was my fault. I should've thought of it before I picked up the camera from the town archives. Must have completely slipped my mind."

Should have thought of what? That one of his students might possibly have a supernatural reaction to a chemical used in an extinguished flash?

Jamie and I stared down at the drinks, at a complete loss as to what to do. It was strange enough that our teacher had handed them to us. Let alone our inebriated teacher whom we'd met at a secret party in the woods. Yeah, not movie material at all.

I was starting to think Jamie was right after all. Maybe the movie audiences would be screaming at us. If this was a book, this would be where readers would start shaking their heads and talking out loud. Probably calling us idiots. Or maybe worse.

Maybe we should just go home.

"Drink up," Barrow urged, taking another one for himself and downing it in a single instant. "You only live once."

Jamie swished the liquid uneasily in his cup, while I peered tentatively down into the dark, trying to discern any distinguishable smell.

"What is it?" I asked, torn between the prospect of being the only one *not* partaking, and the fact that my infamous grandfather would be able to smell a drop of alcohol on me over a mile away.

"It's punch," Barrow answered with a smile. "Special punch." When the two of us still didn't move, he cocked his head suddenly to the side. "Wait a minute, didn't the two of you just have a birthday?"

Jamie blanked as I glanced to the side with a telepathic question. *I didn't tell him that. Did you?*

He shook his head a fraction of an inch, a little frown creasing the center of his brow. *I don't like this, Becka. This feels...wrong.*

I couldn't disagree. From the moment we'd stepped into the clearing, something had felt off about the whole thing. I couldn't explain it. But it was off. Now how did we get out of here without causing a problem, or showing Barrow that our living once lasted forever?

"You *did* have a birthday!" Barrow raised his glass cheerfully, holding it in the air for a toast. "To eighteen! May it be full of surprises!"

Every single person within earshot raised their own glasses as well, and in the end Jamie and I had no choice but to follow suit. We raised our cups with a reluctant smile, and toasted with all the rest of them.

The second the liquid touched my lips, the effect was instantaneous. In a single breath all the tension and hesitation and worry left my body, leaving me feeling strangely numb in its wake. Was this the way it was supposed to happen? Was this why kids our age were always sneaking off to get drunk?

Without thinking, I raised the cup to my lips and took another sip. And another sip after that. I glanced over. Jamie's cup was already empty.

Barrow swapped it out with a full one before Jamie could even notice it was gone, clapping him on the shoulder with an unsettling smile. "So," he leaned a few inches closer, taking in every detail of my brother's face with an attentiveness I didn't understand, "that was quite the football tryout the other day..."

Jamie glanced up suddenly, as if he'd only just realized Barrow was there. His eyes struggled to adjust to the sudden proximity, then he leaned back a few inches. "Uh...yeah. Luca was great."

Barrow chuckled again, pulling him a step closer. "I wasn't talking about Luca, I was talking about you." He flashed a neon grin in the pulsing lights, his teeth alternating with every color. "I would swear you had wings. The way you flew into the air to catch the ball!"

The music cut off with a screech. The lights stopped flashing. I swear even the dancing flames of the bonfire momentarily paused as every person in the woodland clearing turned at the same time to stare at me and my brother.

It was my every nightmare come to life.

A cold chill swept over my skin as I stared out into the darkness. What looked like a hundred glittering eyes stared back at me from the shadows.

Watching. Waiting.

My instincts screamed at me, screaming something important, but I couldn't hear them over the sudden ringing in my ears. I could hardly pull in a breath under the weight of all those hungry stares.

Jamie had frozen dead still, his face deathly pale. A look of sheer panic had swept over him, but like me he seemed unable to move. His lips parted uncertainly, but he was unable to speak. He simply stood there. Breathless.

There was a split-second pause, a second that seemed to go on forever, but it was shattered as Barrow laughed. He burst out so loudly, contagiously. In a way that made the rest of the party suddenly relax into laughter themselves. "Don't look so stricken. It was incredible!" He clapped Jamie on the shoulders with a warm chuckle, flashing me a wink. "Maybe if we get a couple drinks in you, you'll show us again."

My eyebrows lifted slowly as the world around me tilted and spun.

"Um...what?" Jamie tried to smile, but he looked as uncomfortable as I'd ever seen him. Without seeming to think about it, he reached out to take my hand. "Actually, I think we'd better be getting back. We, uh, only came to let you know that we couldn't stay. Family birthday thing...and all that..." His voice trailed off.

There was a quiet murmur behind us, and for a split second I was terrified these people wouldn't let us. The lines on Barrow's face hardened the slightest degree before softening immediately after.

"Of course. I can take you."

"That's all right," Jamie replied as we backed away, polite to a fault. "We can manage."

Barrow stared intently, but didn't say a word as we wove through the throng of restless people and edged discreetly to the end of the field. We'd almost made it back into the trees, when two new faces appeared suddenly in the crowd.

Two faces I realized that I'd been looking for the entire time.

"Bex?" Luca was in front of me the next instant, that intoxicating scent washing over me from head to toe. "Are you leaving already? I just got here."

I tried to focus on his face as the rest of the world blurred in and out of the picture. When that didn't work, I tried to focus only on his smile. "Yeah, we're not..." I lost my train of thought entirely, gripping harder onto Jamie's sleeve. "We need to...we need to get home."

"But you'll miss the whole party." Olivia slipped her hand into Jamie's free one with a coaxing smile. "Come on. Won't you stay just a little bit longer? I still haven't given you your birthday present." She licked her lips as she continued smiling at Jamie.

A flicker of indecision troubled Jamie's handsome face. His hands twitched and he glanced down at his feet, like he was waiting for them to make up their minds, but they stayed rooted to the spot.

Rebekah, what's happening—

"Just stay for one more drink." Barrow threw open his arms, gesturing around the woods with a welcoming smile. "After all, it's not every day we get to raise a glass with the children of angels."

My eyes lifted in astonishment as Luca stiffened dramatically by my side. He turned quickly, like there was something he was dying to get off his chest, but apparently Barrow beat him to the punch.

"Tell me, do the two of you prefer the term 'Your Highness'? Or can I keep calling you Rebekah and Jamie?"

The cup slipped from my hand.

It was instantly replaced with another.

"You...you knew?" I could hardly get the words out. Could hardly manage to string them into a sentence. "This whole time, you knew?"

Barrow smiled and beckoned us closer to the fire. I was fairly sure my legs wouldn't take me, but before I knew it I was there.

"Of course I knew," he replied in surprisingly gentle tones. "It isn't hard to recognize one of our own. And the two of you tend to stand out regardless."

Wait a second...one of our own?

"You?" Jamie's mouth fell open as he took a step forward, staring at his football coach in genuine shock. "You're saying that you—"

"—I'm a Hunter, that's right." Barrow gestured around the clearing, at the thirty or so faces flickering in the firelight. "We all are. Every single one."

My eyes flashed around the clearing in pure astonishment. Coming to rest on each one of the gathered immortals in turn. Such a vast array. Young and old. Rich and poor. An entire community I never knew existed. *Does Caleb know?*

Maybe I'd misjudged them before? Maybe they weren't aggressive...but simply eager? Even Barrow. Hadn't he done nothing but toast us and smile?

Then my eyes came to rest on one face in particular.

"How could you?" I whispered, my eyes welling up with a host of sudden tears. "How could you not tell me? This whole time...you just lied? Every day?" I wasn't sure if I was more mad at him, or at the fact I hadn't figured out he was like me. *I should've known.*

Luca bowed his head, his eyes burning such a hole in the ground it was a wonder he didn't fall right through. "I wanted to tell you. I wanted to tell you every day." Without seeming to realize it, his eyes flickered to Barrow. They *rested* there for a second before returning to my face. "Rebekah, I was...I was scared."

"Scared?" I shook my head, trying my best to understand as the world of logic and reason slipped in and out of reach. "Scared of what? What could you possibly have to risk by telling me—"

"But it isn't just you," he interrupted gently. "It's your whole family." I turned automatically to Jamie, but Luca shook his head. "Not your brother; I mean your parents. Your grandparents. Your aunt and uncle. You come from a family of immortal legends, Rebekah. And based on the fact that they've kept you cloistered away—living in isolation—I'm guessing they're pretty protective."

"So isolated, you couldn't even recognize your own kind," Barrow inserted quietly.

Luca flashed him a look, and Barrow fell silent.

I glanced at Jamie but he looked as lost as I felt. He kept staring around at everyone, his gaze slipping back to me and then Olivia, time and time again.

"I didn't know how to tell you." Luca reached up without thinking and stroked a lock of hair away from my face. "I knew I couldn't just blurt it out, and I was scared that if your family found out—they would take you away." His voice dropped to a rough whisper. "I'd never get to see you again."

I pulled away from his hand, staring in a dazed sort of confusion as the flames of the bonfire danced across his beautiful face. Everything he was saying made some sort of sense, and yet...I couldn't wrap my head around it.

My brother wasn't having any better luck.

"You said...you said you lived with your uncle." His words slurred slightly as he took deep, steadying breaths. "That your parents died in a car crash. But that couldn't be true. A car crash couldn't kill a Hunter. Or are you not a descendent Hunter like us? Are you...an original?" Jamie's eyes grew big as he whispered the words. Even as he asked, though, I knew it wasn't right. They weren't originals. Not Luca and Olivia. That much I was sure of.

Olivia blushed and looked at the ground. She seemed to be having the same problem as Luca. The burning desire to come clean, battling with the acute awareness that the eyes of the village were upon her. "I do live with my uncle," she said quietly, glancing up at Barrow. Jamie followed the gesture, his face lighting up with surprise.

"Coach?" he repeated in disbelief, unable to reconcile the bizarre events unfolding around him. "You live with the coach—"

"It's William, actually." Barrow stepped forward with a smile, waiting patiently for our minds to catch up. "William Barrow. But you can call me Will."

Olivia flinched imperceptibly, too slightly for almost anyone else to notice. She glanced behind her with a look of strained patience before returning to Jamie.

"And my parents didn't die in a car crash. They were killed seventeen years ago. On a beach in Florida." She hesitated for a moment before pushing forward. "Some of the first casualties in your parents' war against Bentos."

Bentos?

Jamie and I shared a look of bewilderment, turning back to the siblings. They stared back with equal confusion, unable to believe it was true.

"Bentos?" I echoed, the name foreign on my tongue. "Who the hell is Bentos? What're you talking about?"

Olivia's mouth fell open in shock, while Luca turned to Barrow with a look of scarcely contained rage. "What did I tell you?" he demanded under his breath. "They're innocent to all this. They know nothing."

Barrow's mouth pressed into a thin line as he just stared speculatively at us across the fire.

A wave of rising panic was bubbling up inside of me, threatening to overpower the numbing paralysis that had taken hold. I needed to get out of here, away from all these new people. Away from all these new names. I needed to get back home to the people I trusted. To a place where things made sense.

And yet...I somehow felt this was exactly where I was supposed to be.

"Rebekah." Luca took my hand in his own, leading me gently towards the fire. "You have questions. Let me answer them. I'll walk you through it, tell you whatever you want to know—"

"Yes, you will," a strong voice interrupted. I looked up in a daze to see Barrow standing right in front of me. He flicked me under the chin with a smile, then pressed a fresh drink in my hand. "*Later*. Tonight, we celebrate."

Luca eyed the drink warily, and suppressed a soft sigh. When Barrow offered him one as well, he poured it out onto the grass.

"Not tonight." His face flashed with an emotion I didn't understand as I tilted dizzily on the grass beside him. "They'll need someone steady."

"It's a party, Luca," Barrow answered softly, handing him another. "We came here tonight to have fun..."

The trees began spinning, and I had the strangest feeling that I wasn't going to remember much of this come tomorrow. I watched as Luca gritted his teeth, but finally accepted a drink. Watched as Olivia downed one as well. Then a second. Then a third.

Things began to get fuzzy after that.

I felt like I might have been walking away, but wasn't sure. No matter how far I tried to go, it wasn't long before I ended up back at the fire. A dozen images flashed before my eyes. People dancing. People laughing. People playing music and singing along to guitars. The air was light and scented with beer and honey. The stars twinkled merrily above us.

This is fun, right? At least, that's what my brain was telling me. *These are good people. People I want to know. People like me.*

That being said, I wasn't exactly in a condition to join in myself. After my third cup of whatever drink they were giving me, my body slowly shut down. At least, I thought it was my third cup; I couldn't seem to keep count.

I need help. I need my brother.

Jamie was swaying where he stood as Olivia pressed drunken kisses into his neck. His eyes were glazed, and he didn't seem to have any better idea what was going on than I did. Instead, I turned to the man standing beside me.

"Luca," I whispered, reaching out a hand for balance as I tried desperately to keep my eyelids from falling shut, "what's happening..."

A pair of strong hands caught me as I slipped to the ground. The smell of fresh leaves and grass tickled my nose as the muscles in my body relaxed, one by one. On the other side of the clearing, Olivia was helping Jamie down as well, laying his head upon a rolled-up sweater by the fire.

"It's okay, honey," she murmured. "Just breathe. Breathe through it."

A familiar smell washed over me and I leaned into it, pressing my face into Luca's chest as he lay the both of us down on the grass. A second later, his jacket draped over me. I cuddled under it, suddenly feeling more tired than I'd ever felt in my entire life.

"I'm sorry."

The words whispered in the air above me. Too soft for me to hear. I tried to lift my head, gazing helplessly into Luca's eyes.

"What did you say?"

He sighed again and squeezed his arms tighter around me, leaning down to press a soft kiss against my cheek. "I said...happy birthday."

Chapter 14

I woke up in that quiet moment just before dawn.

Birds chirping around me. Leaves from the forest tangled in my hair. A lingering cloud of smoke drifted aimlessly away from the remains of the bonfire, and the sky above me glowed pink with the coming sunrise.

Oh—and there was a bird on my chest.

I sucked in a quick gasp of surprise as I stared at it. It stared back at me. For a split second, neither of us moved.

Then it took off with a sudden flap of its wings. Leaving me to wonder if the entire encounter ever even happened.

...what the hell?

I gazed around in a daze, squinting into the light as I tried to figure out what had happened. As I tried to understand why I was covered in dew.

Then an arm tightened around my waist, and I looked up with a gasp.

Luca was asleep beside me. Leaning up against a tree. The early morning sun had painted him in a soft glow, his dark hair spilling messily down his forehead as the shadows of his long lashes stretched across his face. One hand was still holding an empty cup as his other arm wrapped around my ribs. Both of us were still fully clothed—that much at least was clear—but there was a strange intimacy to the way we were lying. A physical connection I hadn't remembered making the previous night.

Come to think of it, I couldn't remember a lot about the previous night...

Moving as quietly as possible I gingerly extracted myself from his grasp, setting his arm back on the ground so as not to wake him. The second I was free I pulled myself shakily to my feet, staring around the field in shock.

I actually slept here last night. I actually didn't go home.

137

A wave of panic crashed over me, followed by a wave of dread. What were my parents going to say?! What was Caleb going to do?! A part of me was amazed they hadn't already called in the U.S. Marshals to search the woods.

Jamie!

There was a soft stirring behind me, and I turned around to see Luca shifting restlessly in his sleep. His breathing hitched as his hand groped blindly around in the leaves, searching for me. Thinking fast, I picked up an abandoned jacket by my feet and curled it into a little ball, slipping it under his arm where I'd been lying just a moment before.

It worked.

His breathing steadied and slowed, and a second later he was fast asleep once again. It was a relief, but Luca Kane was turning out to be the least of my problems. I didn't have time to deal with him; I needed to get home. And before I could do that, I needed to find my brother.

"Jamie!" I called in a whispered hiss before remembering that I was equipped with slightly more discreet ways to get his attention. *JAMIE!*

The telepathy worked. There was a sudden movement on the other side of the clearing, and I saw my brother blink open his eyes.

Oh, thank bloody goodness!

He lay by the smoldering fire with one side of his face pressed into the dirt. His golden hair a tangle of soot and leaves, and as my voice echoed inside his mind he lifted a hand to his temple with a wince, trying like hell to get his bearings.

"...Rebekah?"

He made the same mistake that I did. Speaking out loud. I mentally hushed him as I hurried over across the clearing. The grass beneath my feet was littered with sleeping bodies, all in various states of dishevelment and repose. Some were strewn by themselves beneath the fading stars. Others were tangled on top of each other, searching for a pillow anywhere they could. A trio of kids was tucked safely inside a hollowed-out log, snoring happily, while a girl beneath my feet had passed out with a ring of flowers in her hair.

Becka, what happened? Did we... did we stay the night? Jamie pushed up onto his elbows, only to have Olivia start sliding off his chest. He caught her quickly, looking surprised that she was even there, then lay her gently down on the ground.

Yeah, we did, I answered, staring around me with a touch of fear. *Jamie, we've got to go. I can't even imagine what our family is doing right now...* I trailed off as we both looked automatically in the direction of the house.

Jamie's face whitened several shades before he nodded quickly, forcing himself up to his feet. He swayed the second he was vertical, but didn't fall. I wrapped his arm over my shoulder just in case, and a second later the two of us were stumbling back through the woods, leaving our crazy night behind us.

We didn't talk much on the way back. Neither of us had any idea what to say, and we were both far too nervous about what would be waiting for us on the other side of the trees. It wasn't until we could hear sounds of the main road that I pulled Jamie to a sudden stop.

"Okay. We need to come up with some kind of story," I said in a rush, my eyes nervously darting around. "Some kind of story that doesn't make it sound like we just had some kind of orgy in the woods."

Jamie's face paled even more drastically as he took a step back. "Holy hell, Rebekah...do you think that's what happened?"

"What?! No!" I smacked him on the chest, hoping he would wake up a little bit and help me. "We fell asleep, genius. That's all. We just...fell asleep."

It sounded simple enough, but it opened the door to a whole other world of questions just waiting to be answered. Questions like, why did we go out to the woods in the first place? What happened when we got there? What the freak was in that punch?

"Do you remember anything?" he asked softly, rubbing the back of his neck. However much I'd had to drink, Jamie had at least doubled it. There were dark bruises in the hollows beneath his eyes, and no matter how valiantly he was trying to stand straight the slightest breeze was enough to catch him off balance. "Because I don't. Not a thing. I don't even remember falling asleep."

A shaky breath shook through my shoulders, and I bowed my head. "No, not really. Just bits and flashes." A wave of nausea crept over me and I struggled to breathe through it, trying my best to put the pieces back together. "I remember people dancing around the fire. Singing. Laughing." A sudden memory floated to the surface, and I pulled up my sleeve. "Some kid drew a flower on my hand..."

There was a sudden convulsion, and Jamie threw up on the forest floor.

"Oh crap!" I ran over to him, holding back his hair as he quickly emptied the rest of his stomach. "It's going to be okay. Just breathe."

He straightened up with a ragged breath, looking like some reanimated corpse. "Whatever Caleb does to us...it can't be worse than this."

I snorted sarcastically as the two of us headed back to the main road. "You're worried about Caleb? You should be worried about Dad. Or Mom." I inhaled a shaky breath. "We're dead. So dead."

Jamie scoffed. "Kind of ironic for an immortal, isn't it?"

Chapter 15

We didn't say another word as we trudged miserably down the side of the highway in the direction of our house. Jamie was trying very hard not to get sick, and I kept going over the night again and again in my mind.

There was more that we weren't remembering. More that had blurred away into the fog. Things that were important. Things that were hiding just under the surface, just out of my reach.

A name...There was something about a name...

"Rebekah," Jamie said softly, pulling me to a stop.

I lifted my eyes to see my entire family standing in a line at the base of the hill. Arms folded across their chests. A vicious fire blazing in their eyes.

Oh, this is not going to be good...

They didn't come to us.

They made us go to them.

We did so as quickly as we were able under the circumstances. Stumbling clumsily through the dense underbrush before coming to a guilty stop. The castle loomed up behind them as the two of us bowed our heads. Bracing for what was about to come.

It started with my mother. It was she who drew first blood.

"Did something happen?" she asked in a soft, lethal voice, looking us over in turn. "Or did you do this on your own?"

Jamie's shoulder's hunched as my eyes filled with guilty tears.

"We went out on our own," I answered quietly, mortified to have caused her such worry. "We were upset about yesterday. Mom, I'm...I'm so sorry—"

She left without another word, heading back up into the house. Sarah, Grace, Seth, and Rob were soon to follow. Apparently now that they knew we were both alive and well, they would let Caleb and Michael proceed to murder us.

"Have you LOST your MINDS?!"

My grandfather's voice echoed off the tall trees, ringing back again and again, louder every time. Jamie flinched against the sound, wincing with the mother of all hangovers, and Caleb proceeded to ask the question again, just inches from his grandson's ears.

"ANSWER me! Have the two of you gone COMPLETELY INSANE?!"

"I'm sorry," Jamie answered softly, still looking like he was on the verge of getting violently ill. "We didn't think—"

"NO! You most certainly DID NOT THINK!" When Jamie failed to answer Caleb took him by the chin, jerking up his face to examine his bloodshot eyes. "JAMES ALEXANDER KNIGHTLY! Have you been DRINKING?!"

"That's enough, Caleb." Michael spoke quietly, looking at each of us in turn. "Let him go; we'll meet you inside."

Caleb was livid.

"They are my *grandchildren*—"

"And I'm their father."

The two men stared each other down for a moment before Caleb turned sharply on his heel and headed inside. But before he left, he glanced over his shoulder and dealt one final blow. "Jamie's a teenage boy. I can expect a certain degree of rash impulsivity from a teenage boy. But you...?" He shook his head, looking as disappointed as I'd ever seen him. "Rebekah, I expected better from you."

With that, he vanished into the house. Leaving me feeling so terrible, I wished that the bonfire last night had swallowed me whole. But we weren't out of the woods yet. Caleb might have left, but my father was just getting started.

"Where did you go?" he demanded. "What happened to you?"

"Nothing," I murmured, pawing at the grass with my shoe. "Nothing happened, we just wanted to blow off a little steam—"

"Don't lie to me, Rebekah!" His voice echoed dangerously in the little clearing. "You smell like smoke and beer, and you have the stench of a dozen other people all over you. Now tell me what happened."

Words failed me, so he turned to my twin instead.

Jamie met his eyes only for a second before staring down at the grass. "We got together with a few friends from school. That's all."

He didn't say which ones. A fact my father was quick to notice.

"Who?" When my brother didn't say anything he stepped closer, bringing them toe to toe. "Jamie, tell me right now."

Becka—

Just tell him, I answered miserably. *It's not like he doesn't already know.*

Jamie sighed, bowing his head as a pair of leaves fell from his hair. "It was a few guys from the football team, and...Luca and Olivia Kane."

My father stared at us for a long time. So long that I began to wonder if he was considering disowning us entirely. Then he nodded suddenly and jerked his head towards the yard. "Get in the house."

Jamie and I obeyed without another word. Keeping our eyes locked on the grass as we hurried down the hill and in through the back door. It clicked ominously behind us, and I couldn't help but think that we were never going to be allowed outside the walls again. The sounds of a quiet conversation echoed down the hall from the parlor, but the living room itself was deserted.

"I'm going to take a shower," Jamie muttered, rubbing at a smudge of dirt circling his wrist. "Let things cool down a little."

Yeah, that's never going to happen. I nodded quickly and the two of us headed towards the stairs. We'd just made it to the front door, when I stopped suddenly in my tracks. My hand shot out to grab Jamie as all the hair on the back of my neck stood on end.

"What is it?" he asked, glancing over his shoulder. "What's wrong?"

I didn't answer. I just stared down at the stack of photographs scattered across the floor. A single face was staring up at me, from a million different angles, from a million different points of view. It was a face I knew very well.

"Coach Barrow?" Jamie muttered in surprise. His hand reached out to trace one of the pictures. "Why—"

"*That* is the reason you can't go back to school." Caleb folded his arms sternly across his chest, glaring at us from the other end of the hall. "It appears there was a little more to your history teacher than we thought. The man is a Hunter. He transferred here because of you."

And like the camera that went off in school, everything suddenly clicked.

The inexplicable fog blocking me from remembering what had happened through the night suddenly lifted. The memories of what had happened came rushing back in one fell swoop.

My face paled, and instead of answering my grandfather I turned to Jamie.

He was staring at the picture with a look of dawning recognition, the same dark clarity that had taken hold of me.

It can't be... Even my own telepathic voice was trembling and weak. *Tell me it's not true...*

"For us?" Jamie interrupted, turning suddenly to Caleb. "What do you mean, he transferred here for us?"

Caleb gave him a long look, and chose his words carefully. "That scoundrel of a man has ties to the Lower Coven, Jamie. I can only imagine what he intended by putting himself in a position to get close to the two of you." For a split second, a look of genuine emotion softened the edges of his face. But before I could make heads or tails of it, the parental anger came back and he was untouchable once more. "Fortunately, that no longer has anything to do with you. After tonight, Mr. Barrow will no longer be a problem." He swept away without another word.

I knew where he was going.

He was going to meet with the others and make all the necessary preparations.

I gasped suddenly, realizing what it meant.

"No, no, no!" I whispered. I'd suddenly realized who my family had been planning a Hunt for...

* * *

"Rebekah, this is crazy!" Jamie raced after me down the hall, barely keeping pace as I flew around corners and up flights of stairs. "Please, would you just stop for a second? We can figure this out—"

"They're going to kill them, Jamie." I whirled around on the top stair, right beneath the attic door. It was a door we seldom opened. For as long as I could remember, it had been locked. "Not just Barrow, but everyone else who was with him last night. The kids from school. The others there." My throat tightened as another pair of faces flashed through my mind. "...Luca and Olivia."

Jamie blanched, but held his ground. "They only mentioned Barrow. They only had his picture." I scoffed, but he pressed ahead. "You can't know that anyone else is a target, Bex!"

"You're deluding yourself—"

"Mom and Dad...they wouldn't wipe out an entire community like the one we saw. They just wouldn't." Jamie said the words with confidence, but he couldn't quite hide the faint tremor that lurked underneath. The desperate need for his own words to be true. "It has to just be about Barrow."

A scathing retort rose to the tip of my tongue, but died when I saw the look on his face. The muted fear. The desperate hope shining in his blue eyes. "Okay, so what if it is just about Barrow?" I reasoned, taking another approach. "You really think that the man deserves to die?"

Jamie paused, shifting uneasily back and forth. "I don't..." he trailed off, then tried again, "we don't know his crime—"

"You're assuming there is one," I countered. "You heard what Caleb said—that they could 'only imagine' what he'd intended by transferring over to Port Q. They don't actually know..." I shook my head. "We did this, Jamie. We did. This is our fault. We—"

"So what do you suggest?" Jamie interrupted, his knuckles clenched white on the banister. "That we go charging in, guns blazing, with no idea what the hell's going on? That we go against our own family?! Steal Mom's book—"

"We're not stealing the journal." I crossed my arms defensively. "We're borrowing one spell. Just something to get us out of here so that we can warn Luca and Olivia and get back before anyone's the wiser. That's it."

"That's it?" Jamie shook his head with a look of scarcely contained exasperation. "Yeah, you're right. That's no big deal at all."

His sarcasm wasn't lost on me, but in this case I could see no alternative. This was the only plan that had even a chance of success.

"And what would you suggest?" I put my hands on my hips, and looked him right in the eye. "That we do nothing? That we let Barrow die?"

Saying the name again did the trick. No longer was it a hypothetical scenario. It was a real person now. An actual face burning in Jamie's mind.

His hands clenched into fists before he relaxed them with a curse. "This had better work..."

Chapter 16

The lock on the attic door was no match for our strength.

Jamie simply closed his fingers around it, crushing it to a powder in his hand. A second later we were creeping up the stairs, vanishing behind the forbidden door.

It was a testament to how forgotten this part of the house was, that a thick layer of dust had settled over everything inside. A sight that would have made our neat-freak grandmother lose her mind.

The journal sat on a wooden stand in the middle of the room. Ironic that it was just left out in the open, with no guard to protect it.

I hurried over. Jamie lingered by the stairs to keep watch.

"Hurry," he whispered. "We've gotta go!"

I took a deep breath and touched the journal for the first time. A cloud of dust exploded in the air, and a strange feeling of warmth swept through my hands the moment I made contact. It was as though the book was touching me just as surely as I was touching it. Like it was a two-way interaction. A union between two living, sentient things.

"Bex, find the spell and let's get out of here!"

I snapped out of my trance, and started flipping through the pages. Some of them were in English, but most were in a language I didn't understand. A heavy script that gave me chills just to look at it.

But my mother's handwriting was there as well. Scribbled along the margins and at the bottom of the page. A comforting beacon amongst the rest.

The woman had spells for everything!

To slow time. To vanish a trail. To make bread. From the mundane to the impossible, it seemed there was nothing her magic couldn't do.

The sudden magnitude of the task in front of me suddenly hit home, and I stared down in dismay at the massive book in front of me. Ironic that it was small, yet somehow felt massive now in my hands. How was I going to possibly find what I was looking for in this short amount of time? How could I possibly locate just one little thing amongst the rest?

"I just need a simple spell," I murmured, tracing my hands down a random page. "I just need a way to get out of here..."

There was a sudden yelp, and I looked up to see Jamie staring wildly in my direction. His face shone with panic as he stepped away from the door.

"Rebekah?" His eyes swept over me, then past me, as they roved desperately over the attic. My face screwed up with confusion, but before I could say a word he darted forward, his voice shaking with alarm. "Holy crap! I knew this was a bad idea! Rebekah—"

I clapped a hand over his mouth before he could alert the others.

"What are you doing?!" I hissed. "They're going to hear you!"

His jaw dropped open as his entire body suddenly stilled. "...Becka?"

I stared at him, hoping my look let him know how much of an idiot he was being.

He reached forward and poked me right in the eye.

"Ow!" I slapped his hand away, rubbing furiously at my face "What the heck? Why'd you do that?! What's wrong with you—"

"You're invisible!"

I froze in place, then slowly looked down at my hands. They didn't look invisible to me. Maybe my brother was still a drunk.

"Don't be an idiot," I murmured, trying to keep the fear from my voice. "I can't be—"

He pulled me in front of a mirror in the corner, holding tightly to my hand. My eyes widened in shock. There was only one person standing in the reflection. And it certainly wasn't me.

"...I'm invisible."

"I told you."

This must be it! This must be the way out I was looking for!

"Jamie, go to the book!" I exclaimed, shoving him forward. "Say exactly the same words that I did! Then we can get out of here!"

He dug in his heels against the floor, staring at it warily.

"Wait a second. Do you know a way to get un-invisible?! What if we just get stuck like this, Bex?! Forever?"

"Gimme a break! You know Mom can always set us right! Just do it!"

With a look of extreme trepidation, he headed over to the book. The same look of wonder flashed across his face as he lay his hands upon it; the same little grin snaked up the side of this face as his lips muttered the magic words.

The second he was finished, he looked up at me expectantly.

"Well? Did it work?"

Only one way to find out.

The two of us crossed back over to the mirror, gazing incredulously into the smooth glass. I could see Jamie standing beside me, clear as day, but there was no one looking back at us in the reflection.

"Guess it did." The two of us shared a childish grin before we tore across the room and to the window. "Guess it's time to go!"

* * *

Not ten minutes later, we were already across town. Luca had texted me his and Olivia's address—back when he was hoping I was going to come to work on our history project—and it was still listed in my phone.

Jamie and I sprinted all the way there, then stopped at the same time and stared up in horror at the dilapidated house in front of us.

"This is it?" he asked under his breath. "*This* is where they live?"

It was nothing like how I imagined. Both Luca and Olivia always came off as so polished. There was nothing about them in person that would indicate they lived like this.

The paint was peeling, the tiles were cracking, and even from where I stood I could smell the faint aroma of mildew drifting from the walls.

"Let's just go," I muttered. "We don't have a lot of time."

The two of us marched up the front steps without another word and knocked loudly on the door. As we stood there waiting, I nudged Jamie and pointed to our reflection in the glass screen.

We were both there. The magic had apparently run its course.

He nodded, and when the two of us got no response we pressed our ears to the door. There were people in there, all right. I could hear Luca and Olivia arguing back and forth. They were so caught up in it, they didn't hear the door.

A wave of anger crashed over me, and I flashed my brother a look. He nodded slightly, then took a step back and kicked the whole thing down.

The arguing cut off suddenly as both Olivia and Luca raced into the front room. Luca's hands were raised in front of him, like he was ready to fight, but when he saw Jamie and me standing there he lowered them slowly.

"So you remembered, huh? The drugs wore off."

Jamie and I froze with matching expressions.

"Drugs?" I repeated in disbelief, afraid to hear the answer, even though it was an answer I'd already guessed. Alcohol wasn't as quick and debilitating as what happened yesterday. That was something else. "You drugged us?"

A look of actual pain tightened Luca's face as he took a step back to lean against the wall. "Barrow did. He wanted you docile. Open. Compliant."

Jamie's eyes burned as his fingers curled into fists. "Then he's a dead man."

Olivia flinched, and I gave my brother a quick look. I understood his anger, but it wasn't why we were there. We had come for a reason.

"Have you ever heard of the Hunt?"

Both Luca and Olivia paled at the same time. They shot each other a silent communicative glance before turning back to us.

"Of course," she said, her voice gravelly and raw. "The Hunt is the game the Higher Coven plays when they decide to murder people in cold blood."

"People who threaten the peace," Jamie fired back. "People who would rather see every Grollic or Hunter exterminated than live in peace with them."

For the first time I could remember, her lovely face grew strangely cold.

"What a beautiful story they've told you..."

"Liv, be quiet," Luca warned. His eyes softened a bit as they fell onto me, filled with a sadness and guilt I couldn't begin to describe. "Why do you ask?"

Our eyes locked for a suspended moment.

Then I lifted my chin. "Because they're coming for you."

This time, the words' effect was instantaneous. Olivia let out a little gasp as Luca pulled her automatically into his chest, glancing towards the windows.

"Right now?" His words were sharp, efficient. Practiced. "Why're you telling us? Are you here to help?"

Was I here to help? How could he ask me that? Words failed me as my eyes filled with tears. He recanted immediately, looking like he wanted nothing more than to reach out to me, but my furious older brother stood in his path.

"Not you. Barrow." His eyes flickered briefly to Olivia before turning deliberately to the wall. "But we wanted to warn all of you. We figured that if they had Barrow's name, that would mean—"

"—that they'd hunt down and kill everyone you met last night," she interrupted sharply. "Yes, it does. That's exactly what they're going to do."

I knew it. Everyone we met. Everyone we saw. Laughing and dancing to the music. They were all about to be killed.

Jamie...we can't let that happen.

He abandoned pretense altogether and turned to me, a mixture of frustration and uncertainty battling in his eyes. *What're we supposed to do?*

My lips parted, but I didn't know how to respond. I knew for a fact that Caleb and the others wouldn't listen to us if we tried to stop them. And I knew for a fact that we weren't strong enough to stop them ourselves.

"What about your mother's book?"

Jamie and I looked over suddenly to where Olivia was looking as though a magical life raft had fallen down from the sky. She and Luca shared a quick glance before she took a step forward.

"Legend has it that after the great war, she continued developing her magic on her own time. What if there's something in there that could help us?"

This time, I stepped forward in a rage. "Like what?" I demanded. "You want us to find you a handy bit of magic that'll help you kill our mother? Have you lost your freakin' mind?!"

"Not kill her," Luca said quickly, raising his hands to calm things down. I could tell he didn't like the way Jamie was looking at him, and he was quick to soothe tempers before things got out of control. "Hide *us*."

That...could work.

Jamie and I shared a quick glance. His gave me the slightest of nods as my eyes shone with relief. Yes, that could definitely work.

...if only we could get the book.

"One spell," Jamie said quietly, "something to cloak you. Then you and your friends are out of our lives. Forever. We never see you again. Agreed?"

Luca's face tightened as Olivia's eyes sparkled with tears.

"Is that what you want?" she asked quietly.

Jamie pulled in a deep breath, trying to rein in his emotions and get himself under control. When he was unable, he turned to me instead. I repeated his word from before.

"Agreed?"

It was like a door closed between us.

Luca's face shut down as Olivia turned deliberately to the wall to hide her face.

"Yeah...agreed," Luca said without emotion.

We all stood there a moment, each lost in what maybe could have been, what might have been, and what never would be.

"Let's go," Jamie finally said and turned, slipping his hand around my elbow as he walked outside.

They had to come with us to the house. We could think of no other way. It was a risky move, but there simply wasn't time to split up. We needed to get them off the radar and out of the state as soon as possible.

The plan was simple. They would hide in the woods, while Jamie and I returned to the attic and found a spell that would cloak the group.

A simple plan, but it wasn't going to happen. We never made it inside.

* * *

The door opened a half-second before I touched it, creaking slowly in the soft breeze. "I was wondering when the two of you were going to show up," Caleb snapped.

A moment later, my entire family walked outside.

So much for a stealth attack.

Jamie and I melted away from the door, stumbling backwards down the steps and onto the lawn. At first, the only emotion I had room for was fear. Not fear for myself, but fear for those people we had failed to protect.

It took me a second to realize Caleb wasn't talking to us; he was talking to our friends.

"What're you saying?" Jamie glanced between the two groups, growing more confused with each pass. "You...you know them?"

Caleb's face grew cold. "I don't know them, but we've certainly been watching them. As soon as we found out about Barrow, we investigated his known associates. Why do you think your father was already at the school the day Rebekah was attacked?"

This cannot be happening. This can't...be happening.

"Attacked?" I repeated in a daze. "I wasn't attacked, that was...that was a coincidence. These kids passed around the camera for their presentation—"

"It was an attack," my father interjected, his eyes falling on Luca and Olivia in a way that sent chills running up my spine. "Just like the bonfire."

This time, it was too much. I took a step away from the rest of the group, staring up at my father in disbelief.

"How do you know about that? Were you following us?"

"I was protecting you," he countered fiercely. "I recognized the look in Jamie's eyes. The way both of you were hardly able to stand. You were given a mixture of triazolam and diazepam. A sedative to keep you gentle. To keep you there until morning."

My mouth dropped open in shock, and I glanced over my shoulder at Luca. His face was tense, but he was staring at me with nothing to hide. His hands lifted into the air as he shook his head.

"You know that's not true," he said quietly. "I drank the same punch that you did. It wasn't drugged."

"Liar!" my mother hissed. "Barrow probably insisted you drink it as well to keep up pretenses. To keep them from trying to get home."

"You mean *this* home?" Luca's eyes flashed as he glanced up at the towering castle. "You mean the place where you keep them prisoner?"

Luca! What are you doing?!

He stepped boldly into the clearing, staring up without fear into the faces of the most dangerous warriors the world had ever seen. "Where you refuse to tell them their own history. Repeatedly deny crucial information. So they can never find out who they are. Who they should be."

Michael stepped forward with a little snarl. "Careful, kid. I'm not above killing you where you stand."

"We don't want any of that," Jamie said quickly, eyes flickering between his father and Olivia. Without seeming to realize it, he angled his body protectively in between. "We just want you to let them go in peace. Take Barrow if you want. You have a good reason, but let the rest of them go."

The four of us looked up in silence, waiting to hear what they'd say. Not daring to move. Not daring to breathe. It was the longest few seconds of my life.

Then Caleb shook his head with a chilling smile. "I'm sorry, Jamie. It doesn't work like that."

You could have heard a pin drop.

The entire world seemed to pause around us as we stared up in dismay.

"What?" I asked the single word of everyone around me and Jamie.

We were horrified, but the rest of them were unyielding. Cold. A group of people who had survived too many battles to take any chances now.

"They're in league with Barrow," Seth repeated, not an ounce of humor on his perpetually playful face. "They deserve to die."

Barrow? The way he said it, Seth sounded like he was trying to say that they were in league with Lucifer. That was stupid. And impossible.

Right?

I felt like I was trapped in a dream. A horrible dream. The kind where I couldn't wake up. "You can't possibly be serious." My voice was little more than a disbelieving whisper. "They didn't do anything wrong. They're our age—"

"They're the first connection we've ever made," Jamie interjected, his eyes flashing with the same newly-awakened horror as mine. "Our first ties to the real world. You can't just—"

"You're not supposed to be making connections at all!" Caleb thundered. "You're not supposed to be connecting with anybody! How many times do we have to tell you that?! How many more messes do we have to clean up?!"

A decade's worth of anger came pouring out of me as the walls came down and Jamie and I finally snapped.

"That's not a way we can LIVE, Caleb!" I screamed. "That's not a way that anyone can live! We're eighteen years old! We've tried to be careful! We're not your little science experiments; you can't treat us like that—"

"That's entirely unfair!" Caleb shouted, finally pushed past his limit. "I love you and your brother with all my heart! You have always been my grand-children first, and an anomaly second! You know that! But no matter how much you want to deny it—you and your brother are different! You've been set apart for a reason!"

"And did you ever think that isolation wasn't the best strategy?!" Jamie yelled back, refusing to give an inch. "You can't just keep us locked up the way you do! Never letting us go out! Watching us every second! No one can live like that! It's suffocating!"

"I don't care if you feel suffocated, as long as you're safe!" My father's voice echoed in the clearing, stopping the back-and-forth in its tracks. "Do you have any idea how terrifying it's been? Watching the two of you grow up?"

Jamie and I froze in silence, staring back in a daze.

"At ten years old, you were already doing things that your aunt and I didn't start to do until decades later. At fifteen, you were moving faster than Caleb is able to move now."

Eighteen years of worry and panic came pouring out as my mother stepped forward and slipped her hand into his. "You're a wolf, but you shifted before your eighteenth birthday," she said softly. "No one in the world is sup-posed to be able to do that. You're an angel, but even as children, you out-shone the rest." Her eyes glittered knowingly as they looked us up and down. "And I'm willing to bet that you played around with a bit of magic today. That's how you got out of the house without any of us knowing. All that...and you just turned eighteen."

It was a powerful birthday for those born into the supernatural commu-nity. One I knew my family had been increasingly worried about the closer we got to the big day. Year by year it was building up inside of them as they watched us, waiting. I just never realized how much it was eating them up in-side. I never realized the things they were willing to do.

Jamie and I bowed our heads as my father took a step forward.

"Don't you see? The things you can do, the potential for who you're able to become...it's not normal! There are a million people in the world who would love nothing more than to take advantage. And you just met two of them!"

The explosive argument came to an abrupt pause as I glanced back into Luca's eyes. They might have been right about everything else, but they were wrong about him. He wouldn't do the things they were saying. He couldn't.

"That's not true," I said quickly, shaking my head back and forth as I took a step away. "They wouldn't do that. Neither one of them. They're our first friends. We have a connection—"

"They didn't connect with you," Seth argued. "They targeted you." He looked them both up and down, nothing but pure murder in his eyes. "They did so because you're both sweet and trusting. They wanted to take advantage. But it ends today."

He took a step forward, but Jamie pushed him back. Shaking his head back and forth just as quickly as me.

"No! You're wrong about them. They don't even want us to come with them. They just want to leave—"

"What're you doing here, Jamie?" Sarah asked suddenly. "You came to take your mother's journal. What is the one thing we've always told you that the enemy wants?" She waited a heartbeat before answering for us. "Your mother's journal."

"Two things," Caleb added under his breath. "They've always wanted the two of you as well."

Jamie and I shared a stricken look. Unable to stand against them, but unable to walk away and see the people we'd come to care about ripped apart before our very eyes. It felt like we were being torn in half.

"Just let them go?" I phrased it like a question, my voice as small and frightened as a child's. These people had done a lot of things for me over the years. Surely, they would do this, too. "Please, just let them walk away?"

My father gave me a look supreme pity before he slowly shook his head. "I'm sorry, Rebekah. I would do anything else for you...but not that."

It felt as though something in my chest was literally tearing in half. It was a feeling unlike anything I'd experienced before. I didn't think I'd survive the pain. When my father took a step forward, my eyes spilled over in tears.

But he'd angled first towards Olivia, and before he'd taken more than a few steps Jamie stood firmly in his way.

"I can't let you do this, Dad," he whispered. "I can't let you hurt her. If you lay a hand on her...I swear to you, I'll walk away."

A broken sob rose in my chest, but as my eyes locked with Luca's I suddenly knew that I would do exactly the same thing. The two of us were connected in a way I couldn't walk away from. I would fight to protect it.

...even if it was against my own family.

Michael came to a sudden stop, staring Jamie in the eyes. "What do you think, son?" he asked quietly. "Think you've got what it takes to beat your old man?"

Jamie's face tightened, and his eyes shone with tears. "I don't want to do this." He turned first to his father, and then to his mother. "Please. Just say you won't hurt them."

"Fine," Caleb interjected coldly. "We won't hurt them."

Jamie's face fell in despair as our mother took a step forward. "They want to hurt you. It's the one thing I can't allow."

"No, they don't!" I insisted, looking around for anyone who was willing to help. "They would never do that! You're wrong about them!"

Caleb stepped forward with a sigh. "No, sweetheart, you are." His lips thinned into a hard line as he looked Luca right in the eye. "But don't worry; I have no intention of letting them."

There was a sudden shimmer in the air, followed by a feral growl. The next second Jamie shifted into a wolf, landing on the ground in front of them.

Caleb took a step back. Stunned. Never before had his grandson lifted a hand against him. Not sincerely. Never in anything more than play.

The wolf's giant head bowed in obvious distress but he held his ground, anchoring his body squarely in between Caleb and Olivia. Forever staking his claim.

My turn.

Without another word, I stepped in front of Luca. Hands tensed and ready by my side. Prepared to do whatever I had to, if only to keep him safe.

"I'm sorry," I dropped into a deliberate fighting stance, bracing myself against the hard ground, "but the answer is no."

My father straightened up in shock as a river of tears fell down my mother's face. Caleb was looking at me like he'd never seen me before.

"Don't make me do this, child." One hand clutched at his chest as each word tore away a small piece of him. "Please, just come home."

A wave of sheer devastation flashed through my eyes, but I shook my head, taking a tiny step back towards Luca. "Not if you insist on killing him. You need to make a choice."

His eyes tightened as he slowly shook his head. "It's not me who's making the choice, sweetheart. It's you."

Everyone stood frozen, waiting for someone to make the first move. Finally my father shook his head and clenched his jaw. His eyes locked upon Luca before narrowing with hate. "It's a choice she won't have to deal with very long—"

But at that moment, several things happened at once. My father whipped out a knife and leapt into the air, aiming it straight at Luca's heart, just as I threw back my head with an unearthly scream.

"ENOUGH!"

The sky ripped in two as the ground itself started shaking. Dark thunder clouds rolled in from up ahead, as everyone still standing was thrown violently off their feet. There were shrieks and screams in the mad scramble that followed, but a line had been drawn in the sand.

Everyone on the side of the house had fallen. Everyone on my side was still standing.

Without stopping to think, I grabbed Luca's hand and took off into the trees. Jamie stared after me for a second in shock before picking up Olivia and doing the exact same thing. We heard the distant echoes of shouts and cries as the ground blurred beneath our feet, but before we knew it they had faded completely away.

The sky stitched itself back together. The ground stopped trembling. The forces that had shaken the world apart slowly fell back.

Jamie and I slowed at the same time, then stopped running. He set down Olivia as Luca fell to the ground beside me, trying to catch his breath.

"What just happened?" Luca panted, staring at me with eyes both terrified and completely in awe. "Is it over? Is that the end of the Hunt?"

Jamie and I shared a silent look before I shook my head. The wind picked up around me as I gazed out at the cliff, looking towards the horizon.

"The Hunt isn't over. It's just begun." I sighed, suddenly feeling older than my eighteen years. "And we've just added our names to the list..."

THE END
White Winter – Coming Soon

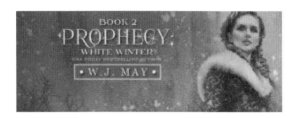

White Winter, Prophecy Series #2

Loved ONLY THE BEGINNING? Find out who Rogue and Michael are in the Hidden Secrets Saga – Read what happened to send Jamie and Rebekah's life into secrecy!
You won't be disappointed!

Seventh Mark part 1 included here FOR FREE!!

Book Trailer: http://www.youtube.com/watch?v=Y-_vVYC1gvo

Seventh Mark – Part 1
Book 1 of the Hidden Secrets Saga
By W. J. May
Copyright 2013 by W.J. May

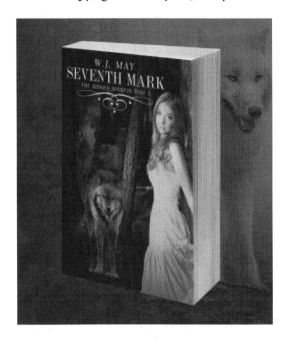

SEVENTH MARK Blurb:

Like most teenagers, Rouge is trying to figure out who she is and what she wants to be. With little knowledge about her past, she has questions but has never tried to find the answers. Everything changes when she befriends a strangely intoxicating family. Siblings Grace and Michael, appear to have secrets which seem connected to Rouge. Her hunch is confirmed when a horrible incident occurs at an outdoor party. Rouge may be the only one who can find the answer.

An ancient journal, a Sioghra necklace and a special mark force life-altering decisions for a girl who grew up unprepared to fight for her life or others.

All secrets have a cost and Rouge's determination to find the truth can only lead to trouble...or something even more sinister.

Warning: There are werewolves in this story... and they are not friendly.

** Warning #2: This book will end on a cliff-hanger. Book 2 picks up where this book ends.**

Chapter 1

Ear buds stuffed in, I cranked the volume on my iPod and clicked my exercise shuffle. I jogged down the gravel driveway and turned to follow the last bit of sunset. *If only I could draw or paint...*

Crossing an intersection, I headed left and let my legs carry me away from the small houses, run-down yards, cracked door screens and broken-down cars into a block of bigger houses. The lawns rolled further away from the sidewalk and the houses grew farther apart. *Maybe one day I'll buy a place like this.* I snorted at the thought.

Even though I'd never admit it to anyone, a part of me is cursed. Like poison running through my veins, I've always believed it would catch up with me. I didn't know the whys or hows, but deep down it seemed inevitable.

Except now fate intervened, and for once in my life, thank goodness. If it hadn't, I wouldn't be here, in this awesome place on the other side of the country. The whole curse thing was probably just in my head.

I gazed straight in front, between the old giant trees lining the roads. The jagged pink and white peaks reflected snow from the remains of the setting sun made me appreciate the beauty of nature. *West coast, oh yeah!* I smiled, unable to keep the giddiness inside. I'd lived all my life in Niagara Falls, but this—words couldn't begin to describe this beauty.

Inhaling real fresh pine scent, not the kind from cleaning agents from the past two days, I savoured the moment. If Family and Children Services hadn't approved Jim and Sally's request, I wouldn't be seeing real mountains for the first time. As quick as the bubble came up, it burst.

Next January I'd be eighteen and no longer at the benefit of the government. Jim and Sally were decent foster parents, but they also made it clear they couldn't afford to help me with college. I quickened my pace. I didn't want to think about where I might be in a year.

You'll be on your own...no family. Nothing. Unwanted again. The imaginary little devil on my left shoulder laughed at me.

Music shouted in my ear, "You're supposed to be alone. Alone...lone...lone..." I glanced at my left shoulder and pretended to flick the imaginary devil off, nearly crashing into the old high-stoned wall lining the neighborhood. Regaining my balance and focus, I pulled the iPod out of my pocket and skipped to the next song.

Street lights flickered on. My eyes had grown accustomed to the darkness without even letting my brain know. *I should turn around before it's completely black.* Didn't want to be out on my own when I barely knew the area.

A gap ahead in the high wall caught my attention. Curiosity won. Instead of heading back, I pushed forward. A public park entrance came into view. Heavy black iron gates led me onto a smooth paved entrance. A large raised garden split the road in two.

A plaque set into the garden's stone wall made me smile. End of an Era. From the raised stones peeking behind the garden flowers, this was a cemetery, not a park. The owner obviously had a sense of humor along with the desire to create one of those resting places with a welcome. A twenty-something looking woman whizzed by on roller blades, waving as she passed.

The pathways were lit up with those new solar green energy lights. I took the first lane along the outer border and slowed my pace. The tall slate and marble gravestones were erected on the left side with an ancient forest lining the right. As I jogged, I passed through a part of the cemetery that must've been the original lot with worn-down, ancient-looking stones. I paused or weaved between the stones to read the odd one: "1886 John Hartzel—18 years of age, 1892 Patrick O'Reilly—died too young, Tammy Fortune 1802 -1822." What's with this place? Can't come here if you're over thirty?

Squinting, I jogged closer to a raised tombstone with a concrete angel resting on top. Using my hand, which carried my iPod, I rested it on the corner of the stone to steady myself. I leaned forward for a better look at the inscription. Poor thing, same age as the others. I straightened and pushed off to finish my run. The cord from my iPod snagged the angel's head, yanking the buds from my ears—the iPod went flying from my hand.

"Crap!" I skidded to a stop on the damp grass and used my palms to hug my ears. It hurt like a bitch. I glanced up at the stone figurine and grimaced. Imagine trying to decapitate an angel. People were probably rolling in their graves right now.

Double crap! My iPod. It better not be busted. Night had fully descended, which didn't work in my favor. I got down on my knees and began groping in the dark, futilely trying to scan the grass. The little solar lights were useless. "Of course, I had to buy the black case," I mumbled and shook my head as I crawled to check under a nearby bench. Cobwebs caressed my face, which had me doing a karate twitch dance as I tried to knock off any possible spiders and remove the webs.

A twig snapped, followed by a muffled laugh.

I froze, waiting, tense, my head cocked to the side. It was dead quiet. *As it should be in a cemetery.* No noise. Not a sound.

"Dummy." I got out from under the bench, sat up and brushed off my sweatshirt. It'd taken months to save for the iPod. I dropped down to search again clawing at chunks of grass. *I'm not leaving till I find it, even if I have to swallow some hairy, icky spiders.*

"You lose something?" A low, gruff voice broke through the dark. "Or are you digging your own grave?"

Chapter 2

My heart leapt to my throat. I smacked my head on the bottom of the bench. "Flippin' heck!" I scrambled back, rubbing the sore spot, paranoid about how high my butt hung in the air. My luck, it was probably some grave-yard rapist.

The stranger said nothing. All I could see was the outline of a pair of dark with white Converse sneakers. I noisily sucked in a rapid breath, not realizing I'd held it.

"Sorry," the husky male voice said, sounding amused. "I didn't mean to startle you. This probably isn't the best place to sneak up on someone." He cleared his throat. "Are you looking for something?"

His voice turned soft, but masculine. Not the kind of voice you expected to hear in a cemetery.

Then again, what kind of voice would one expect to hear?

I glanced up then fell back on my butt. A boy standing a few feet away from me definitely didn't belong in a cemetery. Too tanned, too blond, too...wow, hot.

Very tall, especially from where I sat on the ground. I had to make an effort to drag my eyes away from his face. Even in the dark, his blue eyes flashed against the moonlight. He had the blondest hair I'd ever seen, like a Viking's.

Not a psycho or kidnapper, just a kid like me. I relaxed and stood, brushing my shorts. *Why are you in the cemetery?* I didn't bother to ask. He probably wondered the same about me. With my luck, he'd just visited his girlfriend's tombstone. *Man, I'm awful.*

I quickly shut my mouth, which hung open. Coughing, I spoke a little too loudly. "I-I lost my iPod."

Another chuckle erupted from his lips, sounding like it belonged in the movies. Hollywood-boy walked around me and behind the upright stone angel. He bent down behind it and pulled a long, white string. My eyes widened and for a split second I thought about running. What did he plan on doing? Strangling me?

Then it dawned on me, the white string belonged to my ear buds. A sure sign when the iPod followed along, like a fish on a line. The wind caught behind me and blew escaped ponytail hair into my face. Irritated, I brushed it away from my eyes.

He paused before turning back around. "It smells..." he inhaled "...like liquorice."

I sniffed. "It smells like dead people. Well, like damp grass." The lawn looked to have been cut a couple of days ago. Clumps of old grass lay under the cement bench, emitting a rotten smell like old cheese.

He straightened and flashed a smile, his teeth bright against the dark of night. "You're not from around here, are you?" He held out my iPod and dropped it onto my outstretched hand.

"Got here yesterday." I stuffed the iPod in my pocket. "Thanks. I'm Rouge."

An eyebrow disappeared behind his hair. "Michael." He grinned and held out his hand which I shook lightly.

Pleasantly cool. They'd feel good on my cheeks which are freakin' burning right now. That thought made them flame even more.

"The iPod didn't manage to pull your ears off?"

"You caught that?" Now I wanted to crawl into one of the graves.

"I rounded the bend..." he pointed in the opposite direction from where I'd come, "...when I noticed you trying to decapitate this poor angel here." He patted the figure.

I sensed a smile in his voice.

He cleared his throat and took a step back.

"What're you doing in the cemetery?" I blurted, unable to hide my curiosity.

"Taking a break." He grinned like he'd made a joke. "Are you going to continue your run?" He shifted like he was surprised he had asked the question. He cleared his throat. "Otherwise I can walk with you to the main road."

"I think it's safer if I walk." We started towards the main road. "Do you live around here?" I grimaced at the needy sound in my voice.

"Not too far."

"My place is that way." I pointed to the left.

"I'm that way." He nodded in the other direction.

We continued in silence while I wracked my brain trying to come up with something witty to say.

"Well, maybe I'll see you around." I stared at my runners. Brilliant, Rouge. Brilliant.

"Welcome to Port Coquitlam, Rouge." He started off without a glance back.

I stood admiring his...could jeans really fit that perfect on a rear end? I forced my eyes away. "He's a guy, not a god." My gaze flicked back when a low, bouncy noise sounded. *Did he just laugh?*

His pace never slowed nor did he turn around.

I started slowly jogging home. My heart stuttered and flopped against my chest. I didn't know if it came from the near fright or the closeness of the very hot boy.

Michael was on my mind that night and again when I woke the next morning. *Where did he live? Would he be at school?* He seemed so cool and together. Usually I avoided guys in general, and if one did catch my eye, dark-hair, brown eyes and brooding were the prerequisite.

The next evening, I jogged to the cemetery, grinning when I passed the angel, and gave her a wink. Then I headed north, the way Michael had gone when he left last night. What were the chances I'd actually find his street, let alone his house? I stopped mid-street and turned to walk home—stalker wasn't one of my personality traits.

Friday morning I couldn't stand it anymore. I had to get out of Jim and Sally's house to escape and clear my thoughts. They'd been bickering non stop about fixing the house, Sally's job, Jim's lack of a job and anything else which seemed to pop into their heads.

Through the grey clouds, the air hung heavy with a cool breeze hinting at an end-of-summer storm. The sun kept trying to poke its way through the dark.

As I headed out the front door, I grabbed a baseball cap in case it rained and walked towards the high school. Figuring out where a few of my classes were would save wandering the halls next week.

The limestone near the front entrance of the high school had 1922 imprinted on it... The buildings were created with copper red brick throughout and had large windows on both floors. The school might be small, but its structure was unique. An architectural plaque, showing the school's layout, hung plastered into the brick. In the center lay a courtyard, like that of an old castle.

The very posh building and grounds reminded me of the kind of boarding schools in movies or books. It made me nervous. I hadn't fit into the big high school back in Niagara Falls. What were the chances I'd fit in here, a small school? I kicked a pebble on the sidewalk. It was only one year, so it didn't really matter what happened. I just needed to keep up my grades to score some sort of scholarship. Thank goodness school came easy – science, math, even English – just don't put me in choir or art, and I'd be fine.

Running up the wide steps, I made my way inside the building. The school secretary was busy printing off papers and stuffing them into envelopes. She glanced up as the office door creaked. She wore a frilly dress that matched her horn-rimmed glasses. She might have been here when the school first opened. She smiled and walked towards the front counter.

"You must be Rouge Riding. Welcome to Port Q High. I'm Ms. Graid."

"It's Rouge, like row with a 'g' sound at the end. Spelled R-O-U-G-E; like the way the French spells red." One day, I'd shake the crap out of the person who named me. I smiled. "My last name's actually Rid-ding. Just spelled like your driving in a car." Someone had a good laugh writing my birth certificate. "I thought I should come by before school started to make sure all my transcripts came through."

"Just printed off your schedule." She chirped like a bird. Those glasses gave her owl eyes and didn't flatter her round face. "You don't have any free time this semester, but from the looks of your grades, you won't have a problem."

"Thanks." I took the papers she held out and glanced over the schedule.

Ms. Graid handed me a map of the school, with my classes numbered and highlighted. This woman had too much time on her hands. She'd organized and color coordinated my class schedule with additional highlighting and smiley faces. I made a mental note to memorize the map before I got caught holding it when school started.

"Thanks again." I smiled. I was sure she meant well.

"Be sure and check in any time. I'm always here to help." She hummed some ancient, classical-sounding tune as she returned to stuffing envelopes.

I walked out of the office and decided to follow her little map around the school while it was empty. It didn't take long to find my way around; the set-up of the small building was very basic. I loved the outdoor courtyard in the center. Every surrounding classroom had a view of it.

Stuffing the map in my backpack, I headed down a flight of stairs to make my way to the front entrance. As I passed the front office, a pretty, petite girl walked out. I didn't mean to but I couldn't help staring. She reminded me of someone. I couldn't place who. She had gorgeous blonde hair, long and in a million braids. Her eye color made me think of Niagara Falls. They were bright on her bronzed face. *This girl...definitely one of the popular ones.*

"You new?" Her gaze roamed me up and down.

I nodded. Her voice had a tone of confidence mine would never have.

She linked her arm through mine and steered me towards the exit. "I drove here. 'Bout time someone new showed up." Her leg kicked out and she tapped the handicap button by the front doors, letting the door open automatically. "I'm Grace and we need something fun for Saturday."

"Fun? Saturday?" I tried scratching my head. However, being tugged at an almost sprinting speed, I only managed to tug my fingers through my curly hair. I kind of liked her free spirit and crazy pushiness. Who wouldn't be curious if this girl was nuts or actually fun?

"I forgot. You don't know anything yet." A cascade of laughter erupted from her. "Sorry. The senior class has a party the weekend before school starts. You'll come, right?"

It wasn't like my plans were laid out for the weekend. I might get to see Michael if he attended the high school. Except, in the few moments I spent with him, he seemed older somehow. Grace was like one giant fireball of energy. Someone who chattered, so I wouldn't have to. "Sure. Sounds nice."

Her vice-grip on my arm released when we came to the world's tiniest car.

"It's a smart car. Awesome, isn't it?" Grace patted the bonnet.

I pointed my finger at a pair of pink fuzzy dice hanging off the mirror. "I think they're bigger than your car."

Grinning, Grace unlocked the doors. "My brother got those for me." She rolled her eyes but patted the dice affectionately. "Oh shoot, I didn't even ask." She smacked her head. "Do you need to stop by your place before we head to the mall?"

"Probably a good idea." A change of clothes seemed required. I felt un-derdressed. I didn't have loads of money, but it wouldn't hurt to check out the mall.

Grace zoomed out of the school lot and headed in the direction I point-ed. She swung the little car on my street and then slammed on the brakes right in front of the house. Freaky, as I'd only pointed and never said the house number.

She jumped out of the car faster than I could get my seat belt off. I stepped out and pulled at my shirt, not in a rush to go inside. Grace just seemed a lot classier than my dilapidated house.

"I, uh, live here with my foster folks..."

"No way! My brother and I are adopted. I totally know the feeling." She smiled. The sympathy in her eyes too much for me.

"Maybe similar, but trust me, it's completely different." I pulled out my house key. "I get the feeling your folks are pretty well off. Jim and Sally are, well...they just are...They work hard, but..." Not knowing what else to say, I turned and headed towards the front porch. The neighborhood and house spoke better than I could.

Grace followed on my heels, but I didn't miss the funny look on her face. When I opened the front door, she pinched her nose. Her face screwed up tight.

"Sorry. It's bleach. We've been cleaning and painting."

She coughed, politely covering her mouth and dropping all expression from her face. "It's fine. It just caught me by surprise." She glanced around. "The place is, uh, cute."

Jim lay on the couch watching TV in dirty jogging pants and a paint-stained shirt, one of those ugly wife-beater tank tops. He lowered the volume with the remote and waved before looking over. Then his thumb hit the wrong button and channels started flickering past when he noticed Grace. Obviously at a loss for words, Jim sat up, his mouth hanging open. In the past three years, I'd never brought anyone home, and Grace was probably the pret-tiest thing he'd ever come in contact with.

"My room's upstairs," I mumbled.

"Hu-llo there." A weird smile crossed his face as he stared at her.

Is he actually trying to flirt with her? Gag! Any minute he'd be salivating like a dog – all I needed was a bell.

I grabbed her wrist and pulled her towards my room. Her eyes were wide and bright blue. She didn't say anything, but as soon as we got into my room, she went straight to my open window and took a few deep breaths.

"Sorry 'bout that." My cheeks refused to stop burning. I grabbed my black miniskirt and threw a turquoise shirt over my white tank top. Pulling my pony holder out, I shook my tangles out, ran a finger through my hair and then clipped a small barrette to hold most of my bangs away from my face. Far from stunning, but at least it looked decent.

Thank goodness Jim was absent from the living room when we left. Hopefully to shower and change.

Two steps outside, I started laughing.

Grace stared at me, one eyebrow raised. "Sorry. I just wasn't expecting...I don't know what I expected."

"Not taken personally." I grinned. "He's never acted like *that* before. He's harmless, honest." At least she hadn't taken off running. If she could handle that, she was definitely friend-worthy.

Both giggling, we got into her car. "How did you end up with them?"

"I didn't have much of a choice." I shrugged. "The system kept me stuck inside it. I got bounced around a lot back in Niagara Falls, and when I landed with Jim and Sally...I've been with them through most of high school and when Sally got the job transfer, she an' Jim asked if I wanted to come with them. I said yes. I have to stay until I graduate." I tried not to let my frustration and disappointment leak into my words. "I never got adopted. It supposedly took the system forever to try and locate either of my parents, which they never did, and by the time they stopped searching, I wasn't the newbie baby parents wanted to adopt." I absently stared out the window as we drove. *Why did I just tell Grace my sob story?* It'd never been a self-pity point for me and I turned eighteen in January, so it wouldn't matter much longer.

"Screw shopping. Do you want to come over to my place and watch a movie instead?" She swung the little car around, doing a one eighty. "We can dig through my closet and find something for each of us."

We passed End of an Era cemetery. I held my breath, something I'd always done as a kid whenever I drove by one. Michael crossed my mind. I quickly pushed him out. "Sounds good." My breathing resumed as the car travelled by houses and left the cemetery behind.

The road became more hilly, the houses sparse. Grace made a sharp turn, the little wheels squealing in protest. The long driveway lay between luscious green grass and red maple trees with the biggest leaves I'd ever seen.

House wasn't the right word to describe where she lived. Church or castle seemed more fitting. Built out of limestone with beautiful architectural detail, there were unique carvings in the bricks. *Gorgeous.* It took my breath away.

Grace mumbled something I didn't hear. She parked her car between a dark blue Mustang and a black Mondeo.

A sudden wave of nervousness flushed through my veins. Some weird urge to jump out of the car and run nagged at my insides. Chewing my pinkie fingernail, I tried to squash the jitters. Why in the world did it feel like I wasn't supposed to be here?

Chapter 3

"Are you coming?" Grace held my door open as she peered in the little car. Her forehead creased then quickly disappeared when she smiled. "Caleb's a bit dramatic." She laughed at some private joke as I stepped out.

I frowned. "Caleb?"

"Yeah...*Yeah,* my adoptive father." She gave her head a slight shake, her hair sparkling in the porch light's reflection against the now growing darkness outside. The sun must have given up trying to get through the clouds, and called it an early night. "There's a *royal air* about him. It's hard to explain. You'll see when you meet him."

"Air?"

"Bad joke." She giggled. "I meant h-e-i-r, like he pretends to be a king." She rolled her eyes. "He designed the house."

I didn't get the joke, but I'd never been great with parents or any adults. Probably why part of me wanted to stay outside. Another part begged to step inside and find the peace this place had to offer.

The front steps led to large wooden doors with multi-colored stained glass insets. Grace pushed one open and ushered me in. "My room's upstairs. Let's check out what I've got to wear for Saturday." She kicked off her ballet flats and started up the stairs, turning to wait for me.

The place screamed rich. I bet old money since everything looked antique. Grace said Caleb built it, but the house seemed from before this century. Maybe the guy dug reproductive stuff and had it all done to look ancient – like the stuff belonged in a palace somewhere. The cool windows probably made rainbows on the walls. They ran all the way to the second floor with an open concept view. *A great room.* I remembered studying it in an architecture class at my old high school.

Grace led the way up the winding staircase to the first door on the left. *Why am I so comfortable around her? Like I've known her forever and yet we've barely just met.*

Grace chattered at the top of the stairs, "I know what it's like to be the new kid. If I'd had someone to show me around, it would've made things a lot easier."

Her massive room had a king-size bed and four matching dressers, everything painted with bright and fresh colors. Stepping into her closet, I barely made it two feet. It was easily three times the size of my bedroom. Hundreds of clothes dangled on hangers, organized by color and type. Dresses hung on one side, skirts, pants, tops and blouses on the other. Massive shelves, with more shoes than I dared count, climbed to the ceiling. "Maybe you need to seek professional help." I laughed, setting my bag on one of the shelves. "Too bad you're so tiny, or I'd borrow a third of your clothes. You wouldn't even notice them missing!"

Grace bounced up and down, like an elegant ballet dancer. "Tiny? That's your polite way of saying I'm short? Ha!" She grinned. "You're just tall. Everything'll fit but my pants." She twirled around the closet. "Sleep over on Saturday. We can get to know each other. It'll be fun."

Her face looked so hopeful. Even with the weird nagging feeling still pulling at my gut, I couldn't say no. "Twist my ar—" I stopped mid-sentence when her door flew open.

"Gracey. You smell something? I smelled it all the way down—"

My heart stuttered a few beats before racing out of control. There, in the closet door frame, stood Michael.

His head whipped from Grace to me. Heat rose on my face. I dropped my gaze to my hands. Grace's brother. It suddenly felt like I'd unconsciously used her to find him. They looked exactly alike. Why didn't I put it together sooner?

Grace ran over to him. "Michael, knock before coming in. *I tell you that all the time.*"

"No you don't. It's nev—"

"This is Rouge." She rubbed her neck. "She's new. A senior at Port Q."

"Hello." His voice made me melt and freeze all over—like fire and ice.

"Ha-hello." I cleared my throat. "It's, uh, nice to see you again."

"You know each other?" Grace's head swung back and forth between the two of us.

"We ran into each other the other night – that's all." Michael's eyes never left my face. He inhaled, stepped out of the room and disappeared down the hall. A door slammed shut and, seconds later, loud music hit the air.

I wanted to disappear. Could his disgust be any more obvious? "I went running in the cemetery. I didn't know he's your brother. We just met one time...he helped me find my iPod."

Grace came over and waved her hand. "Michael's, like, kind of abrupt. He's lousy with socializing. What were you doing running in a cemetery at night?" She paused then held up a finger. "On second thought, don't answer."

A burning between my shoulder blades reminded me I needed to relax. I took a deep breath. *Screw it. Not worth the time.* I'd be out of here after graduation so it wasn't like I had to hang out with him or try to be friends. *Nice try, Rouge. You still think he's cute.*

"Don't you dare change our plans for Saturday." Grace must have thought my silence meant I didn't want to be here. She picked out some clothes, led me out of the closet, then flipped the light off. "I'll tell Michael to get lost for the night. He could do with getting a life."

"No. Don't worry. I'm still coming." I swallowed, glancing down the long hall as we headed for the stairs. "How old is Michael?"

"Just slightly older and trust me, he never lets me forget. I hate to admit it sometimes, but he's actually my real brother. Sarah and Caleb adopted both of us."

She took me through the living room, which had a huge flat screen TV and an awesome sound system. One of those wireless ones. The furniture looked antique and expensive, but very comfortable, like it was meant to be sat in. The beige and bright white accents of the room made the abstract artwork on the walls seem like they were painted right where they hung.

A woman, as stunning as Grace, sat at a desk near the window. They could almost pass as sisters. Both had similar features—the same perfectly tanned skin and beautiful ocean blue eyes. She also had the same extremely feminine physique, but more muscular. She probably did Yoga or Pilates ten times a day.

She had to be Sarah, Grace's adoptive mom. Sarah's blonde hair skimmed her shoulders. She grinned and leaned against the desk, her chin fitting perfectly into her little hand. "Hello."

"Sarah, this is Rouge."

"Nice to meet you." I was jealous of her perfect-sounding voice. Bold, sensual and like she feared nothing.

Grace pointed to a burnt red colored door on the other side of the living room. "That's Caleb's office."

The room fell silent at the mention of his name. The butterflies in my tummy started dancing again. I'd never met the guy, so why should I be nervous about his office?

"He's out this evening." Sarah stared at Grace. "A meeting out of town."

The butterflies settled a little, or maybe one managed to escape. I clenched my teeth together. Urrgghh...I hated being nervous.

"Is it okay if we watch a movie in here? If you've got work to do..." Grace spoke oblivious to my inner battle.

"Go ahead. I'm going to clean the kitchen then run some errands." As she stood, a beautiful silver pendant caught my eye. I leaned slightly closer to see the detail but never got the chance. Sarah tucked it inside her blouse.

We settled in to watch the movie. I didn't remember half of it; my mind kept wandering back to the boy upstairs.

When it finished we both stretched and headed to the hall. "I'd better get you home. Heaven forbid I get you in trouble."

I laughed. "You won't. Jim and Sally aren't much bothered when I come or go." I sighed when I realized I didn't have my key. "Shoot! I left my purse upstairs." I pictured it where I'd dropped it in her closet on one of the shelves. "Just let me run up and grab it."

"I'm gonna grab a bottle of water. Want one too?" Grace turned back towards the living room and the kitchen beyond.

"Sure." I darted up the stairs two at a time, counting my steps. I sneaked a quick peek down the empty, door-closed hall.

My purse lay right where I'd left it. Head down I checked for my keys as I ran out of Grace's room. I glanced up in time to bump straight into someone's chest. *Michael's.* His hands reached for my elbows. I froze. He smelled so good – husky, masculine and something that made me want to close my eyes and inhale so deeply the scent saturated my lungs.

It took all my willpower to step back. Why he didn't move away first skittered across my mind.

"Sorry," I whispered. "Didn't see you."

"It's fine." His voice came out husky.

"Did you find it?" Grace called out from the bottom of the stairs.

Michael flinched and dropped his hands. He stepped aside to let me by. "Sorry."

For bumping into me? Or for earlier? I had no idea.

"Good night, Rouge," he spoke quietly. The way he said my name, I would have done anything he wanted. No one had ever put that much meaning into one little word.

Chapter 4

"Folklore." Something about the cover made me stop working. The leather was warm in my hands, even when all the other books were cool from being in storage.

It was Saturday morning. I'd gotten a job at The Eclectic Bookstore. Liza, my new boss, asked me to sort through inventory which needed filing. Liza had a natural Goth appearance and couldn't be older than thirty.

The store sold new and old stuff. She handed me a cardboard box of books and asked me to enter the bar codes into the computer or create titles in her system if they didn't have an ISBN number. Not as confusing as it sounded. Once I typed in the number, the title would show up and if it didn't I just entered the title and author, her computer did the rest. It wasn't the most exciting job, but at least I'd have spending money and hopefully be able to put a bit away for after graduation.

Halfway through, I'd found the leather book.

Everything around me melted away, except the raised contours of some kind of beasty animal on the cover. So lifelike I wondered if it'd been hand drawn from a photo instead of being some made-up creature. Gingerly, afraid I might crack the leather, I opened the front cover and checked for a date. Apparently it had been written pre-copyright days. I flipped through, my fingers running across thick parchment and ink blotted pages. A noise inside the shop snapped me out of my reverie. I set it aside, figuring I'd ask Liza how much it cost.

The rest of the morning I spent sorting and stocking books. They all seemed to cover stories about witches, warlocks and other immortal legends. Liza had mentioned she loved old fairy tales and their history. She dressed the part and seemed to have that eerie, far-away thought and conversation process. She had the personality to suit it as well. I loved it.

When we finished mid-afternoon, she picked up the leather book I'd set aside. "Interested?"

I shrugged. "It looks old."

She tossed it at me. "Keep it. A bonus for your first day."

Catching it like a football, I hugged it to my chest. "You sure? I can pay for it."

Shaking her head, she laughed. "It's okay to accept a freebie once and a while. Trust me, it always feels better to give than to receive."

"Except if you give everything away, you'll go broke." I tried to stop a grin but it managed to escape. "Thanks. See you later." I stuffed the book into my backpack and headed out the front door.

After the dimness of the shop, the bright sun blinded me. I squinted against its glare. Slipping my other arm through the backpack strap I froze momentarily when a car sped behind me. I jumped to the other side of the sidewalk when it screeched against the curb.

"What the –"

Grace's little Smartcar stopped within inches of my feet.

"Need a lift?" The fuzzy dice still swung from her crazy driving.

"You're nuts!" I pounded my chest, trying to restart my heart.

She chuckled and grinned. "You're fine. I stopped in plenty of time." She revved the sewing machine engine. "You heading somewhere or all finished?"

I opened the passenger door and got in. "I started a part-time job today."

"At The Eclectic Bookstore?"

"Yeah, how'd you know?"

"I saw you leave the store and swung the car around. Ready for tonight?"

"Sure. Just need to grab my stuff."

We drove to my place. Once there, she played with the car keys and glanced towards the house.

"I'll just run in and grab my stuff." I opened the passenger door and tossed my backpack in the back. I dashed inside, thankful Jim and Sally weren't home to question me. I left a note on the fridge: "Sleeping at a new class-mate's. Text my cell if you need me." Throwing my already packed bag over my shoulder, I was out again in less than three minutes.

Grace leaned across the seat and swung the car door open for me. I tossed my bag with my backpack and then jumped in. "Ready."

"Awesome. Let's get outta here."

At her house we went straight to her room. Grace ran down and grabbed a fruit tray so we could snack, chill on her bed and listen to music.

"I wonder what the weather's supposed to be like tonight." I glanced out the window toward the clear blue sky.

Grace jumped off the bed and strolled to the closet. "Cloudy by the lake. It'll be cool, but I've got the perfect scarf for you."

"Do you know the forecast after the weekend?" I joked.

"It'll be nice, not too sunny, typical weather for the beginning of September."

"Thanks, weather woman." I laughed. "Didn't know you were such of fan."

She smiled. "I like to be able to coordinate my outfits to match the temperature outside." Making a face, she tossed a scarf at me.

"Fair enough. Where's the rest of your family?" I tried not to sound like I cared if her brother was home.

"Caleb and Michael are probably working, and Sarah's getting some groceries. She's very excited you're sleeping over."

"What does Caleb do?" Rob banks? The house was freakin' huge.

"He's...uh...He's head of a big, important company...uh...dealing with medical stuff." She disappeared back into the closet.

At least the guy had a job. I had no intention of prying as I knew the feeling too well. "What're you wearing tonight?" The perfect question to entertain Grace.

"I went shopping today. Got an amethyst colored top and black skinny jeans." She came out dressed in new clothes. Her pants enveloped her toned legs and the top was glued to her skin in all the right places. Even the color of the fabric made her skin glow. I wished I could look like that. An outfit hung neatly over her arm. "Here's yours."

"I took the clothes held out to me, catching the price on a silver tank top and awesome matching black half-jacket. It was over a hundred bucks. I'd have to work three weeks to afford it. "You bought me stuff? I thought I was just going to borrow something to wear. I'll have to pay you back."

"You won't. It's a gift and it'd be rude if you didn't accept it." The corners of her mouth twitched like a playful kitten's and her eyes sparkled.

"That's not the point." I didn't know how to explain I didn't want hand outs.

"Please. I wanted to." She signed. "I promise I won't do it again."

Far from an expert in gift receiving, I did know what to do or say.

My silence must have been an okay for her. She grinned. "Just check the sizes and ignore the prices tags."

I slipped on the pants and top, somehow not surprised she'd guessed my size perfectly.

"Full-length mirrors in the closet." She followed close behind as I went to the mirrors. "Hey, cool birthmark." She lightly touched the bottom corner of my left scapula. "It looks like some kinda shape."

I'd never paid much attention to it. As a kid I wondered if my birthmother noticed it when, or if, she ever held me. I reached behind, pulling the top's strap to try and cover it. "It's in one of those awkward spots. I can't really see it." I stared at my strange, but pretty, reflection in the mirror.

"You look great." Grace beamed from behind me in the mirror's reflection.

I'd personally never bought something in this style, but Grace had taste. The outfit made my long skinny arms and legs look muscular and sexy. Turning sideways, I checked to see how the pants fit my butt. I actually had one in them. "I owe you big time."

I searched the mirror for her face. Focussing past her, my breath caught as I noticed Michael behind her, leaning against the closet doorframe. He'd slipped quietly into the room unnoticed. He stared at me in the mirror, his eyes bright, but his expression closed off when his gaze met mine.

He cleared his throat. "You, uh, you're...pretty."

"Oh no you don't!" Grace shouted at him, waving her hands wildly in his direction. "She's coming out with *me* tonight. If you want to hang out with Rouge, you ask her out when she's available. After tonight, I don't think that's going to be for a very long time. You might as well get in line!"

Michael frowned, deep lines etched in his forehead. They quickly disappeared when he smirked. "No probs. Caleb asked me to drop you two off and pick you up."

Why? The strange, secretive look that passed between them kept me silent.

Grace leaned forward and pulled the price tags off of my clothes. "Caleb just worries." She turned to Michael. "If you're driving, you aren't planning on staying, are you?"

"Not really." His eyes flitted back and forth as he looked at Grace. "Just let me know should you need me."

Was I somehow missing part of the conversation?

"Fine, then." Grace cleared her throat. "Shall we go?"

Outside, we walked single file toward the parked cars. Grace climbed into the back of a Mustang and pulled the seat back so I had no choice but to sit in the front.

I scowled at her. I was nervous and had no skills around guys. I'd be better hiding out in the back, listening and pretending to participate in the conversation.

Michael must have caught my expression because he chuckled as he got into the driver's seat. Nervous, I plopped down in the seat beside him and fumbled with the seat belt. He reached over and took it from me to click it in. I let out a small gasp as our hands touched. His hand went from ice cold to searing hot.

A current of hot and cold seared up my arm, all the way to my shoulder. My free hand instinctly went to my shoulder. I rubbed it. The weirdest hot and cold sensations assaulted my palm.

Grace chattered the entire ride out to the park. I kept trying to listen, but Michael's close proximity made it impossible to concentrate.

"Rouge?" Grace tapped my shoulder, making me jump. "Are you going to get out or just stay in the car?"

I glanced out the window. We'd parked along a line of trees with a sandy beach off to the right. "Sorry." I fumbled with the catch in my seat belt, trying to get out as fast as I could, heat burning my face and neck.

Michael got out and held his seat back forward so Grace could crawl out, their heads bent close, talking quietly. His face was etched with concern, but I couldn't miss Grace mutter, "I can take care of myself—and Rouge."

Michael set his lips in a thin line. "Fine. Have fun." He jumped into the Mustang and sped away.

"Everything all right?" Too bad they fought. I wouldn't have minded trying to talk to him, or simply having him near would've been fine with me.

"We're good." Grace pulled on my jacket and pointed toward the noise on the beach. "Michael's a little, um, overprotective. Caleb's made him that way. Michael worries way too much about me, and it's obvious he doesn't want you to get hurt either. He likes you. He just won't admit it yet."

"What?" I stopped walking and put my hand on her forearm. My heart skipped every other beat.

"He's my brother. Trust me, he likes you." She rolled her eyes. "The look on his face was priceless when he walked into my room. You're definitely going to make some first impressions this evening too."

I'd rather hang out by the shadows. However, if Michael might be interested, I think could handle a little spotlight. My face scorched. "You sure about Mi—"

"Positive." Grace laughed. "Come on. Let me introduce you to our senior class, and I'll point out the cute boys. We might as well make Michael jealous while we're here."

We made our way through the parked cars towards the music. Someone had attached huge stereo speakers to a pickup backed onto the sand. Outdoor lawn torches, which also seemed to keep the bugs at bay, were set up to maximize lighting the area. Lawn chairs lay scattered around the fire pit and small groups were all over the place.

"So, which one of these cliques is yours?" I wished I'd just worn a sweatshirt and no makeup.

"I kind of float around. We've lived here three years, and I still kind of feel like the new girl."

Definitely a popular girl. Grace had no idea what being the new girl actually meant.

Skipping the pathway, we climbed over large boulders and jumped the three foot drop onto the beach. Somehow, Grace had gotten her shoes off before we landed, her feet barely making an impression in the sand. My Mary Janes filled instantly with the cool particles, but I chose to keep them on.

"Heads up!"

A football flew in our direction. I ducked out of the way while Grace caught it with one hand, not even pausing in her stride. A cute, dark-haired, athletic-looking boy came jogging up.

"Nice catch, G!" He skidded to a stop. "Whoa, wait a moment. Who's the new hot-chick?"

"Simon, your ball." Grace tossed the football expertly. "This is Rouge."

Simon bowed dramatically. "Welcome to Port Q High's unofficial before-school-starts official party night." He held out his hand.

"Hey." This guy babbled like a girl back at my old high school who drank Red Bull all the time.

"Let me introduce you to the rest of the gangstas." He grabbed Grace's and my hands, pulling us over to the group of guys waiting for the football. "This is Tommy, Damon, Sean and Jake." Except for one, all were similar build to Simon. The other guy was absolutely huge with these dark, almost black eyes. He seemed to be shooting daggers at Grace.

I stepped close to Grace. "What's with the big guy?"

"He's interested. I'm not." She rubbed her forehead with the back of her hand, making an "L" shape with her fingers. "Loser," she whispered.

Simon stuck close by me, trying his best to entertain. Twenty minutes later, I needed space to breathe. I tried to catch Grace's attention, but she was chatting away with Sean or Jake, I couldn't remember which one. "Bathroom break. Where are they?"

"Up the hill. Over there." He pointed in the direction. "Do you see the line of trees? Just follow them and where the one big tree is, they're just behind there. See a few people heading back? I can take you."

"No!" I'd rather die. "Uh, no thanks, I'm pretty sure I can find my way." I stood and made a beeline for the trees. Glancing back, Grace stood by Simon, blocking my view of him. Quickly sneaking into the forest, I figured I had about four minutes before Simon came looking for me.

Simon was nice but a little overbearing. He seemed the long-term kind of guy. I planned on bolting after graduation. Now, Michael, he might be an interesting short-term thing. I scoffed. Who was I kidding?

The thick grass and leaves muffled the music and noise from the beach, making it peaceful. I walked farther into the trees. Enjoying the moment, I leaned back against a large oak tree, closing my eyes.

The cicadas, crickets and every other insect around me abruptly went quiet. A strange, hushed silence. The hairs on the nape of my neck rose. Holding my breath, I strained to hear something, anything, around me. Opening my eyes, I stared into the forest. Eyes not adjusted to the dark, I couldn't make anything out but trees and shadows.

My heart hammered over-adrenalized and fight or flight screamed. Stumbling, I suddenly couldn't remember the way back to the beach. Muffled music seemed to come from all around. Placing the sound grew impossible. The blood rushing in my ears made it even harder to concentrate.

Swallowing hard, I took a tentative step forward and froze. In front of me, a pair of large amber-yellow eyes with obscenely black pupils shone crystal-clear in the dark. A low, guttural growl escaped from the darkness. Hot putrid breath slid across my face. I nearly gagged.

Whatever the freakin' thing was, it was mammoth. I couldn't find an outline of its body, just a shadow. Terrified, I was positive if I screamed the thing would jump out and attack me before I could get the sound out.

"Crap, crap, crap..." Body still frozen, I looked left to right and tried not to move my head. Hadn't Grace said she could take care of both of us? "Grace...Michael?" I whispered. Shuffling slightly around the tree, my eyes never left the spot where the wicked monster stood. Tears of fear ran down my cheeks when I bumped into the rough bark of the tree behind me.

This is it. There was nothing I could do. I'd walked straight into this den of death. Realizing the certainty, I exhaled a slow breath, willing my heart to calm. I began to hear and think more clearly. Someone called my name. The monster's eyes shifted slightly, as if it too listened.

I managed a hoarse whisper, "Over here."

A snarl filled the air and the yellow-eyed beast disappeared too fast for anything that size. Suddenly, Michael appeared, lifting me like a feather and cradling me tight against him. His hot chest, cool breath and husky scent distracted me from the terror behind us. In seconds, we were out of the forest, in the lightened area by the bathrooms. Grace came rushing over.

"What the heck happened?" Her brows crushed together and chest rose with fell in quick bursts.

Too soon, Michael set me down on the grass carefully, like a flower that might break.

The horrible eyes wouldn't clear from my memory. "I, um, I, damn it! Sorry. Just give me a sec." I pressed my hands on my knees, bending over and trying to fill my lungs with the air I'd forgotten to breathe. "I stepped into the edge of the trees to give myself a break...from Simon. Everything went all voodoo quiet, a-and this *huge* thing with funky eyes showed up!" I shivered, looking behind them to the trees and darkness. It had happened, right?

"Stay here. I'm going to have a look." Michael disappeared into the forest.

I reached out. "You can't –" I sputtered, but Grace held me back. "He can't go in there. It isn't safe."

She pressed a finger to her lips. "Shh...It's all right. Michael's going to see if he can catch it." She gripped my hand.

"Catch it? Are you crazy?" My voice rose and I pulled away. "I couldn't tell where the thing ended or where the shadows began."

Michael emerged from the tree line.

Relief flooded through my veins. Shaking his head, he looked ticked.

He grabbed our elbows and started to steer us towards the parked cars. "Time to go, ladies. This party's over." He turned to Grace, whispering, but I caught everything. "It's gone...caught the scent but it took off as soon as it heard us." His pace picked up.

Grace jumped in the backseat. Michael patiently, but not looking so patient, helped me into the front and clicked my seat belt in.

We pulled out of the parking area.

"Wait! The rest of the kids. Someone needs to warn them."

"It won't be back."

"You don't know that for sure."

"Positive." Michael's curt reply stopped me from asking again.

I didn't argue. For some reason, I believed him. We drove the rest of the way in silence.

Parking the Mustang with the same annoyingly-crazy driving skills as Grace, Michael shoved the car into park. As he ripped the keys out of the ignition, he glanced into his rear-view mirror. "I need to talk to Caleb. Take Rouge inside. Get her something sugary to drink. It'll take the edge off."

"I'm fine."

"You're in shock. Head to Grace's room. I'll come up later when I'm finished." His fingers raked through his hair, he gave me a quick smile and then he ran into the house.

Grace and I made our way at a much slower pace into the house and up the stairs. I struggled into a pair of jogging pants and a tank top, my body too numb to function properly. Dropping onto the bed, I lay on my back, dazed.

"I'll grab you something to drink." She slipped out the door.

I thought about the creature and curled up on my side, hugging my knees. My heart thumped hard and fast again my chest. "What kinda creature were you?" I mumbled to myself. Something escaped from the zoo? A wild animal from the mountains? I kept seeing the weird, amber-yellow eyes flash against the white walls. They continued to stay there, except set against blackness.

Popping my eyes open, I forced them to blink and focus. I'd fallen asleep. The lights were still on in the room, but the house was quiet. Glancing at my watch, it was after two. I crawled out of bed to find Grace.

As I walked out of the room, Michael came up the stairs.

"You should get some more sleep." The concern on his face made me melt a tiny bit.

"Is everything okay?" I was paranoid I might wake someone. "I hope I didn't cause any problems?"

He smiled and turned me gently back towards the bedroom. Dazed, I crawled back into bed and watched him sit down on the edge. My gaze followed the outline of his body. I didn't realize he'd spoken. "I'm sorry. Can you repeat that one more time?" I whispered.

"Everything's fine. We've been downstairs in Caleb's office. You didn't cause any problems. That's silly thinking. You don't need to worry anymore."

"Do you know what that *thing* was?"

He sighed then finally nodded. "I've a pretty good idea."

"Would you care to enlighten me?" I tried to read his face but, apart from a tiny frown, it remained expressionless.

"Not at the moment, but I'll explain it when I can." His answer was loaded with implications which only created more questions.

"Would it have killed me?" My voice was calmer than my insides.

He sat silent for a moment, his knuckles cracking as he squeezed them. "Yes."

"And you tell me not to worry?" I straightened, tucking my legs under me.

Forced air pushed through his nose. "It was hunting, and you were in its path. It'll not happen again. I promise you."

The determination in his voice made me stare at him. His head bent slightly forward, his eyes intently watching his fingers pick at his clean nails.

"I don't know why it went for you. I think you just happened to be in the wrong place at the right time." His words came out slow and punctuated, like he'd been rehearsing them. "You need to rest." He gently helped me lie back down.

As I drifted off to sleep, I hoped so hard he was right, even though I didn't believe him.

Chapter 5

Something warmed one side of my face. My head instinctly moved towards it and the other side of my face cooled against the pillow. Fluttering my lids, the sun shined through the window, creating the heat. Burrowing deeper into the heavy duvet, I drifted, not asleep, but enjoying that wonderful half-awake feeling when you know you don't have to get up and rush off to school. The scent of delicious male cologne filled my nostrils. I moved closer to the smell.

"You know, you're very cute when you sleep."

My eyes popped open. Michael lay on the bed, his head leaning against the headboard of Grace's bed, arms crossed, hair perfect and an unbelievably sexy grin on his face. Last night's memories came crashing through my mind.

I sat up, very conscious of my heavy, tired eyes and morning breath, positive the back of my head had a rat's nest tangled in it. *Why do guys always have to look so perfect?*

His face lost its humor. "Are you okay?"

"I'm, uh, fine." Just in dire need of a brush and a bottle of mouthwash. Maybe throw in some kind of manual on crazy beasts living in the forest.

"You feel like getting up and going for a drive?"

With him, no human would say no. *Except...* "I should find Grace, and see if she's planned anything."

Michael let out an intoxicating laugh. "She's fine." He paused, staring at the ceiling a moment. "Grace and Sarah are out running an errand. We've plenty of time to go for a ride and still be home before they get back. I promise. She's not mad." His hand came up in a Scout's honor position.

"If you're sure..." Guilt washed over me for preferring to hang out with Michael rather than Grace. However, if she'd gone out with Sarah, a short drive wouldn't be so bad. "Give me ten minutes."

I waited. Michael didn't move. My only way off the bed would be to crawl over the top of him. Kicking the blankets off, I shuffled to the foot of the bed. Still unable to avoid not touching him, I edged over his legs and let my toes reach for the floor. My hands brushed against his shins, enjoying the hot and cold feeling his body gave off. Once off the bed, I stood in the middle of the room not sure where I'd left my backpack or what to do.

"I'll meet you downstairs." He dropped his legs over the bed and stood, relaxed and confident. He walked by me, his arm brushing against mine. When he opened the door, he turned. "I'll make some breakfast while you get ready." He pointed at the ground beside Grace's closet and disappeared down the hall.

I looked down where he'd pointed. My bag. The door behind it led to a bathroom. Alone, I grabbed my backpack and dumped it on the bed, hoping I'd packed something decent to wear today. The leather book from the bookstore slid to the floor. I leaned over and grabbed it then tossed it on the bed, more concerned about dashing to the bathroom, showering and getting dressed in record time.

I did manage to get ready in a decent amount of time. Unfortunately, my sneakers decided to play hide and seek. Michael knocked on the door just as I was crawling around on the floor looking for my right shoe.

"Do you remember where I tossed my shoes last night when we got back?" Near the corner of the bed, a sparkle caught my eye. "Forget it. Found you." I grabbed it and held it up triumphantly to Michael. He wore a pair of blue jeans and a long-sleeved black shirt. Incredibly hot without even trying to be. *Okay. Enough with the oozing over the guy*. I was starting to annoy myself with my inability to let it go.

"I made coffee and Sarah bought muffins. She bought like ten different kinds. Are you almost ready to–" He stopped mid-sentence, dropping the travel mug on the nightstand, and muffin bag on the floor. He swiped something off the bed.

I reached out to stop the wobbling mug.

"Is this *yours*?" He held the book at arm's length, by the corner.

I nodded.

He snorted.

In disgust? "I got it from The Eclectic Bookshop yesterday." Pulling my shoe on, I peered at the cover. *Why's he acting so weird?* "I haven't had a chance to look at it. It looks really old."

"Yesterday?" He glared at the book and mumbled something.

All I caught was "...makes sense now." I had no idea what he meant.

"We need to get this out of the house before Caleb gets home. He'll freak if he sees it."

"Why? It's just an old folklore book."

"Let's go." He reached for my elbow and steered me toward the hall. "You can drink your coffee in the car."

Gravel sprayed as we spun out of the driveway. Michael finally slowed the car when he turned onto a scenic route to the mountains. He sat rigid and quiet, so I sipped at my coffee and ate my muffin. I picked up the book and flipped it open to the middle. "Holy friggin' smokes!" The hand drawn picture was of the ugliest, crudest looking thing I'd ever seen—some kind of ancient scary mythical creature. I traced a finger along the charcoal ridges. Some kind of fountain pen ink had been used in tracing it.

I turned to the first page and read the single sentence on it. "Grollic Monstrum. An aberrant occurrence that has the ability to produce fear or cause physical harm. Can the beast be tamed? Or controlled?"

I flicked through some of the drawings scattered throughout the book. Large, dark, omniscient animals had eyes that stared directly at you from the paper. A page on the left showed a drawn photo which had been painted in. Amber yellow eyes.

I gasped and then tried to catch my lost breath. What knocked the wind out of me was cold, hard realization.

"That animal last night, it..." I couldn't finish the sentence. It couldn't be. This kind of stuff was all myths and legends, folklores.

Michael continued to stare at the road, his knuckles white against the wheel he gripped. His posture confirmed what I didn't want to believe.

"It can't be. It doesn't exist."

The silence drove me crazy."

"It isn't real."

"They are."

What? Wait a sec. "Not just one, there are more? H-How do you know?"

"I just do. The grollic's smell was all over the forest."

Turning to face him, I studied his tense profile. "You could smell it? I didn't even hear that thing until it was three feet in front of me. A grollic?" The word was foreign to my tongue. I needed to concentrate but it all seemed ridiculous. What normal human could hold a conversation on real-live monsters seriously? "You're not one, are you?" I giggled. He did seem to have some peculiar habits, obviously not spooky, but, in my anxiousness, I couldn't resist teasing.

"Never!" He snapped like I'd whipped him.

I exhaled, letting my head fall against the back of the seat. "Sorry. I'm only kidding." Michael obviously wasn't. I'd hit a nerve with my crappy humor. A reminder of why I should never use it.

He pulled over on the side of the road at a lookout point. Something about the intensity in his blue eyes captivated me. I didn't bother glancing out the windows at the scenery. I had all I needed in the car.

Michael shoved the car in park and drummed his fingers against the steering wheel. "This is real. There are things I'm not allowed to say," he scoffed, "and other stuff you wouldn't understand."

Crazy alert. Get out of the car and walk away. My brain seemed to think it knew better than my body. I sat silent, unsure what to do.

He stomped a foot against the car floor. "I'm not sure what to tell you."

"The truth." I barely knew the guy and here I sat, in his car, demanding he spill his guts. I crossed my arms, ticked at my inability to keep my mouth shut.

His eyes ran up and down me, obviously misreading my body language. "I tell you a hideous creature went after you, and you barely bat an eye. You just turn and ask if I'm one."

"I was joking."

"Yeah, you said that." He shifted, turning back to the wheel and staring straight ahead.

My right thumb traced the pad of my left hand. If I told him my feelings, I'd step over a line I'd never crossed before. *Totally risky, but is it as dangerous as the animal in the forest last night?* Swallowing hard, I hesitantly laid my fingers on his wrist. When he looked at me, I stared back into his ocean blue eyes. "I...We haven't known each other very long, but there's something...I li-like you." I wanted to add it was different, not like anything I'd ever felt before. Instead, I babbled. "This may sound weird, but I can't get you out of my head. I hardly know you, but I trust you with my life." Horrified at what I'd admitted, I pressed my lips closed tight. When Michael didn't say anything, I sat back against my seat. Crap! I've just screwed up royally. I dropped my face in my hands.

"*Trust* me when I say I'm not right for you." Michael's voice took on that husky rasp which made my breath catch. "I'm no good for you."

My heart sunk. Grace had been wrong last night when she said Michael liked me. My brain kept sending my heart mixed signals. I responded the way I always did. I got defensive. "Isn't it up to me to decide what's good or bad for me?"

"I was afraid you'd say something like that." Without another word, his hands pulled at my wrists, forcing me to look at him. The anger in his face softened as his eyes danced back and forth. His face close, he leaned forward and as he opened his mouth to speak, he brushed his lips lightly against mine. Fire and ice. Like dynamite exploding inside my head.

Without thinking, one of my hands touched his face and the other went behind his head, its fingers curling in his soft hair. Then he kissed me, this time with intention. It was intoxicating, left me completely breathless.

As quickly as he'd begun, he pulled away, heaving. "Sorry. That wasn't supposed to happen." His eyes were shut tight.

"I didn't mind at all." Could my mouth, for once, keep up with my brain and shut up?

"Rouge," he whispered. I loved the way my name rolled off his tongue. "This can only end badly."

"How do you know? We've barely started. Why not give this a chance and see what happens?" Terrified he'd push away, I reached out and grabbed his wrist. I'd never wanted someone like this. I'd been content to live my life on my own and suddenly it seemed the loneliest option in the world.

Michael rubbed the light stubble on his jaw. He appeared torn, trying to wrestle his version of good versus evil. He sat perfectly still for a few minutes and finally turned, his blue eyes boring into mine. "Screw it. I can't fight this. Just promise you won't hate me in the end?"

"As long as we don't burn in hell, we're good to go," I joked.

His jaw dropped and his eyes grew big. Then he laughed, a deep throaty one straight from deep inside. "Alright. Let's head back to my place. Grace is already bugging me, wondering where you are. And," he swallowed, "it's time you met Caleb." He squeezed my hand and turned the car around.

The way he spoke made me anxious. I thought about those terrible yellow eyes again. Thankful now it'd been too dark to see the thing properly. "What are they?"

Michael sighed. "Grollics? They're human but biologically messed up. Something's wrong within their natural order. It's impossible to explain."

I had no reply. I didn't get it nor could I fathom it. If I hadn't seen those freakish hollow eyes last night, I wouldn't believe a word Michael said.

We drove for a bit in silence. My mind raced at the thoughts of a possible relationship, of monsters and of why in the world my hormones were all jacked up. Why did Michael know so much about grollics? A sudden thought crossed my mind. "How old are you?"

He glanced at me out of the corner of his eye. "How old did Grace tell you I was?"

"She dodged answering the question, like you are now."

"You asked her about me?" He grinned. "I'm...nineteen."

"I'll be eighteen in January. However, I think I'm seventeen going on thirty. I've been grown-up for so long."

He chuckled. "I know the feeling."

Another thought hit me. "How old's Grace?"

The question took him by surprise. He appeared about to say one thing but seemed to change his mind. "We're twins."

Totally weird. Now how'd I have a hunch on that? "How come you're done with school?"

"I work with Caleb."

"Did you drop out? Or skip a grade?"

"No."

That didn't answer anything. He obviously didn't want to talk about it – yet. "Why the pretense she's younger than you?"

"She is younger, by a bit."

"You born first?" Grace had said he was older. Too many weird secrets. "Are you guys in some kind of trouble?"

"Questions, questions." He grinned. "Has anyone ever told you, you talk a lot?"

"Never." I shrugged, feeling giddy. Not once in my entire life. "One more question, and I promise I'm done."

Michael raised an eyebrow.

"Why was one of those monstery-things after me?"

"Now *there*'s a loaded question. Caleb might know the answer." He glanced down at the book sitting between us.

"One more question." He opened his mouth, so I quickly added, "Can we stop at Starbucks and grab a latte? Sorry to say this, but you make lousy coffee."

Chapter 6

Rocking slightly side to side, I now hesitated outside the house. Maybe the reason my body didn't want to go in had to do with the horrible memory of the beast. If we went inside and talked about it, I'd be admitting it was real.

Michael reached for my hand and squeezed it, giving me the courage to cross the threshold. Little currents of hot and cold raced across my skin.

Does Michael have them too? I blinked, trying focus on the task ahead. This was serious. I really didn't want to be some monster's dinner.

In the middle of the living room, Michael stopped. Grace and Sarah relaxed on the couch and a man sat at the desk Sarah had occupied yesterday. My heart stuttered.

Caleb.

He was older than I thought he'd be. Maybe late fifties or sixties. The tightness in his face and posture made him appear ready to pounce. Or overreact? The kind of guy who shot first and asked questions later.

Where everyone looked tanned, Caleb was pale like me but even more so. Almost pasty white against the dark, expensive clothes he wore. He had the same intense blue eyes as the others, but with years of knowledge behind them, like he'd been through the wars. He was handsome, in a strange way, with strong facial lines. He sat almost regal.

When he glanced at me, his eyes darted from my feet to my head to my feet again, a harrumph escaping his lips.

I wanted to disappear.

"'Tis a pleasure to meet you." He spoke with an English accent – very proper – and polite. However, his words sounded automatic—years of being taught what to say.

"Hello, Mr...." I paused. I didn't know their last name and it seemed wrong to call him Caleb without permission.

"Knightly."

"Hell-Hello." Should I curtsey or kneel?

He leaned back in his chair, fingers clasped tightly together, resting on top of the desk. "It seems you had an altercation last night with a grollic."

Wow. Straight to the point. "Michael's been trying to explain." I played with a loose strand of hair which had escaped my ponytail. "He seems to think there's a...a grollic after me."

He tutted. "Possibly, but not confirmed. That's the first sighting of one in a very long time. We assumed they'd become extinct in this area. It seems they may have just burrowed underground." He twirled a large ring on his right hand. "Do you have the slightest inclination why one would fancy you, of all people?"

I shrugged, suddenly conscious of the book lying in Michael's car. I shook my head. It made no sense the two were related. "I just moved into town. I haven't done anything since I got here. Met Michael and Grace, got a job...normal stuff. Last night, I stepped into the trees on an off-chance. It wasn't something planned."

"Maybe you caught it off guard. Maybe it was curious about the noise from the kids," Sarah said.

Good point. Maybe I was in the wrong place at the wrong time.

"Perhaps..." Caleb rubbed his chin, his eyebrows drawn close together. He stood. He was a lot taller than I originally thought, at least half a foot taller than Michael. "We must remain aware of our surroundings and be cognisant of any possible threats. Grace and Michael will keep an eye on you, and we shall see if this grollic has any other intentions. Perhaps it was hungry."

The way Caleb looked at me—or through me—I felt like some carnivore's dinner, nothing more. I gasped and took a step back. He strode by me, without a second glance, to his office, the antique door closing with a cold click from the brass doorknob made me jerk.

"It's just some freak of nature, some kind of wild animal. Caleb talks as if the thing can think and plan an attack. Animals can't do that." I spoke to no one in particular. *Who're you trying to convince? Them or yourself?*

Michael slipped an arm around my shoulders. "Nothing happened last night and nothing's going to happen to you. I promise."

"It was definitely a one-off." I loved it that I believed him. He made me feel...safe.

Thank goodness school started without a hitch. No monsters came knocking at my door. I did joke with Grace, with me practically sleeping at her place all the time, a grollic could've come but bolted when it got to my neighborhood.

It sucked but I barely saw Michael. Caleb apparently had him travelling for work.

Simon made it his priority to introduce me to everyone at school. While the weather stayed warm, a group of us sat in the courtyard every lunch break.

One Friday, near the end of October, the guys, being their usual rowdy selves, started a game.

"Rouge," Simon said. "Are you going to come with me to the Halloween Masquerade?"

Before I could think of an excuse not to go, Damon dragged Simon to a desk chair he'd set in the middle of the courtyard.

"Help me set this up. Then let's jump over it." Damon pointed at us gals sitting together. "You ladies keep score." All the guys scrambled over to join them, each one easily clearing the chair. Soon two, then three chairs were lined up. When a few guys knocked out, Damon dragged a picnic table to replace the chairs. He scraped his foot in the grass to make a line ten feet away. He declared they had to stand behind the muddy line. The remaining three cleared the table sideways. They turned the table long. After Damon and Simon barely cleared it, they pulled two together.

I leaned toward Grace. "Maybe they should fill their pants with rolls of toilet paper."

"What's that Red?" Damon paused in his work and grinned at his nickname for me. "Chumming up to your little pal?" He glared at Grace. "It's obvious Red's you're new little Barbie doll. Poor new-gal didn't stand a chance once you sunk your claws in her."

How old was this guy, nine? "I have a brain, thank-you. I'm not a Barbie. Maybe you're just jealous she wouldn't let you be her Ken?"

He stepped forward and leaned down, his face inches from mine, hot breath hitting my cheeks. "What'd you just say?"

My courage flew out the window. I dropped my gaze. His eyes were red, nostrils flared, lips curled in a nasty smile. I locked on his neck where a birthmark, which also looked angry, peeked out from the edge of his polo shirt near the buttons.

Simon pulled Damon back. "Leave her alone. You're scaring the poor girl."

I gasped for air, not realizing I'd held it. With a shaky hand, I covered my mouth, not sure what else to do.

Damon blinked and jerked his arm out of Simon's grip. "Whatever. Sorry, Red."

"You're such a jerk, Damon." Grace grabbed my arm and led me inside by the elbow. "You okay?"

Leaning against the cool, cement bricked wall, I tried to calm my nerves. "Bit insecure, isn't he?"

Grace laughed. "I usually just try to ignore him."

"How do you ignore someone so big?"

"And ugly?"

I grinned, feeling better. "You so missed your chance when you turned him down."

"I guess he never got over it." She pretended to clutch her heart. "It started the first week I was here, but he was just so big—"

"An' ugly."

"An' smelly. It turned me off."

"I don't blame you."

The bell rang. I had chemistry and she had art on the other side of school.

"See you after classes. Try not to pick anymore fights." She laughed and disappeared down the hall.

Afternoon classes flew by. At the end of the day, I made my way out to the parking lot to Grace's car. My heart skipped a beat when a dark blue Mustang sat parked beside the Smartcar.

Michael stood waiting between the two cars, leaning against his door.

"Hi." I hadn't seen him for two weeks and he looked awesome. I made tight fists, warning my fingers not to reach up to his blond hair begging to be tamed. His blue eyes piercing with their intensity, his lips and slight stubble – all of it made my blood rush.

He nodded a hello, but his face remained serious. "Grace told me what happened. I thought I might have a word with this Damon boy."

Boy? Damon was like a year younger than him. I waved my hand. "It's nothing. Damon probably took too many steroids and had some reaction." Bummer. I had been hoping for: *I missed you.*

Michael's head shot up and his body tensed. I turned around to where he looked.

Damon pushed through the school front doors, strutting across the grass with Simon in tow. They headed to the other side of the parking lot. He kept glancing our way with an irritating, cocky smile, but he continued to his car. He gassed the engine and sped out of the parking lot.

"Michael!" Grace's singsong voice made both of us turn. "What a surprise." Her cheeks and most of her face burned slightly red.

"Really? You contacted –" Michael stopped mid-sentence.

Something passed between the two of them, but I couldn't figure out what. It might take a bit of patience, but I intended to find out. Why would Grace call Michael and tell him about lunch? It was no big deal. Then it dawned on me. "It seems your old flame's still holding a bit of a nasty grudge."

Grace shrugged. "You win some and, in his case, you lose again. The guy's a meat-head."

"Maybe it was good I wasn't here." Michael turned and smiled at me. "Well, if my knight-in-shiny-armor services aren't needed; is there anything else I can help you with?"

"Well..." I said. "There is this Halloween Masquerade. We are actually required to go for drama class. I could really use a date."

Chapter 7

Of all the Halloween themes, we got stuck with famous couples. Grace convinced Simon to go with her and she took charge of all our outfits. She bought a Spartacus costume for Michael and a Roman slave one for me. I'd come to trust her and she made me laugh with her charity shop and eBay shopping.

The night of the dance I sat in her bathroom on a stool, letting her curl my hair and pin it up. "Doesn't Spartacus's wife get murdered?"

She dropped the curling iron.

I swore she caught the hot part in her bare hand but didn't even flinch.

Setting the curling iron on the counter, she grabbed a few bobby pins. "Aren't all famous couples tragic?"

Her hand was obviously not burned. I pointed at her in the mirror. She was dressed as Fashion Fairy Tale Barbie. "I don't think Barbie and Ken have a tragic ending."

"Touché. But if Damon sees the outfits, he might change that." She giggled at my shocked looked in the mirror. "I'm just kidding. He's the one who gave me the idea." She pinned the last bobby pin in my hair. "Stand."

We stared at my reflection. The faded grey-blue slave's dress had tattered sleeves and hem but I was willing to bet, no slave ever wore a dress this form-fitting. Grace had tied a black scarf around my waist for a belt. She'd bought the gorgeous pair of strappy sandals from a second-hand shop.

She traced her fingers along her collar bone. "Something's missing." Snapping her fingers, she disappeared out of the room.

I stared down at my red polished toe nails and leaned against the doorframe. Grace had found a gladiator costume on eBay in Michael's size. The thought of his body in a fighter's outfit created a tingling in my lower abdomen. I was willing to bet Spartacus had nothing on Michael. Hopefully I didn't embarrass myself with staring, or even worse if I'd start salivating.

"Wear this." Grace held something shiny in her hand. "It's not a choker, but we can link the clasp on a shorter part of the chain and make it look like one.

The necklace, beautiful and obviously antique, was made of sterling and shone like Grace had just polished it. "I can't wear that."

"I know Roman slaves wore copper, but this is so perfect. It's—"

"Too expensive." My fingers had a will of their own and reached for the silver. The chain was cool, but the aged Celtic pendant had a unique feel. Heavy but...different. I couldn't tell if it was hot or cold. I held it up to the light. The pendant turned out to actually be some sort of vial with a ruby inside. "Is this some kind of family heirloom?" *I'm not wearing this—my luck it belonged to Caleb's mother.*

"Just try it on." Grace took it from my hand and clipped the chilly metal around my neck. Against my skin, the pendant gave me goose bumps but warmed instantly. How in the world did it do that?

"Don't you look adorable, little sis," Michael said sarcastically from the hall doorway. "Apparently your idea of tragedy is quite different than the rest of the world's."

Grace's bouffant hairdo blocked my view of Michael's face. A round shield covered his body, except for his bare legs and sandaled feet.

"Hardy-har-har." Grace faked a girly laugh. "My shopping helped you though. You're quite dashing."

"Half naked in October? Don't you th—" He froze as I stepped beside Grace.

Grace grinned, a wacky, I-got-you-good smile totally meant for her brother. "Come on, don't look so serious. It's Halloween! Let her be your slave for a night."

Hot. Very hot. Muscles and flesh and metal everywhere. No wonder the Romans loved their gladiators. He could have been a god. However, the scowl on his face stopped me from sharing my thoughts.

He glanced back and forth between the two of us. His face then broke into a half-smile. "You do make a sexy slave." He walked over and reached for the necklace's pendant. It seemed to burn with his touch. His fingers cooled the skin against my collar and neck.

My breath caught. "This isn't Caleb's, is it?"

He chuckled. Leaning forward, he gave me a tender kiss on the forehead. "It's definitely not Caleb's." He tucked a stray curl behind my ear.

My head spun. I wasn't sure if it was from the moment as it seemed like something deeper than just words were being said, or if it was Michael's close proximity, or the fact I'd forgotten to breathe.

Grace sighed quietly. I guess we should get going."

We headed down the stairs. I stared at Michael's almost bare back. Nice tight muscles, smooth skin with slightly protruding boney shoulders. The guy probably had zero body fat.

Sarah waited at the bottom with a digital camera. She snapped a photo and looked at the screen. "There's a back flash from Rouge." Sarah glanced up and stared at my neck, her eyes grew big. "Michael, did you put the *Siorghra* on her?" She sounded...almost hopeful.

I stopped on the second to last step. *What the heck's going on?* These people seemed to be leaving half their sentences inside their heads. *What's a Senora, or whatever they called it?* There was obviously some hidden meaning. More strange secrets. I intended to find out, after I knocked the necklace against the back of the head of Grace.

"Grace put it on." Michael winked.

At me or Sarah? I couldn't tell.

"It suits the outfit, doesn't it?" Grace, grinning like a madman, finally spoke up.

"It looks gorgeous. Rouge looks gorgeous." Sarah opened a closet door. "Sweety, take this scarf wrap, in case you get cold." She held a sapphire blue scarf out to me.

"Thanks." I wrapped the pretty scarf around my wrist not sure if I'd need it. *Better to have it and not need it.*

We drove to the school in Michael's car. My gladiator would never ride in a tiny Smartcar. The music could be heard from the parking lot. I climbed out of the car, setting the scarf on top as I flipped the seat forward so Grace could crawl out.

We walked around the side of the school and found Simon leaning against the wall outside the gymnasium, dressed as Tuxedo Ken.

He grinned when he saw Grace. "It's about time. I was beginning to think you were going to stand me up! Damon said—"

"He here?" Michael glanced around.

"Damon?" Simon's eyebrow's mashed together. "No, he had some family function or something."

"Probably couldn't find a date." Grace whispered.

We headed inside. The gymnasium had been transformed. There were flickering lights set against the walls to look like fireplaces, roughly hand made tables and benches lined one side and students sat drinking, snacking and laughing. Painted brick patterns covered the walls and floors. A pair of thrones sat on the stage with stage. An ancient castle made to look present day. A big cauldron filled with fruit punch stood to the left of the stage.

"I'll get us some drinks." Michael gave my hand a light squeeze before disappearing into the crowd.

I shivered. The janitor had probably put the fans or air-conditioning on in the gym. Realizing I'd left the scarf on the hood of the car. I leaned toward Grace. "I'll be right back."

Jogging to the car, I hoped it hadn't disappeared. It wasn't on the top where I'd left it. Bending down, I looked under the car and frowned. Not there. I straightened and checked the top of the trunk and hood. The wind had blown it against the wiper and luckily it had caught on the end. I wrapped it over my shoulders.

I turned around to head back to the gym and nearly jumped out of my skin. Damon stood before me, his arms crossed tight over his chest.

"Sheesh. You scared me." I swallowed. "I didn't hear you come up."

"Did you come with *her*? Simon said he was going as her flippin'—Ken." He spat on the ground and then leaned forward, his pitch black eyes and hot breath smacked against my face like a slap. "I'm obviously concerned for his safety."

This guy's freaking nuts. "I've no clue what you're talking about." Was he drunk? As I looked into his eyes to see the tell-tale red on white, Damon stepped back, like *I* terrified *him*.

"You are so going to burn in hell for this one. You think you can squirm your way into that family?"

He was crazy. "You're the stupidest person I've ever met, and believe me I've met some real idiots."

"Listen, bi—" he stopped mid-sentence and reached for my neck.

Jammed between him and the Mustang, I had nowhere to go. My hands curled into fists and rose by my neck, trying to protect it. Was he going to strangle me right in the school parking lot?

Instead, he stepped back again, pulling one hand back like I'd burned him. He swiped at my throat with the hand still in the air.

He's trying to grab my necklace. I clutched the pendant, worried he'd lean in and rip it off.

Instead, he kept his distance, but the venom in his voice couldn't be missed. "So help me, Rouge. If you ever come near me again, I'll destroy you. I know exactly what their *kind* are. And I'm not alone. More know. Lots more." He snorted, pointing at me. "Yeah, you tell your precious Michael that. Let him know we're going to annihilate him." He turned and ran off into the darkness.

He's definitely crazy. I couldn't move. I'd forgotten how to breathe. My brain told my body to walk back to the gym, to get there as fast as I could, but I stood frozen, clasping the pendant protectively in my hand.

"You okay? What's taking so long?" Michael walked around the front of the car.

I jumped. Dazed, I stared at him. What had Damon meant about Michael's kind. "I, um, left Sarah's shawl on top of the car and came out to get it. D-Damon stopped by..." my voice trailed off.

"What?" Michael swung around, doing a three sixty. "Where'd he go?"

"I dunno." I raised my hand and twirled my fingers and then snapped. "One moment he was here and the next, gone." I stared into the darkness where Damon had disappeared.

"Let's get outta here." He unlocked the car doors.

I blinked, trying to focus. "We can't just leave Grace." Damon could go after her.

"I'll let her know."

"No. You wait here and I'll ask Simon to drive Grace home." I needed a moment to catch my breath and my nerves.

"I can – never mind." He shook his head. "Go. I'll make sure Damon's sorry ass isn't poking around."

"I'll be right back." I sprinted off to the gym. My wobbly legs needed to run out the adrenalin stuck inside them.

Grace wasn't hard to spot on the dance floor. She looked like she'd been expecting me. Simon seemed to be dancing on his own.

"Do you mind driving Grace home?" I asked him.

He replied before Grace had a chance. "Love to! What kind of Ken would I be?"

Grace shook her head, looking directly at me. "What'd he want?"

Did she mean Damon? I hadn't mentioned a thing. I swallowed. Damon had taken off in the other direction. He wouldn't come back tonight. "Michael and I just want to hang out."

Simon put his hand up for a high five, which I slapped, not understanding why.

"You go, girl!"

"You're still sleeping over, right?" Grace asked.

"Yeah, I'll see you back at the house." I gave her a hug and went to meet Michael waiting in the car.

We sat in silence as Michael drove. Staring absently out the window, I tried to figure out Damon's weird behavior. Maybe he was on drugs. Maybe he had something wrong with the processes in his brain. The lack of cars and streetlights stopped my train of thought. A bluish hue covered everything from the bright night sky. "Where're we going?"

"We have a cabin by the lake. I figured we could hang out there for a bit." He let his foot off the gas. "That doesn't sound right at all. We could hit a Starbucks instead, if you wanted."

"Should I be scared?" I teased. "You're taking me to a hidden cabin in the woods and next week will I be the front headlines in all the national papers?"

"Ha-ha." He laughed sarcastically. "The place is like fifteen minutes away. I just thought it'd be easy to talk there. I go when I want some peace and quiet."

"Then let's go. We're almost there now." I trusted Michael and I had a few questions myself.

He flipped the blinker on and headed onto the exit. "It's just a couple miles down the road from here."

Ten minutes later he pulled onto a gravel lane. He drove the car easily through the dark forest. A cabin stood in the distance with a glass lake stretching behind it. The cabin was the kind you saw in those country magazines. Modern, with a vintage look but absolutely gorgeous. Michael, still in his Spartacus outfit and oblivious to the cool air, opened the door and switched lights on as I followed him in.

Simple shades of beige colored the walls, mixed in with wood and brown leather furniture. My gaze caught on the six tall windows facing the lake. The lack of style inside the cabin disappeared by staring out those windows.

"I'll get a fire going." He opened a brass ornately decorated box and started to toss the wood into the brick fireplace. He had the logs snapping and flames dancing in moments.

Taking my hand, he pulled me over to the couch.

My legs barely touched the leather, and he leaned in to kiss me.

I returned with frantic kisses while his hands roamed down my back, his fingers finding their way to rest along the spaces between my ribs, his nails scraping against my shirt. Everywhere he touched shocks of longing started on my skin and ran through my blood to my heart. I swear I was going to explode.

Groaning, Michael gently, but firmly, pushed me away. I didn't want to stop, he tasted like I needed more of him. I leaned in to fill the space between us. The fire's reflection danced against his bare shoulders.

"Rouge," he whispered, "we need to talk. If you keep doing this, we're not going to get anywhere."

"I really don't have anything important to say." If we talked, something would change. Don't know why I knew it, but I did. Couldn't I just have this moment—for like ten minutes?

"Rouge." The warning tone in his voice made me straighten and watch him. He was right. We needed to talk.

Michael stared into the fire, resting his elbows on his knees and rubbing his hands together. He sat quiet, both of us trying to catch our breath.

Finally, he sighed. "What did Damon want?"

I shrugged. "He doesn't like your family much."

Michael sat rigid. "Tell me exactly what happened."

"It was stupid. Total loser. He acted all worried about Simon. Then he looked at me like *I* scared him." I paused, waiting for Michael to stop clenching and unclenching his hands. "The guy's psycho. I thought he was going to steal the necklace."

Michael inhaled and exhaled loudly, his nostrils flaring.

Something about Damon's comments gnawed at me. I tapped a finger against the top of my knee, not sure if I should ask Michael or just ignore Damon's useless babble. *Honesty or nothing.* I took a deep breath. "He said he knows what you are. What the heck's he talking about? Is Caleb part of some sort of mafia?"

Michael snickered then covered his mouth. "Sorry. That was rude of me. Trying to picture Caleb eating spaghetti like some TV mafia-guy..." He shook his head. "If you knew Caleb, you'd get it." He moved, and shifted me as well, so we sat facing each other. He took my hands and rested them on his knees, laying his on top.

More strange talk. Maybe there was something wrong with the water here. I pulled a hand out of Michael's and touched the pendant. "What is this necklace?"

Ignoring my question, Michael stared at the window behind me. "Damon knows what the pendant stands for. He knows who we are." He removed his hands from mine and began picking his perfectly clean fingernails.

Why the sudden nervousness? "What?" I'd get answers tonight, if I had to shake them out of him. "Whose necklace is this?"

"Mine," he whispered, not looking up.

I slid the pendant along the chain. *Not really a surprise, is it?* "What's inside?"

"Blood...my human blood."

Wha-? I didn't expect that as a reply. The pendant dropped with a clunk against my chest. "If it's you're blood, why wouldn't it be human?"

Michael rubbed his face. "It's complicated. Grace has one as well. We all do. It's called a *Siorghra.*"

"Siar—a what?" Crazy alert—again. Get out of the cabin and start running through the forest. *Nah, you know what happens in horror movies.* I ignored my own warning, too curious about the necklace and what Michael might say. I held my tongue, waiting for Michael to wrestle with whatever demons he was fighting and explain what on earth he was talking about.

"The *Siorghra* was created as a link. It's Gaelic, a term for eternal love. Sarah and Caleb wear each others. Once on, it can never come off."

I reached for the pendant. *I'd be wearing this for the rest of my life?* "What! Never?"

"I didn't put it on you, so it can be taken off." Michael sighed. "I meant it won't fall off or be broken unless specific things happen."

"Like what?"

"I have to put it on you, it's my blood."

Freaky—but kind of romantic at the same time. "You're sister's pretty gutsy."

"Yeah, she likes pushing me when she can." He chuckled and relaxed. They obviously had sibling affection I'd never experienced.

"Is this something Caleb's family created?"

"In a way."

I hated how he was answering my questions with bits and pieces. Sighing, I blew the bangs away from my forehead. "What's going on? You want to talk, but you're not really telling me anything."

Michael pushed off the couch and began pacing in front of the fire. His costume clinked and sparkled against the flickering light. I kind of hoped it would irritate him and he'd pull the top off. He paced back and forth about ten times. Just when I was about to suggest we head back, he began talking.

"That—" He pointed to the pendant on my neck "—is the last bit of me that still holds life."

"What?"

He stopped pacing. "I'm not who you think I am."

Ah, double crapper. I didn't know what was going on, but after seeing that beast a few months back nothing would seem unbelievable. "You acted all scared about the book I got, but then got ticked when I asked if you were one of those Grawlics." I started laughing, the nervousness inside of me escaping.

"Grollics," he corrected. "I'm not one. We are in no way related. But... we are the same in a sense."

"You're kidding."

"I wish I was." He sat down beside me.

The sadness in his eyes tore little bits off my heart. "What're you trying to tell me?"

He stared at the necklace. His eyes were bright blue against the reflection of the fire, almost aqua-green in color. "I'm not like you...anymore."

I couldn't get my head around this conversation. "It doesn't make any sense. You said this is your blood."

His eyes closed. "Grace and I, we were...like you... about a hundred and forty years ago. The man I knew as my father wasn't my... my biological father. Grace and I never knew."

This was jacked up. "What happened?"

"Our...My mother was raped before she married my father. On the day of their wedding, just before they took their vows. She never told us, we learned about it after her death."

My mouth fell open. "That's awful." What a secret to carry. "Maybe your dad really was your father." I felt I was grasping at straws. "You know, fifty-fifty chance."

"No," he spoke sharply. "Mother was raped by someone you could never imagine."

"What do you mean?" I couldn't believe I was actually having this conversation, and believing it.

"You know those Greek mythology stories about the gods coming down and having children with humans?"

My eyes grew huge. "You're the son of Zeus?"

"No." He shook his head and dragged his fingers through his hair. "Shit! I'm screwing everything up. I was trying to use it as a comparison. The Greeks used these folklore stories because they are partially true, they just got the heavenly participants mixed up." He waited, obviously wanting me to guess.

"Okay," I said slowly. "You're a soul returned back to earth. Or, you're living some reincarnated life?"

"No. I'm part..." He began pacing again.

Something clicked in the back of my mind. "Angel?"

"Sort of." He threw his hands in the air. "This is so hard to explain. Grace used to joke about angels, saying we were distant third cousins, once removed."

"An angel raped your mother?" That didn't make sense. *Impossible.*

"I know what you're thinking, but not all angels are good. They come from both ends of the spectrum. We're not angels. My mother was not an angel. We still don't know the entire process or what exactly created us. We think it may have something to do with fallen ones but aren't completely sure. One thing for sure, Caleb is different than us."

"Caleb's one, too?" This was unbelievable.

"We all are. Sarah found Grace and me. She met Caleb later and they gave each other their Siorghra." He tapped his head, as if trying to knock out a noise.

I thought about how similar Sarah, Grace and Michael looked with their tanned skin. *Except Caleb's so... so dark.* Well, he was pale, but he seemed... I didn't know. Maybe he came from the bad guys. The only thing he had in common was – "You all have blue eyes." So they're some kind of immortal.

Michael's brows went up in surprise. "Grace and I had brown. They turned blue when we died."

"What? Dead?" I rubbed the heel of my palm against my forehead. "Slow down a bit. I think I'm missing something here."

He sighed. "Grace and I didn't know until we were killed."

Killed?

Chapter 8

"What?" My back burned near my left shoulder blade. I reached behind and rubbed the muscles. Could this conversation get any stranger? Was I actually starting to believe him?

"That's the worst thing about being one of us, being a slightly Nephilim. You don't know until you're dead."

"Nympho?" *Wait. That didn't sound right.* My cheeks went hot.

Michael laughed. "I'm not a nymphomaniac – at least, I don't think so. We're sort of Nephilim. Fallen angels. Only a small, tiny part, we're also something else." He paused. "It's really complicated."

I opened my mouth, but nothing came out. What could I say?

"You know, I've never told anyone." He swallowed and rolled his eyes at the ceiling. "Caleb's going to peel a layer of skin off me when he finds out I've told you."

"That's horrible!" Caleb was a monster, probably related to the Grollics.

"Not literally. He's just going to be pissed."

I stood, feeling the need to get my bearings. Everything felt backwards. I rolled my shoulders trying to get the burning muscles on my left side to relax. "This is way too much." I rubbed my eyes, not caring if my makeup smudged.

"I'm sorry. I shouldn't have said anything. The world's complicated enough and I just threw more confusion into it." Michael checked his watch. "It's getting late. I guess we should probably head back to the house." He pulled his ear. "Sheesh! Grace won't let up. She wants to know where we are and if everything's all right."

"Say what?"

He chuckled, breaking the intensity of the moment. "Might as well spill it all. It's different between Grace and me. We're twins, born *and* killed at the same time. Caleb's never seen it before. And he's seen a lot."

I basically filed most of what he said into my brain to try and think about later. I stuck to the basics. "So, you can read her mind because of it?"

"Sort of. Grace and I are kind of unique - like talking on the phone without the phone. We can tune each other out whenever we want. I can't read Grace's private thoughts anymore than she can read mine."

Despite the seriousness of the situation, I giggled. "I got a feeling you tune her out a lot more than she does you."

"A little." He smiled, his eyes flashing.

"Why do you all have the exact same eye color?"

Michael glanced at the pendant around my neck. "Caleb figures when we die, our blood loses its oxygen. Blood turns blue without oxygen."

Like our veins. "You don't age? If you've been around for a hundred and forty years and Caleb's been around for, like, forever..."

"You remain the age you were at the time of your death."

"But you and Grace are so young."

"Long story." He checked his watch again. "Too long to get into tonight."

I planted my legs and crossed my arms. This was way too fascinating to have him just tell me a little and say it's time to go. "I'm not finished. I have more questions." I hadn't even started to scratch the surface. "What's with Caleb?"

Michael began pushing the logs around in the fire with a cast iron stick, trying to get it to die down. "He's an original of the Coven."

"Coven?" I sounded like a parrot. It sounded like some vampire story. Next he'd be telling me they existed as well.

"Kind of like royalty...original bloodlines. That's another very complicated story. There are not many of his kind. He's extremely powerful and much respected in our world. No one crosses him. He's monumental to all of us." Michael shook his head, his hair falling forward. "We really need to get back to the house. I didn't take my phone and Caleb's bugging Grace now."

"Fine." I grabbed my shawl off the couch. "We'll go, but you're driving slowly. I have a million questions."

Michael smiled. "I've a feeling they're never going to end." He killed the fire and we left.

My brain wouldn't stop humming as we drove. "If you and Grace were together when you... when you..." I couldn't finish the sentence. "Did Caleb find you after?"

Michael focused on the road, his tanned knuckles white as he squeezed the wheel. "Sarah found us. We had no idea what was happening, but she knew." He was silent for a moment, either concentrating on the stop light, or reliving what happened. He cleared his throat. "Caleb met Sarah a bunch of years later, after she'd adopted us. He saw her and immediately gave her his *Siorghra*. She did the same without question. They were simply drawn to each other. Caleb had been alone before he met her. She was his first."

I stared at my Spartacus sitting so close, but seeming from another world. There was so much information to sort through. It didn't scare me, but rather fascinated me. It was like I'd been waiting all my life for him. I'd never fit in anywhere and this all made sense, like it was a part of me or my ancestry. I don't know why I felt the ties, but another part of me was horrified at the thought. What I did understand: I wanted to wear Michael's *Siorghra* more than anything. It also made me wish I had one to give him.

We pulled into the driveway and walked silently to the house. Doubt began to fill my head. What if his family was angry I knew their secret? *What would Caleb say?* Michael took my hand and pulled me closer to him as we reached the front steps.

Brushing close, his silk skin touched mine and I groaned. "I need to change. I can't talk to your family wearing this."

Inside, Michael led me straight upstairs.

"I gotta change, too." He kissed my forehead and turned toward his room. "Take your time. I'll meet you downstairs."

I walked into Grace's empty room. Changing into a pair of jeans and plain long sleeve top, I kept Michael's *Siorghra* on and slipped it inside my shirt. Time to head into the lion's den.

First, I needed to pee. I slipped into the bathroom.

"You okay?"

I nearly jumped ten feet when Grace spoke. I switched light on. She sat on the counter, her bare feet swinging in the air.

"You scared the heck out of me!" My heart felt ready to explode, and there she sat, all chipper and smiley. "Why're you sitting in the bathroom, in the dark?" I punched her shoulder.

"Wasn't sure if Michael would come in the room too. Didn't know if you needed some privacy." Grace tilted her head. "Sooo, you know our dirty little secret."

"Kinda."

She slid off the counter and staring at me. Then suddenly she lunged at me and swung her arms around me, hugging me tight. It was a moment before she let go and it took me a moment longer to catch my breath. "I knew you were special the moment I saw you. I knew you'd totally get it."

"You're crazy. Even nuttier for putting the *Siorghra* on me." I touched the necklace, loving the feel of it but not wanting to admit it.

"You needed to know. I figured Michael would tell you tonight if I did. I've no idea how, but you're involved in this as well. I feel it." She stepped back and stared at me intently. "You don't care about what we are, do you?"

Me? Involved? How and in what? "Why should I judge you? I liked you before and nothing's different."

She squealed and hugged me again, shorter in length but still enough to knock the wind out of me again. "It's about time Michael met someone. You are so worth keeping around."

I wanted to ask if I might be like them. Maybe I was some sort of fallen whatever they were. *It kind of makes sense.* I didn't know my parents and always had the feeling of needing my freedom – that there was something more out there.

"They're waiting. You ready?" Grace interrupted my thoughts.

My throat suddenly dry, I nodded. "Wait. I need to pee."

Like a best friend, she waited in the hall and we headed downstairs together. Heavy silence greeted us in the living room. Michael sat on the couch, dressed in jeans and a white shirt. Grace pulled me into the room and set me between her and Michael.

Caleb sat by the desk. Sarah stood behind him, her hand on his shoulder. They made a stunning couple, and also frightening in a way I couldn't quite grasp.

"Rouge knows," Michael said in a low voice.

Caleb's eyes narrowed as he stared at me. He didn't say anything for a few minutes. Then completely ignoring me, he turned back to Michael. "I never considered you an idiot."

My breath caught in my throat. I figured he'd be angry, but I didn't think he'd act like I was some kind of insignificant fixation. I opened my mouth to say something and then closed it. *It's not my turn to speak.* This conversation was between Michael and Caleb.

"I'm not." Michael's jaw twitched. "Rouge's not what you think. She's trustworthy."

"It goes against the Coven and its plans." He cleared his throat. "This'll only bring trouble upon all of us –*your family*. You need to consider this very carefully. I will ask once, what are your intentions?"

"I'm not sure. I need time to think things through."

"Think things through? Do you think you should have considered that before you went and told her? Decide, Michael. I am not willing to risk our safety for this child. A girl, who you know nothing about. Do you know her past?"

My past? I had nothing to hide. I literally had nothing.

"I understand your concern."

How did Michael stay so calm sitting on the couch? I couldn't stop my right knee from bouncing.

Michael leaned forward. "Rouge's not the issue. What happened tonight is. While we were at the school, a boy approached her. He saw my Siorghra on her neck. He threatened her, threatened us."

"You put your Siorghra on her?" Caleb screamed.

Grace spoke matter-of-factly, "No, I did...to go with the costume."

Caleb threw his hand up to stop her. "I'll speak with you later." His eyes whipped over to me. "Who's the boy?"

I swallowed, trying to push the butterflies back down my throat. My shoulder blade began burning again. "Damon said... he knew what you are..." I took a deep breath. When Caleb didn't reply I added, "He plans on destroying you."

"He what?" Caleb roared. His nostrils flared, and faster than I'd ever seen anyone move, he flung the desk across the room. Papers flew everywhere, as if trying to get away from him. "A boy? A damn boy tried to intimidate my family? Impossible!" He glared at all three of us on the couch. "Is this the first time?"

My butt clung to the couch beneath me and I leaned against Michael's shoulder. How could someone toss a desk like it was a book? Forcing courage, I made myself sit straight.

Grace didn't even flinch at Caleb's outburst. "Damon hit on me a while back and got no where. He's nothing, just a boy who's jealous. He doesn't know anything. It's a bloody game." She glanced at me before shifting back to

Caleb. "He's got a bit of a grudge and took it out on Rouge at school when were we hanging out in the courtyard a while back. He's not worth it."

Caleb paced, his hands clenched behind his back. "This boy threatened you?" He turned and glowered at her, his eyes shone a brilliant blue. I pressed myself closer to Michael as he continued, "And you did nothing?"

Sarah interrupted, "He's human?"

Michael nodded. "He's young. Too young to be—"

"He's just an idiot on a steroid rant." Grace met Caleb's stare and then purposely turned to the overturned desk.

Caleb's angry voice rang across the room. "Is there anything about this person you *do* know? Who's his family? His friends? Is he a serious threat? What does he know? Something's being missed. A random nobody doesn't get what the pendant represents. Does he need to be eliminated?"

Sarah touched his shoulder. "We can't get rid of him until we understand what he knows. Who he's with. Kill without questioning him and we accomplish nothing. We must remove the threat–all of it."

She sounded military. What kind of lives had each of them led? What had they done in order to survive undetected to the human eye?

Caleb stood statue still. "Michael, find out about this idiot, and if he and his little posse are any hindrance to us. Get rid of the girl, she's of no use." He dismissed us with a wave of his hand and stomped to his office, the slamming blood-red painted door reverberating throughout the house. Some kind of crystal shattered in the kitchen.

Sarah touched Michael's shoulder. "I'll talk to Caleb." She kissed him on the top of his head, and went into the office.

"This isn't good," Grace whispered, more to herself than us.

"Michael," I said, my world crumbling and knowing I had to do what was right. "I don't want trouble with Caleb. He's right, your family comes first." I reached and squeezed his hand before standing. "Take care of what you need to. I'm going to head home."

He stayed seated on the couch, looking confused.

Grace jumped up and ran to the hall. "Take my car."

I caught the keys she tossed me automatically, like a robot, and watched her run up the stairs. Michael sat still frozen on the couch. All of a sudden my heart began tearing. *He's not going to fight for me. There's no such thing as a white knight.* After everything I'd learned, he hadn't told me everything. I wasn't supposed to be here.

I walked the few steps back to him and leaned forward to lightly brush my trembling lips against his cheek.

He whispered in my ear, "It's not safe for you to be with us. I knew this was too dangerous. I should never have talked to you that night you were running. This is all my fault." He gently traced my lips with a finger. "I'll try and come for you, but it's better if you just forget about us. Act like we never existed."

In dead silence, I left the house. *First there's Grollics and now...* It was too much for my little head to comprehend. Driving home I realized I still had Michael's Siorghra. I snorted. *Well, at least he'll have to see me one more time.*

I couldn't shake the terrible sense of doom. We'd just been on the edge of something that felt so real. For the first time in my entire life, I was crying for someone I loved.

Chapter 9

The next morning, I couldn't tell if my head or heart hurt worse. My eyes stung from the tears I'd shed and my throat killed from the crying it had tried to swallow. However, my shattered heart made the thought of getting out of bed almost too hard to bear. Tempted to skip school I only went because I hoped to see Grace.

Pulling into a parking space at school with the Smartcar, I wondered if Michael might drop Grace off. No such luck. I waited near the entrance of the school and reluctantly headed to class when the buzzer went.

Her empty desk in first hour made my stomach drop. The only plus side of the day was Damon's absence as well. I trudged through classes optimistic I might see Grace after school... only to be disappointed.

I drove home after school, parked in the driveway and locked the door. I had no intention of driving it again. After the incident last night, returning the car without being asked didn't seem likely. There was no way I would go to the house without being invited.

Neither Michael nor Grace contacted me through the week or weekend. Three weeks past, and Jim and Sally began to grumble about me hanging out in the house. For the first time since moving in with them three years ago they didn't want me around. I avoided them by staying in my room.

In the darkened bedroom one evening, I lay staring at the cracked ceiling and wondered how to bring Grace's car back. Did I have enough courage to drive to their house, knock on the door, and hand the key back? No way. I thought about parking it at the school and mailing the keys back but my luck, it would get towed away.

"Get to the point, dipstick," I mumbled to myself. I was pretending to wrack my brain only as an excuse to see Michael. It killed me that he hadn't tried to contact me. No effort. Whatsoever. The guy spilled his guts and told me to leave. So much for liking the good guy.

It's all I had been thinking about, night and day for almost a month. Now I just didn't want to think anymore.

In a huff, I jumped off the bed and grabbed my backpack off the floor. I'd bought a calendar for the New Year. Flipping to January, I stared at the box with the number seven in it. My birthday. Eighteen. All that was left after that would be graduation, and then my freedom from the system.

Which meant I'd be on my own.

Slapping the calendar shut, I turned away and tapped my fingers against my leg. I needed distraction, something to do which didn't require thinking about the future. Staring at the walls around my decrepit room, my eyes rested on the mess inside my closet. *Perfect.*

I dropped to my knees and began tossing dirty clothes into one pile, others that needed to be hung into another and shoes to be paired to the side. While digging, I grabbed something rectangular and soft half buried in the clutter. I pulled it out and gasped.

The Beast book. *Grollic Monstrum.*

The worn leather felt comforting against my fingers. I flipped it open to the beginning. The first pages were written in some foreign language so I skimmed them, simply glancing at the drawings. *Funny, I thought the first page had said something in English...like a definition or something.*

The closet mess forgotten, I crawled onto the bed. About a third of the way through the book, the words turned to English. It talked about a war between Grollics and their worst enemy, and how it all began. It turned into a narration and the beast in the forest seeming like a distant memory now, I settled into the pillows to read.

An aged Grollic tried to help a young woman lost in a forest looking for a cottage. She seemed afraid of the beast but dainty as she may have appeared, the woman had strength inside of her beyond any human ability. She threw the old man aside and attacked the others with him, killing all but him. She claimed she'd spared him as he'd tried to aid her, even though she had no right to save him.

The eye for the eye. The old Grollic planned his revenge. He watched the woman and learned where she travelled. He waited for the day when the white-caped girl returned to the cottage on the other side of the woods. He raced ahead to the clearing and easily killed the unknowing man inside, then waited for the girl.

The girl approached and the moment she entered the house, he attacked. Claws reaching to rip her neck just missed, but as the Grollic stumbled he sank his teeth into something warm. The girl grabbed a chair and smashed it over the Grollics back. They fought through the small cottage, breaking almost everything inside, including themselves.

Near death, the girl barely managed to escape through a narrow window. How she managed to race away in to the forest, the Grollic thought he'd never know the answer. Her now red cape –covered in blood— flapped behind her as if nodding it knew the truth. The Grollic had killed because of what she had done to his family.

The stunned Grollic stared. What he had thought was a cape, had actually been wings. Weak and shattered, he fell back against the wall. The fight between the two had nearly killed them both. He then understood their bloods could not mix. They shared unique powers, but those powers could never be blended. They each had the ability to destroy, as if they'd been born to battle against each other.

Thus began the war as both vowed to never find peace until either race was obliterated. The Grollic may not have understood what he met that day, but he did learn the blood running inside his body could poison hers and vice versa.

Holding the book between my fingers, I sat back, eyes wide. My favorite nursery story as a child was Little Red Riding Hood. Boy had this story changed from the original version.

I turned the page. Both sides of the book had hand written, in point form, notes about the girl and possible ways to kill or stop her. Other questions asked if there was more than one girl and how they came into existence. Simple sketches filled the pages. I couldn't make heads or tails of those any more than the handwritten stuff.

Bile rose in the back of my throat when I flipped to the next page. The right side displayed a crudely hand drawn Grollic. A disgustingly ugly one. A series of diagrams showed a man turning into the Grollic. Each picture had detailed anatomy and notes along the sides. Interesting, the Grollic's heart was actually on the right side of its body, higher up than on most animals or humans. In human-form, the heart rested on the left side but as he shifted into Grollic-form, the heart would also shift.

It was the last picture my eyes kept flitting back to - the mammoth size of the beast, the ferocious face with yellow eyes and snarl of sharp teeth. The drawing so life like, it kept bringing me back to that night in the forest.

I shivered, and tried to swallow. An eerie scraping noise against my window nearly had me screaming. I closed my eyes, willing the noise to stop.

It didn't.

Inhaling a long, slow breath, I then opened my eyes and focused on the window, too scared to get up and look outside. *Don't be such a freakin' wimp.* Squinty, I realized the wind had picked up and a broken branch hung onto another limb. It scraped against the window as the wind blew the still connected limb. A big gust knocked the loose branch down and the ting against the roof of Jim's car told me it'd landed.

My heart still in my throat, I shook my head in disgust. *Wimp. Loser.* I chided myself. *Get back to reading.* Except I now had to put my hand over the monster's picture to focus on the other side of the book. I stared at the human drawing. A small marking caught my attention, above the right aorta of the heart near the collar bone. It showed a detailed drawing of the tattoo on the corner of the page. I squinted. Somewhere in the back of my mind I recalled seeing it before. Scratching my scalp, I couldn't place where.

The remainder of the book switched back into the weird foreign writing. I shut it and tossed it onto my nightstand. *Enough stupid monsters for one night.* The clock radio read 1:30 a.m. Before switching the light off, I glanced at my messy pile on the floor. It would give me something to do, a reason to get out of bed since tomorrow was Saturday.

Weird dreams visited me throughout the night. Grollics and angels killing each other, cutting themselves and letting their blood drip into the enemy's cuts. Girls in red dresses and capes running through forests, with white monsters in pursuit. Tattoos on everyone to mark if they were Grollic, angel, or human. Angels morphing into beasts scarier than a Grollic.

I woke early with the feeling I never really slept. Covered in sweat, I threw a pillow over my head and tried to fall back asleep. The sun had not yet risen, and I didn't want to get up with nothing to do but put my shoes and clothes away. After forty minutes, a few tiny little rays of light began peeking through my window.

Throwing on my red-hooded sweatshirt and a clean pair of jeans, I turned to leave. I ran back to the nightstand to grab a ponytail holder and saw the Grollic book. I grabbed it too. If I was going to go see the sunrise, I might as well have something to look through. *Less scary in the daylight.*

It was cool enough that no fog or mist had come in during the night. I walked to the cemetery-park Michael and I had met, buying a latte at a Starbucks along the way. At the park I sat on a bench, drinking, as I watched the sun make its way over the horizon. *Beautiful and peaceful.* The world kept turning even when it felt like mine had stopped.

After an hour my bladder told me it'd had enough. I jumped up to throw my empty cup into a garbage on the path when a sudden realization hit me like a punch in the gut. I stumbled back to the bench and sat dumb-founded. *The mark!*

I'd seen it before on somebody. That day in the courtyard.

Could the beast be human?

Damon.

Damon's a Grollic.

When he'd threatened me during Halloween, he thought I was the same thing as the Knightlys. *Impossible!* Michael, Grace or Caleb would know. *Right?*

I thought back to my encounter with Damon in the school parking lot. I'd worn the necklace. Michael's *Siorghra* had blood inside which could kill him. He thought I could kill him. Another thought hit me like a wave of nausea. *It was Damon in the woods the night on the beach.*

He said there were more of his kind.

Michael and his family must know. But what if they didn't? What if Damon's pack was ready to attack Michael's family? What if they already had? And I'd done nothing.

Running home as fast as I could, I took the stairs two at a time and grabbed the keys to Grace's car. Jim hollered something at me as I raced out the door. I ignored him. There wasn't time to argue or explain.

I unlocked, tossed the book on the seat and stuck the keys in the ignition. The car started and revved as if it knew I had to hurry. I shoved the gearshift into drive and flew down the roads, fingers crossed for no police. They were the least of my worries. Hopefully Caleb wouldn't kill me and ask questions later.

Or maybe, he would and I'd find out I'm one of them.

The car slowed to a crawl when it came to their driveway. My foot could not press the gas pedal. *Maybe this is a mistake.* How could a simple human figure out something useful to a family, especially one like Caleb? If they were okay, they probably were planning some counter-attack.

"Stop being such a wimp," I hissed at my reflection in the review mirror. "Just go up to the house and bang on the door. Hand the book to whoever opens and tell them Damon's a Grollic. Then leave." I'd have to walk home but at least I could return the keys and necklace and try to forget them and move on with my life.

I parked beside the mustang and marched towards the house, forcing through the urge to run away. Hand in the air, ready to bang on the door; I realized I'd left the book on the passenger seat. About to turn around to grab it, the door swung open.

Michael.

My body froze, but my heart hammered at record breaking speed. Dressed in a white shirt, his tanned skin looked perfect. I couldn't stop myself from staring. My thoughts over the past few weeks had left so many details out. The rush of feelings caught off guard.

If he was surprised to see me, he didn't let on. "Hello, Rouge."

Stuffing my hands into my jean pockets, I cleared my throat and tried to sound normal. "I know you told me not to come, but there's something really important I need to tell you."

"Has something happened?" He stepped onto the porch and glanced behind me, most likely scanning for hidden monsters.

"No...Yes...Maybe." I blinked a bunch of times, ticked my eyes burned.

"It's dangerous you're here."

His words or posture gave away nothing. I couldn't read his thoughts. "I know." I swallowed, my eyes darting inside as I tried to calm the anxiety inside me.

His expression broke. He wavered and looked as lost as me.

I stepped toward him and stumbled, unable to keep my knees from buckling. His arms surrounded me and he held me tight. My head instinctively went to his chest and I left it there, inhaling his wonderful masculine aftershave, the taut muscles under his shirt, his warmth, all of it. *Would it be wrong to want to stay here forever?* I then remembered the real reason I'd come. Putting my hands on his shoulders, I pushed him back a few inches so I could think. "We *really* need to talk. Can I come in?"

"Maybe it would be better out here." He paused and his eyes shifted back and forth at mine.

I shook my head and exhaled a long breath. "I think I'd better come in and you should get Caleb, Sarah and Grace."

He raised an eyebrow, but said nothing.

I paused, thinking I might need a bullet proof vest and remembered a better devise for protection. "Just need to grab something from the car."

I ran to get the antique book, letting the fresh air cool my flushed face. It was my only chance to convince Caleb I was worthy of being with Michael. I took a deep breath, squared my shoulders, and headed into house.

THE END
of Part I

Seventh Mark Part II

Prophecy Series

Find W.J. May

Website:
http://www.wanitamay.yolasite.com
Facebook:
https://www.facebook.com/pages/Author-WJ-May-FAN-PAGE/141170442608149
Newsletter:
SIGN UP FOR W.J. May's Newsletter to find out about new releases, updates, cover reveals and even freebies!
http://eepurl.com/97aYf

More books by W.J. May

The Chronicles of Kerrigan

    Book I - *Rae of Hope* is **FREE!**
    Book Trailer:
    http://www.youtube.com/watch?v=gILAwXxx8MU
    Book II - *Dark Nebula*
    Book Trailer:
    http://www.youtube.com/watch?v=Ca24STi_bFM
    Book III - *House of Cards*
    Book IV - *Royal Tea*
    Book V - *Under Fire*
    Book VI - *End in Sight*
    Book VII – *Hidden Darkness*
    Book VIII – *Twisted Together*
    Book IX – *Mark of Fate*
    Book X – *Strength & Power*
    Book XI – *Last One Standing*
    BOOK XII – *Rae of Light*

PREQUEL –
Christmas Before the Magic
Question the Darkness
Into the Darkness
Fight the Darkness
Alone the Darkness
Lost the Darkness

SEQUEL –
Matter of Time
Time Piece
Second Chance
Glitch in Time
Our Time
Precious Time

Hidden Secrets Saga:
Download Seventh Mark For FREE

Like most teenagers, Rouge is trying to figure out who she is and what she wants to be. With little knowledge about her past, she has questions but has never tried to find the answers. Everything changes when she befriends a strangely intoxicating family. Siblings Grace and Michael, appear to have secrets which seem connected to Rouge. Her hunch is confirmed when a horrible incident occurs at an outdoor party. Rouge may be the only one who can find the answer.

An ancient journal, a Sioghra necklace and a special mark force life-altering decisions for a girl who grew up unprepared to fight for her life or others.

All secrets have a cost and Rouge's determination to find the truth can only lead to trouble...or something even more sinister.

NEVER LOOK BACK

The wise learn many things from their enemies.

My name's Atlanta Skolar, and I'm a huntress. No, not the vampire-slaying type, or like the ever-brooding Winchester brothers from *Supernatural.* I live a relatively normal life—during the day at least. I go to school, have friends, and try my best to survive Uncle James' horrendous cooking.

However, the nights in the city of Calen are not always calm. There's a thin veil between our world and the world of monsters, the good and the bad. I'm one of the few who stands between the two. With the help of my uncle, who's taken me in since my parents' deaths, I spend the nights making sure the balance is maintained and that each side keeps to their respective places.

At least, that was until something rattled the cages and everything hit the fan. There's a new evil in town, an evil that's been here before, and it may be responsible for my parents' deaths. An evil that isn't satisfied with the balance. It'll do all it can to make sure darkness falls over Calen and the rest of the world once again.

Scary? That ain't the half of it.

It's particularly interested in me.

Why? No idea.

But it's my job as a huntress to make sure the evil is stopped, no matter what.

RADIUM HALOS - THE SENSELESS SERIES
Book 1 is FREE:

Everyone needs to be a hero at one point in their life.

The small town of Elliot Lake will never be the same again.

Caught in a sudden thunderstorm, Zoe, a high school senior from Elliot Lake, and five of her friends take shelter in an abandoned uranium mine. Over the next few days, Zoe's hearing sharpens drastically, beyond what any normal human being can detect. She tells her friends, only to learn that four others have an increased sense as well. Only Kieran, the new boy from Scotland, isn't affected.

Fashioning themselves into superheroes, the group tries to stop the strange occurrences happening in their little town. Muggings, break-ins, disappearances, and murder begin to hit too close to home. It leads the team to think someone knows about their secret - someone who wants them all dead.

An incredulous group of heroes. A traitor in the midst. Some dreams are written in blood.

Courage Runs Red
The Blood Red Series
Book 1 is FREE

What if courage was your only option?

When Kallie lands a college interview with the city's new hot-shot police officer, she has no idea everything in her life is about to change. The detective is young, handsome and seems to have an unnatural ability to stop the increasing local crime rate. Detective Liam's particular interest in Kallie sends her heart and head stumbling over each other.

When a raging blood feud between vampires spills into her home, Kallie gets caught in the middle. Torn between love and family loyalty she must find the courage to fight what she fears the most and possibly risk everything, even if it means dying for those she loves.

Daughter of Darkness
VICTORIA
Only Death Could Stop Her Now
The Daughters of Darkness is a series of female heroines who may or may
not know each other, but all have the same father, Vlad Montour.
Victoria is a Hunter Vampire

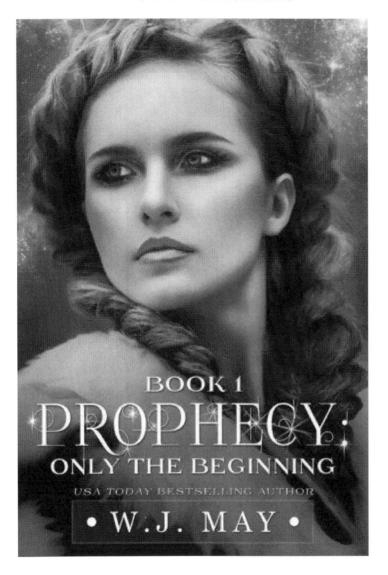

Don't miss out!

Click the button below and you can sign up to receive emails whenever W.J. May publishes a new book. There's no charge and no obligation.

https://books2read.com/r/B-A-SSF-XLON

Connecting independent readers to independent writers.

Did you love *Only the Beginning*? Then you should read *Rae of Hope* by W.J. May!

USA TODAY BESTSELLING AUTHOR, W.J. May brings you a series you won't be able to put down!

How hard do you have to shake the family tree to find the truth about the past?

Fifteen year-old Rae Kerrigan never really knew her family's history. Her mother and father died when she was young and it is only when she accepts a scholarship to the prestigious Guilder Boarding School in England that a mysterious family secret is revealed.

Will the sins of the father be the sins of the daughter?

As Rae struggles with new friends, a new school and a star-struck forbidden love, she must also face the ultimate challenge: receive a tattoo on her sixteenth birthday with specific powers that may bind her to an unspeakable darkness. It's up to Rae to undo the dark evil in her family's past and have a ray of hope for her future.

Join Rae Kerrigan in this bestselling series and the start of one amazing adventure!

Also by W.J. May

Bit-Lit Series
Lost Vampire
Cost of Blood
Price of Death

Blood Red Series
Courage Runs Red
The Night Watch
Marked by Courage
Forever Night

Daughters of Darkness: Victoria's Journey
Victoria
Huntress
Coveted (A Vampire & Paranormal Romance)
Twisted

Hidden Secrets Saga
Seventh Mark - Part 1
Seventh Mark - Part 2
Marked By Destiny

Compelled
Fate's Intervention
Chosen Three
The Hidden Secrets Saga: The Complete Series

Paranormal Huntress Series
Never Look Back
Coven Master

Prophecy Series
Only the Beginning
White Winter

The Chronicles of Kerrigan
Rae of Hope
Dark Nebula
House of Cards
Royal Tea
Under Fire
End in Sight
Hidden Darkness
Twisted Together
Mark of Fate
Strength & Power
Last One Standing
Rae of Light
The Chronicles of Kerrigan Box Set Books # 1 - 6

The Chronicles of Kerrigan: Gabriel
Living in the Past

The Chronicles of Kerrigan Prequel
Christmas Before the Magic
Question the Darkness
Into the Darkness
Fight the Darkness
Alone in the Darkness
Lost in Darkness
The Chronicles of Kerrigan Prequel Series Books #1-3

The Chronicles of Kerrigan Sequel
A Matter of Time
Time Piece
Second Chance
Glitch in Time
Our Time
Precious Time

The Hidden Secrets Saga
Seventh Mark (part 1 & 2)

The Senseless Series
Radium Halos
Radium Halos - Part 2
Nonsense

Standalone
Shadow of Doubt (Part 1 & 2)
Five Shades of Fantasy
Shadow of Doubt - Part 2
Four and a Half Shades of Fantasy
Dream Fighter
What Creeps in the Night
Forest of the Forbidden
HuNted
Arcane Forest: A Fantasy Anthology
Ancient Blood of the Vampire and Werewolf

Made in the USA
Middletown, DE
10 July 2017